APPLAUD THE
HOLLOW GHOST

Also by David J. Walker

Fixed in His Folly
Half the Truth

APPLAUD
THE
HOLLOW GHOST

$$\equiv$$

D AVID J . W ALKER

ST. MARTIN'S PRESS
NEW YORK

WEST BEND LIBRARY

Library of Congress Cataloging-in-Publication Data

Walker, David J., 1939–
    Applaud the hollow ghost / David Walker. —1st ed.
        p.   cm.
    ISBN 0-312-18041-1
    I. Title.
PS3573.A4253313A86   1998
813'.54—dc21   97-39917
                                                                     CIP

First Edition: February 1998

10   9   8   7   6   5   4   3   2   1

To Ellen, stealth-helper indeed

This is a work of fiction in its entirety, which means I made it all up myself. I hope, therefore, that it is true.

Along those lines, I owe special thanks to Patrick Reardon, for counsel as to criminal procedure and a statute obviously put together by committee; to Michele Mellett, M.D., a trauma surgeon (enough said); to Eric K. Wagner, D.V.M., for care for our real-life spaniels and advice about an ill-fated fictional stray; to Caesar and Betty Vitale, for a touch of Italian; to my editor, Kelley Ragland, for her enthusiasm and judgment; and—most of all—to the members of the DeMello group, allies on the adventure.

"You don't believe in me," observed the Ghost. . . . "Why do you doubt your senses?"

"Because," said Scrooge, "a little thing affects them. A slight disorder of the stomach makes them cheats. You may be an undigested bit of beef, a blot of mustard, a crumb of cheese, a fragment of an underdone potato . . ."

—CHARLES DICKENS, *A CHRISTMAS CAROL*

It is—last stage of all—
When we are frozen up within, and quite
The phantom of ourselves,
To hear the world applaud the hollow ghost
Which blamed the living man.

—MATTHEW ARNOLD, *GROWING OLD*

APPLAUD THE
HOLLOW GHOST

CHAPTER

1

LAMBERT FLEMING WAS BARELY *fifteen years old—and trying very hard to fit in—on that bright, sad afternoon in October when he suddenly became invisible. I was about the same; fifteen years old and trying hard to fit in, that is. Not invisible.*

It happened on the basketball court, and the scene must have replayed itself a thousand times in my mind since then—and that's not counting the dreams. Sunlight streamed down through a row of high, narrow windows along one wall of the gym, striping the air with bright rivers of light, each river teeming with clouds of swirling, rising bits of dust, like millions of tiny, panic-stricken fish trying to swim their way up and out to somewhere else.

Lammy had known he had absolutely no chance to make the basketball team. He wasn't even really interested. But I'd encouraged him, thinking I was doing him a favor, and he came to tryouts only because of me. Then, probably because the coach thought Lammy was my friend and I seemed like a possible future star, Lammy ended up as a team "manager." That meant he gathered up sweat-soaked towels and counted balls and became a handy target for a constant barrage of hauntingly cruel taunts from most of the players.

Lammy wasn't handicapped, exactly, or even unintelligent. He was just a sad-faced kid, rounded and plump and soft all over, without the slightest clue about how to relate to other human beings. He reminded everyone of that giggling Doughboy in the Pillsbury ads, except he never laughed and his mannerisms seemed a little more feminine than the Doughboy's. So most of the kids called him "Doughgirl."

1

I called him "Lammy."

On the first day of school, the alphabet had put us together—slump-shouldered Lambert R. Fleming in the homeroom desk just in front of the big new kid, me, Malachy P. Foley. I was a sophomore transfer to Saint Robert's, a small, coed Catholic high school on the northwest side of Chicago, and I'd started talking to Lammy before I really noticed how greasy his hair was and how his grimy fingernails were so long they curled over the tips of his fingers. Pretty soon, though, I noticed that he hardly ever talked to anyone, and nobody ever talked to him.

I was in a miserable, angry mood those days, anyway, mostly because of the way things were going at home. So even after I found out how uncool it was to treat Lammy as anything other than the outcast that he was, I made it a point to keep on talking to him. Not that I really liked him. I understood much later that he was just a convenient way to tell everyone else they were jerks and I didn't give a damn what they thought.

But by that October afternoon, when the coach left us alone to run twenty laps while he went back to lock up his chem lab, things had already started changing for me. Basketball was my sport, and I was strong and fast and tall for my age. In a school with no football team, those were perfect credentials, and I'd started making friends. That meant giving up my lone-wolf facade and adjusting my behavior to match what the other kids thought. I did give a damn, which was unfortunate for Lammy—and for me.

Things went bad that day when all of us finished our twenty laps before the coach got back. Someone got the extremely funny idea that Doughgirl ought to run laps, too. It probably would have blown over if Lammy had had the sense, or the strength, to flat-out refuse. But maybe he was afraid, or maybe he actually thought it would earn him some respect. Anyway, he got up and gave it his best, chugging around the perimeter of the gym in his

2

manager's shirt and his baggy gray sweatpants with elastic around the ankles.

Most of the players—about a dozen—gathered in a group, laughing and shouting and clapping their hands rhythmically to the beat of the soles of Lammy's cheap basketball shoes slapping flatly against the wood floor.

Their shouting quickly turned into a chant. "Dough-GIRL! Dough-GIRL! Dough-GIRL!"

I stood off to the side with a couple of other guys who didn't have the heart to participate in the ridicule, but lacked also the courage to do anything about it.

Lammy himself made a sad, hopeless attempt to join in with the humor. Waving his hands above his head and waggling his butt as he ran, he grinned as though enjoying this wonderful opportunity to entertain the troops.

The clapping and chanting grew louder. "Dough-GIRL! Dough-GIRL! Dough-GIRL!"

By the time he finished only two laps, Lammy was already winded and he tried to sit down. This, of course, simply stirred his audience to new heights. They pushed him back onto the floor. Barely able to sustain a trot, he stumbled along, gasping for breath.

"Dough-GIRL! Dough GIRL! Dough-GIRL!"

Foolishly, he kept trying to pretend he was part of their game. He shook his behind more provocatively and even twirled around once, clumsily. He couldn't have done anything worse.

Because the chant changed then, became meaner, more ominous.

"Dough-GIRL! Take it OFF! Dough-GIRL! Take it OFF!"

I moved farther away, pretending to concentrate on stretching my leg muscles. But I couldn't take my eyes off Lammy. I felt sorry for him, embarrassed by him, furious at him—all at once. Finally, in his own ever-increasing stupidity, he accommodated the stupid chant, pulling his sweatshirt off and twirling it above

3

his head while he kept moving, in scarcely more than a walk now, his belly and chest one plump mass, heaving beneath a thin white T-shirt.

"Dough-GIRL! Take it OFF! Dough-GIRL! Take it OFF!" gave way to a simple "Take it OFF! Take it OFF!"

But by then Lammy was completely exhausted. With a hapless wave toward the chanting group, he stopped, looked around, then turned and cut diagonally across the gym floor . . . and straight toward me, for God's sake.

His taunters had turned into a teenage version of a lynch mob—hooting and mindless. The only boy on the team bigger than I—a mean kid with a face every mother loved, but the conscience of a hyena—ran out and grabbed the bottom hem of Lammy's T-shirt and yanked it up over his head and off him.

The group cheered. "Take it OFF! Take it OFF! Take it ALL off!" they howled, clapping and stamping their feet.

Grinning slyly, the hyena bowed low to his audience, then spun back around and yanked Lammy's sweatpants down to the floor before he ran back to join the crowd. Lammy just stood there then, his pants puddled around his ankles, a fold of soft fat half-covering the wide white elastic waistband of his jockstrap. He clasped his arms across his pale, hairless chest. He was hugging himself, all alone at mid-court. His forced smile had turned into a grimace. Tears ran down his cheeks—and he kept looking straight at me.

I wanted to do something. But I was just one of the guys. I looked everywhere around the gym, except back at Lammy. Where was the coach, for God's sake? I was just one of the guys, damn it. It was Lammy's fault that he'd acted so stupid, not mine. What did he expect me to do about it?

What I did was turn my back on Lammy and the rest of them, and walk off the floor and into the locker room. As I pulled my street clothes on over my practice uniform, I discovered I was crying, too.

4

I ran all the way home. But there was no comfort there, no one to talk to. My mom was busy starting supper and talking on the telephone. My dad was in the basement watching TV. He was still with the police department at the time, working midnights behind the desk, sitting around and drinking too many Old Styles whenever he was home. There was no help for me there.

I never asked anyone how it had ended. If the coach caught them, or what. A week or so later I got into a fight over nothing with the big kid who'd pulled down Lammy's pants. The coach had to pull me off him because I had him down and was pounding the back of his head on the tile floor of the locker room. The coach made me apologize and the hyena sneered at me when I did, and I hated him. But of course that had nothing to do with Lammy.

Lammy never showed up at practice again. He became invisible. Sometimes I'd know he was nearby, shuffling through the cafeteria line with a tray full of desserts, or standing all alone against a wall somewhere, hugging himself and staring down at the floor. But I never looked at him. I never saw him.

And I never told anyone how much of a coward I was.

THAT WAS OVER TWENTY years ago.

Now I was standing in a stuffy, noisy corridor outside Branch 66 of the Circuit Court of Cook County, at Twenty-sixth and California, about eight and a half miles south of where Saint Robert's High School used to be before they tore it down. Lambert Fleming was there, too. I saw him. He was backed up against the wall, breathing hard, hugging his soft body, and staring down at the floor. Ten yards down the hall, sheriff's deputies were pushing back a group of about a dozen angry people.

The little mob was shouting at Lammy—chanting actually: "Filthy pervert! Lock him away! Filthy pervert! Lock him away!"

Lammy's lawyer, Renata Carroway, took one of his arms and I took the other and we led him away from the crowd. Renata and I had laid low until after his bond was set. The judge never dreamed that a loser like Lammy, a maintenance worker at an animal shelter who had lived with his mother all his life on the second floor of a two-flat, could hire private counsel, much less come up with bond money. Otherwise, with that crowd in the spectators' seats, he'd have set a higher bond. No one had been more surprised than Lammy when we showed up.

But about a year or so earlier I'd been drinking brandy with the Lady in front of the fireplace at her home on the lakefront in Evanston. She's old enough to be my mother and she has a name—Helene Bower. But everyone calls her "the Lady." She's great to talk to, and that evening, although she hadn't asked, I'd been trying to explain—again—why I acted the way I did sometimes, and I'd spilled the whole sad Lambert Fleming story.

The Lady's the sort of person who actually hears what you're saying and remembers an awful lot of it. She must have remembered Lammy's name, anyway, because she'd cut an article about his arrest out of the *Chicago Sun-Times* and left it at my door with the supermarket coupons she clips for me every Thursday. No note. Just the newspaper article.

So now Lammy was free on bond and I'd hired one of my favorite criminal defense attorneys for him. He even had his own private investigator now, to help his lawyer find out what had really happened.

Because this time, damn it, I wasn't going to walk away on him—no matter what. Although I sure hoped I wouldn't help his lawyer find out he was really as guilty as everyone thought. I was going to help him this time, but I certainly didn't want to learn that Lambert Fleming really *had* exposed himself and sexually assaulted that cute little girl—like she said he had.

Renata and I walked Lammy out to her BMW and I watched as she drove away with him. He hadn't said one word to me. He acted like he couldn't even see me.

CHAPTER

2

ON TUESDAY MORNING, THE day after Lambert Fleming was let out on bond, the weather wasn't bad for January in Chicago: temperature in the mid-twenties and snowing like crazy. From my place in Evanston I drove south on Sheridan Road, into and through the city's East Rogers Park neighborhood, then west on Foster. If traffic was slower than usual it wasn't due to the snow, but the salt trucks all over the place. This isn't Louisville, or D.C., or even Philadelphia, after all. When it snows here, entire political regimes are at risk, so we smother the stuff in salt before it can even hit the pavement. That's why my Chevy Cavalier was on its fourth muffler in eight years.

Putting up Lammy's bond had exhausted what remained of my share of the $40,000 Breaker Hanafan left in a gym bag on my doorstep the previous October. Breaker's a crook, but it hadn't surprised me when he'd returned the bag after I'd carelessly left it at his place. The forty grand had been paid me by a very pretty, but drug-addled, former investigative reporter for a local TV station. Actually, "paid" isn't the right word. But she certainly wasn't about to ask for it back.

Anyway, now it was gone, but as long as Lammy didn't jump bail, there'd be a bond refund at the close of his case, whatever the disposition was. I wanted to get it over with in a hurry and get my money back, which is why I was ignoring Renata Carroway's order not to do anything without checking with her first. I hadn't actually *promised* her, after all.

The victim of Lammy's alleged sexual attack was eight-year-old Patricia Connolly. From the newspaper reports and some checking I'd already done, I knew that everyone called her "Trish." Her mother was dead and she lived just down the street from Lammy, with her grandmother and her father. The grandmother, Rosa Parillo, went to Mass every day of the year and usually stayed after to recite the rosary in Italian out loud with her cronies. Trish's father—Rosa's son-in-law—was Steve Connolly, who'd parlayed his performance as a precinct captain into a job as a senior snowplow driver at O'Hare Airport from November to April. Steve played a lot of golf the other six months, when he wasn't getting out the vote or hanging out with cronies of his own—mostly Italian, like Rosa's, but hardly the churchgoing type—at Melba's Coffee Shop on North Avenue.

I was on my way to talk to Lammy, but as I got closer I changed my mind. Whether that was because it would *really* be better to look around a little first, or whether I just wasn't ready to face him yet, I'd leave to my analyst—if I ever needed one.

The snow regulations prohibited street parking, but I found a plowed lot beside a grocery store. The sign said "For Customers Only," so I went inside and bought a quart of chocolate milk and found a pay phone.

"D'par'men'AviationO'HareSnowR'moval." The way he said it, it was one word.

"Steve Connolly, please," I said.

"Steve ain't in today."

"But it's snowing like hell. I thought he—"

"Steve ain't here. Personal day. Wanna leave a message?"

"No thanks, I—"

"Good." He hung up. Probably busy. And shorthanded at that.

I unfolded the ear flaps of my wool cap, zipped up my jacket, and walked four blocks through a beautiful swirling snowstorm to the Connolly house, a well-kept brick bungalow on a corner lot just a half block south of where Lammy lived. It was a safe bet no one there was anxious to talk to me, and I didn't bother to knock on their door.

8

In the alley, tire tracks that were rapidly filling with snow still showed that someone had backed out of the Connolly garage within the last hour or so, and hadn't come back. It wasn't likely that Trish or Rosa would be driving anywhere, so it had to be Steve. I continued on down the alley to the rear of Lammy's place. The owners lived on the first floor, but were retired and spent the winters in Florida with their son. Lammy's mother had been renting the second-floor flat for over thirty-five years. Her other child, a daughter ten years older than Lammy, was divorced and lived somewhere else.

Most of the homes that backed up to the alley had garages, but not this one. A waist-high chain-link fence enclosed the backyard, its gate trapped half open by the snow. The two-flat building itself was brick but, like so many others in the city, its once-open back stairs and porches had long ago been framed in and enclosed in wood siding. Through the blowing snow, I could see the faded blue-gray paint that was peeling away from the vertical boards. Ninety percent of the enclosed porches in the city must get the same blue-gray paint. Most of it starts peeling off in a year or so.

I went through the gate and into the backyard. If anyone saw me, they kept it to themselves. The ground was covered with snow, but I imagined a sidewalk that ran from the gate to the enclosed porch, and I followed it.

According to what the state's attorney told the judge, this was where Lammy had dragged Trish. It had been cold out and she was hurrying home from her cousin's house. She'd been watching TV and gotten bored and decided to walk home when her father was late picking her up. It was less than two blocks and she'd taken the alley and wasn't paying much attention. She tried to scream and get away but he grabbed her from behind and put a gloved hand over her mouth. Then he dragged her inside the porch enclosure. He tore open her coat and pulled down her jeans and her panties. Then he pushed her down

9

onto her back and . . . about that time she blacked out. The medical report Renata Carroway had seen spoke of contusions on Trish's jaw and cheek, and lacerations inside her lips—from her own teeth. There were bruises and scratches on her lower abdomen, and on one of her thighs, too, but no other significant wounds, and no lacerations or abrasions on her buttocks or the backs of her legs. The findings were inconclusive as to penetration. There was no sign of ejaculation, no blood traces other than her own.

She'd apparently identified Lammy, even if it was too dark for her to get a good look at him. He had his pants open and exposed himself. She saw that. He was white, and he had on a dark blue coat with a hood over his head, "like that Mr. Fleming always has," she'd said.

I tried the door to the porch enclosure. It wasn't locked and I stepped inside and stood on a slab of rough, cracked concrete. Out of the snow, it took a moment for my eyes to adjust to the semidarkness. Wooden steps led up to the first and second floors, and a cement stairwell led down to an exterior basement entrance. I looked down . . . and locked eyes with the man staring back up at me.

It was Lammy, all right, standing at the bottom of the short stairway in his shirtsleeves. He didn't move, and somehow it looked as though he'd been standing in the same spot for a long time. I yanked off my cap and his eyes widened with sudden recognition, then quickly shifted away from my face. He opened his mouth as though to speak, but closed it again and lowered his head.

He held a dog cradled in his arms like an infant lying on its back. The dog was a mutt with no collar and a ragged coat. Almost certainly part German shepherd. Very certainly dead. Its body was stiff, and dark blood stained and clotted the fur around where its genitals used to be.

CHAPTER

====

3

"HE WAS ALREADY DEAD," Lammy said.

"Of course he was. Jeez, I didn't think *you* killed him."

"No, I mean he was already dead when they . . . when they cut on him."

"What are you—"

"A stray. I been tryin' for a week to catch him, take him to the shelter." He spoke in a monotone and never looked up at me. "Musta got hit by a car and died and somebody saw it and . . . and then they did this."

"How do *you* know?"

"I know stuff about animals. He didn't feel anything, I don't think. Dead already."

My guess was he didn't really know, but was trying hard to convince himself the dog wasn't conscious when it was cut. Even though I hadn't talked to him since he was fifteen years old, my problem wasn't believing that Lammy might "know stuff about animals," but that he might know anything worthwhile at all—about *anything.*

". . . rang and I answered it," he was saying. "A man said I should go downstairs and see what they oughta do to . . . to me. That was real early. I was scared and I didn't go down for a long time and—"

"Is that basement open?" I asked.

"Uh-huh. But there's no heat in there."

"That's even better. We'll put the dog inside for a while, and go upstairs and make some phone calls."

An hour later I'd learned the police weren't much interested

11

in a dead dog, castrated or not, but Lammy was welcome to go into the station and make a report if he wanted. I'd also had Lammy's telephone calls rerouted through a service that would try to trace any calls he got, and I loaned him a cellular phone I sometimes use that's listed to Barney Green, who'd once been a partner of mine—back when I used to have a law license.

Lammy said that after his arrest his mother had been kept awake all night with threatening phone calls. The next day his sister, Elaine, picked her up and took her to Elaine's house in Cicero. It was a tiny house and there wasn't much room for Lammy's mother, and there certainly wasn't room for Lammy to come, too—even if Elaine would have invited him. Which she didn't.

"No room," Lammy repeated. "Besides, she said she's worried what her neighbors would say, you know, 'cause she's got daughters, and—"

"Right. I got it." We were standing in the kitchen. I wanted to leave, to get away from there. I wanted to help him, but I didn't want to have to talk to him. It was too depressing.

"I'd rather stay here, anyway," he said. "I'll lock the doors."

"Have you ever stayed anywhere else overnight in your life, other than right here?"

"Just when I was in jail. That's all. I never been anywhere." He was looking out the window. "I read a lot, though."

"I know. I heard all about what they took." The cops had confiscated a stash of what the newspapers described as "sexually explicit, lewd, and pornographic materials" found in Lammy's room.

"No, not that," he said. "I mean . . . history."

"Oh?"

"Yeah, mostly books about war. The other stuff—the magazines—it's just, you know . . ."

"Yeah, I know," I said. "Look, I'll go get my car and come back and pick up the dog. I'll see that it's buried, okay? Or cremated or whatever they do. Come to think of it, is there a veterinarian at the shelter where you work?"

"Different ones, on different days. The one I like is Doctor Daniels." He gave me the vet's office address.

"Everything'll be fine," I said. "I'll call you every so often on the cellular phone, see how you're doing."

"Uh-huh." He stared down at his shoes. Except when I'd startled him with the dog in his arms, he hadn't looked straight at me once.

I was halfway down the back stairs when I thought of something else. I went back and stuck my head in the door and found him still standing in the same spot in the kitchen.

"I knew you'd come back," he said.

"Oh?"

"Yeah, 'cause you didn't ask me yet."

"What are you talking about?"

"You wanna ask did I do what that girl said. That's why you—"

"Wrong. I came back to ask where you get the books about war. I mean . . . do you buy them, or what?"

"Uh-uh. The library. In the neighborhood. They order 'em from downtown."

"One other thing. You promised me you'd lock the doors. But I just walked right in."

"Oh . . . okay. But—"

"Good-bye."

I retrieved the Cavalier and drove back to pick up the dog. The snow had stopped and the temperature was falling fast. I laid the dead dog in my backseat and drove a half hour to an animal hospital on the edge of Old Town without turning the car heater on. I handed the dog over to a slightly bewildered Doctor Lynette Daniels. I was a little surprised when she said she might talk to a veterinary pathologist. I never even knew there was such a thing.

13

"We'll have to consult a specialist like that if I can't tell what he died from," she said. "I practice general veterinary medicine, and one day a week I go to the shelter where your friend works." She smiled. She was very attractive.

"Not really a friend," I said. "More like a client."

"He's so . . . pathetic, isn't he? But he's very good with the dogs."

I hadn't wanted to ask Lammy if he'd done what Trish Connolly said he did. I didn't want that to get in the way. I wanted to know first if he was right about the dog. I wanted to find out if he really knew "stuff about animals," and if he really read lots of history books. I wanted to talk to people at the animal shelter where he worked, and maybe to the local librarian.

I wanted to discover that Lammy was just another one of us human beings that eats and takes a crap and rides the el to work and has good days and bad days—and even *knows* things. I wanted to think of him as a flesh-and-blood person, not that goddamn disappearing boy that kept showing up as a ghost in my dreams, standing in his jockstrap in the middle of a river of his own tears and calling to me over the sound of rhythmic applause even as he turns transparent, hollow, empty—and I practice jump shots on the bank and pretend not to hear.

THE TEMPERATURE MUST HAVE been down to the lower teens when I left the animal hospital. There was a parking ticket on the Cavalier. I tossed it in the glove compartment, figuring this one *had* to be a legitimate business expense. Even the IRS wouldn't expect a person to park in a lot and carry a dead dog two blocks along a slippery sidewalk. *Would* they?

On the drive to Melba's Coffee Shop I wondered what income there'd be during the rest of the year to credit that expense against. I always report every penny of income. First, because I don't really mind paying what little taxes I owe, figuring I get back probably more than my share of basic services, no matter which set of scalawags is at the trough. Second, because I get audited pretty regularly. Not because they ever find anything. but because a while back I made some people unhappy. They just don't seem to get over their ill feelings—and I just don't seem to want to go back to jail.

Of course, when I did my time—first in Cook County Jail, and then downstate for a while—it had nothing to do with taxes, or even with a real crime. I was a lawyer then and a difference of opinion arose between me and the Illinois Supreme Court about whether a conversation I'd had with a client was privileged or not. The court said it wasn't, held me in contempt, and ordered me locked up until I'd reveal what the client told me. The justices have to run for office every so often, but the fact that almost every voter in the state believed my guy was a cop killer and I should tell, privilege or not, certainly wouldn't have affected the court's judgment. No way.

They finally let me out, but in the meantime they'd suspended my law license, too. When I inquired about getting it back they told me I'd have to "show remorse" for my contemptuous conduct. I figured I'd do that right after the court apologized to *me*.

So now I didn't make much money, but I sure had lots of time. And it was my own. I could run, and work out at Dr. Sato's dojo, and practice the piano. The income from a small trust I'd funded a few years earlier with my one-and-only big-time attorney's fee—from a case for the Lady—wasn't enough to live on. But I had friends as well as enemies, and they helped contort my resume to fit into the requirements of the Illinois Private Detectives Act well enough to get me a license, and even a firearm authorization card. With an occasional paying client, and a few gigs here and there in barrooms where people don't listen too closely to the piano player, I got along.

I couldn't park on North Avenue because of the snow regulations, and I finally found a spot beside a funeral home. I finished the quart of chocolate milk and walked back to Melba's.

You couldn't miss Melba's. It was the nondescript little hole-in-the-wall with the full-size Ford conversion van parked at the fire hydrant out front.

It's funny how the local cops, the Feds, the Chicago Crime Commission—and maybe Geraldo and Oprah, too, for all I know—can identify the hangout of just about every player in the syndicate lineup. Sometimes you wonder what good it does. But, when you're walking into the coffee shop where the father of the girl who says she was attacked by your client hangs out, it can be helpful to know that an old-time hood like Gus Apprezziano happens to hang out there, too. It makes you aware that there may be lots of fire power in the vicinity.

The sign hanging inside the window said "CLOSED," but the hasp they must have used to padlock the door from the outside whenever they left was hanging open and there were lights on inside. I pushed the door open and went in.

The place was warm and full of the odors of overheated coffee and stale bacon grease and corned beef and garlic, and there should have been laughter and the jovial banter of regular customers and lots of local good cheer. Maybe Melba's was that way sometimes. But this was three o'clock in the afternoon and what laughter and banter and cheer there'd been, if any, must have gone out with the lunch crowd.

It was an old-fashioned room, four times as long as it was wide, with a Formica-topped table squeezed into the space in front of the plate glass window to the left of the door and a row of identical tables lined up straight ahead of me along the right wall, with four chairs at each one. A counter with stools ran along the left wall, then turned and made an L before it got to the back. A swinging door and a service window both opened into the kitchen in the rear.

A large-breasted woman somewhere past sixty, with a pockmarked olive complexion and a long, narrow nose hanging over a beginner's mustache, sat behind the near end of the counter. As I entered, her right hand drifted absently toward a stack of menus beside the cash register. When she looked up, though, her hand dropped down onto the menus. Meanwhile, her left hand was full of dollar bills, and there were little stacks of more bills set out in front of her.

Farther down the counter, on the customers' side, a woman sat on a stool with a pencil in her hand and a coffee mug and a *Sun-Times* on the counter in front of her. She wore a black leather coat and bright red pants tucked into black leather boots with very high heels. She glanced up at me, then returned to her crossword puzzle. Three men in shirtsleeves—all of them large and none of them over forty years old—huddled over the table farthest from the door. Their heads turned my way and I recognized one of them as Steve Connolly. His reddish-brown hair was thick and wavy, and he had the head and broad shoulders of an all-pro linebacker. He wasn't as wide lower down in the body as a linebacker, but he was tall and well-built, with maybe a hint of flab starting around the middle. I'd noticed all that the day I'd seen him in court. He hadn't come out into the corridor to join the group yelling at Lammy, and there was no reason he'd know my face.

The men returned to their conversation, leaving no one looking my way now except the money counter. I stared back at her. She must finally have decided I wasn't going to turn around and go away. "Sorry, mister," she said, "we're closed."

I could have said I was looking for Steve Connolly. I could have said the apple pie looked good and could I have a piece. I could have said any number of sensible things. What I did say was, "Sign says coffee shop, doesn't it? Maybe I'll have a cup of coffee then." I said it so loud that even someone in the kitchen could have heard.

The three men raised their heads and craned their necks to

stare at me. The woman in the red pants gazed down at her crossword puzzle, then flipped her pencil around and erased one of her answers.

"Sign also says breakfast and lunch only," the money counter said. "Closed at two-thirty."

I dropped one of my business cards on the counter. "I don't want coffee anyway. I have a message to deliver." I kept my voice up, and my hands out and away from my pockets.

"Hey, buddy!" It was Steve Connolly who called out. "She said she's closed."

Ignoring Connolly, I said, "It's a message for Mr. Apprezziano." I didn't know what he looked like, but Apprezziano had to be close to seventy years old, so he wasn't there. "A message to Mr. Apprezziano about one of his flunkies who cut the balls off a dog and left the body at my friend's house." I picked up a heavy soup spoon lying on the nearest table and waved it for emphasis. "My friend loves dogs, so that was a mean, chickenshit thing to do. Stupid, too."

"Hey!" It was Connolly, getting to his feet now, and his friends with him.

I backed up and pulled open the door, very happy that it opened inward. "You tell Mr. Apprezziano if something like that happens again he's gonna read about his chickenshit boy in the newspaper—and about himself, too."

Connolly and company were halfway up the row of tables, but by then I was outside the door. I pulled it shut, flipped the hasp closed over its U-shaped staple, and dropped the handle of the soup spoon down through where the padlock would go.

I don't know just how long it took them to get out of there, but it wasn't before I was around the corner.

CHAPTER

4

FOUR HOURS LATER I was standing in my kitchen, rinsing the remnants of a bowl of chili into the sink, and talking on the phone with Lammy's lawyer, a very irate Renata Carroway.

"Hey, slow down," I said, as soon as Renata paused for breath. "That's a prosecutor's typical bullshit threat, and you know it."

"Call it whatever you want, damn it. But the state's attorney calls it 'witness intimidation.' Claims he's got four witnesses who'll testify that you, acting on behalf of Lambert Fleming, barged into property that was clearly marked 'closed,' refused to leave when asked, then shouted obscenities and threats against Steve and Patricia Connolly if they don't, quote, 'leave Fleming alone.' He says if anything like that happens again, he'll charge both you *and* my client with intimidation of—"

"I heard you the first time. But who is this state's attorney, anyway?" I stuck the bowl in the cupboard over the sink. "Somebody you can halfway trust?"

"Are you kidding? His name's Cletus Heffernan, and he's a full-blown, first-class, certifiable—"

"Asshole?" I tried.

"I was going to say Nazi."

"Whatever. So . . . a guy like that, we know he's bluffing. Three reasons. *First,* if he thought they'd stick, he'd have filed his charges without wasting time talking to you. *Second,* neither you nor Lammy has given me any authority to act on Lammy's behalf. I'm the one paying your fee, but you have no control over what I do. Fact is, *you* work for *me,* come to think of—"

19

"Wrong. Who pays my fee makes no difference, and you know it. I work only for my client." She paused. "But you're right about the control part. It's pretty clear even *you* don't have much control over what you do. Anyway, I've warned you. Now I have to hang up, because there's—"

"Wait. There's a third reason we know Heffernan's bluffing, and—"

"Good-bye."

Renata hung up, but I told the phone anyway. "The third reason," I said, "is that there were *five* witnesses at Melba's, not four."

I dropped two empty beer bottles in the orange recycling bin outside my kitchen door at the top of the back stairs. The Lady was working on improving my dietary habits, so the homemade chili she'd sent over—five quarts of it, frozen, in plastic containers—was vegetarian. I'd added way too many hot peppers, trying to give it some flavor, which had made that second beer a necessity. But I'd finished one whole quart of the chili. For that I deserved a reward.

So I popped the top off a third bottle of Berghoff, thinking maybe I should throw out the rest of the chili—for the sake of my liver. Instead, I called the Lady.

"Could you use a gallon of your vegetarian chili back?" I asked, when she came on the line.

"Why certainly we can. But I was rather hoping you'd learn to like it, Malachy."

Malachy. The Lady always says *Malachy.*

Lady Helene Bower, the widow of the late Richard Bower, who'd been a lord of the British Empire—or a knight maybe, I never got it straight—never calls me Mal. Her upbringing makes using nicknames uncomfortable for her and, as far as I can tell, she simply doesn't want to waste the effort trying. Not that the Lady can't change. For example, most people, even after I correct them, keep right on pronouncing my name so the last syllable rhymes with "sky." But just one mention to the Lady that it rhymes with "key," and she never made the mistake again. I told her once—when she was being especially annoying about something—that it amazed me how quickly she'd made *that* switch, given how slow she is to change sometimes. "Oh," she'd said, "I just rhymed *Malachy* with smart-*alecky* . . . and never forgot." She'd said it with such a straight face, I couldn't—

". . . far too much red meat," the Lady was saying on the phone. Then, "Malachy? Are you there?"

"Oh. Yes. I guess my mind was wandering. Anyway, I just called to tell you I'm trying to help Lambert Fleming."

"That's nice," she said, "if that's what you want to do."

"Well, *you* sent me the newspaper clipping. So that's what *you* think I should do, isn't it, Helene?" People only call her "the Lady" when she's not around, because she insists on being called "Helene" in person. I never said she was any more consistent than the rest of us.

"I don't really have an opinion," she said, "except that I believe unresolved issues such as that can often—"

"What unresolved—" I started, but then thought better of it. "The point is I'll do what I can for Lammy, but I have a feeling I might regret getting involved."

"From what I saw in the papers," she said, "I'd be surprised if you don't come to regret it very *much*—in the short run. But you may eventually find you're glad you did—in the long run."

I promised to deliver the rest of the chili back to her, and we said good-bye. I knew she'd want to spend the evening meeting with some of the battered, abused women who live with her, or in one of her other homes.

I took a long pull on the Berghoff and opened the refrigerator. Except for the beer on the bottom shelf, it looked pretty barren in there, with margarine and mustard and a package of generic bologna pretty much covering the food supply. But there were also two twenty-six-ounce cans of coffee. I took the opened one over to the counter by the coffeemaker.

The Lady's house is just a little north of Northwestern University's Evanston campus. My wife, Cass, and I helped her find it, back when the Lady decided there was nothing for her to go back home to in England. It's a mansion, really. And as you drive in, up a curving, very classy crushed-stone drive, there's a long garage with six sets of very classy folding doors, with windows. The doors had been built tall enough to accommodate carriages in an earlier era. The garage has a not-very-classy second-floor apartment that Cass and I leased from the Lady and called our "coach house."

From the coach house kitchen windows I could see Lake Michigan as I measured out the Folgers, because the moon was up and it was winter and the leaves had abandoned all the tall oaks and maples between me and the shoreline. The moon, the lake, the leafless trees—even the Krups coffeemaker she'd gotten for ten bucks at a garage sale—all urged me to think about Cass. But thoughts such as those weren't helpful, because I hadn't seen or heard from Cass for far too long just then.

So I thought about the Lady, and how odd it seemed that not everyone liked her—at least until they got to know her well. They'd start out suspicious anyway, thinking she sounded too good to be true. Then, at first meeting, she seemed so . . . well . . . so *British*. Stiff, maybe. But the Lady simply was the way she was, and it never seemed to occur to her to care very much anymore about what people thought of her.

As for me, I liked her—very much. I'd given up trying to explain the Lady without sounding sentimental, but to me she was like an eccentric, lovable aunt—often irritating, impossible to ignore. At any rate, she was right about things more often than it was comfortable to admit.

I programmed the timer to start my morning coffee, hoping

the Lady was right this time and that I'd be glad about trying to help Lammy in the long run.

The phone rang.

The caller identified herself as a trauma unit social worker, and wasn't far into her message before I canceled the timer and started the coffee brewing right away. The long run would have to take care of itself.

The short run had just taken a sharp turn down a very steep hill.

CHAPTER

5

THE TRAUMA CENTER CLOSEST to where it happened was about a half mile due south of Wrigley Field, and I knew it well. When I got close, there were police cars swarming all over the neighborhood, many of them unmarked—although perfectly obvious to anyone with a vested interest. Blue-and-white squads, strobe lights flashing, blocked off traffic at intersections. So I had to park on Belmont Avenue, just slightly intruding into a bus stop, and hoof it four bitterly cold blocks to the hospital. I made my way unmolested all the way to the main entrance, where a security guard blocked the way. Another guard stood just inside the plate glass doors, head down, talking into the radio attached to his collar.

The outside guard, young, probably Puerto Rican, raised a gloved hand. "You need a city star or hospital ID to get in. Sorry, sir."

"But a social worker called. My friend—"

"Can't help it, sir. There's too much going on right now."

Just then the other guard, a middle-aged, pleasant-faced man who would have looked like the neighborhood grocer if there still were such a creature, pushed through the door toward us. When he saw me his face lit up. "Hey, big guy!" he said. "Long time no see."

Sometimes the gods *do* smile on us.

I couldn't recall his name, and even if he knew mine he'd have called me "big guy," like he called every other male person in the universe, regardless of size.

"Long time," I said, "three years, anyway."

"But hey, you're lookin' great, big guy." He turned to his partner. "This here guy's an okay guy. He was a patient here. You shoulda seen him in the ER. Him on one stretcher, half his damn body parts on another."

"Not exactly," I said, but before I knew it he was escorting me down the corridor, bringing me up-to-date on his baseball card collection along the way.

In the emergency room, it turned out Lambert Fleming was already old news and the trauma team's attention had turned to a pair of shooting victims who'd arrived together within the last hour. That's what all the excitement was about. The victims were members of rival street gangs—one a Latino group, one a mixed bag. The army of cops had been mobilized to keep both victims' outraged and oh-so-courageous fellow gang-bangers from storming the hospital and shooting at each other inside, where it was warm.

The guard got Lammy's room number and steered me to the proper elevator. "A medical floor," he said, "not intensive care or anything."

I rode up and stopped at the nurses' station, thinking maybe it was too late for visitors and someone might challenge me. But the ward clerk found my name listed on Lammy's chart under "next of kin." She said he might be drowsy—from painkillers—but pointed me down the hall.

One of the two beds in the room was empty, and pictures flickered and flitted eerily across the screen of a soundless TV set high on the wall. The head of Lammy's bed was raised, propping him into a sitting position. Both his arms lay motionless on top of the thin white bedspread, the left one wrapped in bandages from above the elbow down to his hand, with just the fingertips sticking out, and held in a slightly bent position. His right arm, pudgy and hairless and pale—except for the bruises and scrapes and ragged cuts—stuck out below the short wide sleeve of a hospital gown. An IV line was taped to that arm.

I stood there silently a while and stared at him. They'd shaved off his eyebrows, and most of the hair from his skull. The facial and scalp lacerations were too many to count, with a few that had needed multiple stitching. The upper half of his face was already turning purple and yellow, the flesh puffed with fluid and the eyes like slits in the smooth swollen flesh of a terribly discolored lump of bread dough.

Finally, I cleared my throat and his head jerked as though he'd been dozing. He must have seen me through the slits, because he opened his mouth. But he closed it again, and if he said anything it was drowned out by the chorus of adolescent male voices that had risen up inside my head, uninvited, in a jeering, sing-song chant I'd replayed too many times over the years: *Dough-GIRL! Dough-GIRL! Dough-GIRL!*

Anger tightened up in my chest at whoever had done this, and along with it came apprehension, the urge to forget about the whole thing, to just turn around and go home. But there'd be no more comfort at the coach house now than there'd been the last time I ran away from Lammy's problems. So I just stood there and let the hard, hot desire to retaliate fight it out with the urge to walk away.

"I'm sorry." Lammy's voice had a far-off sound and took a while to break into my consciousness. "I mean I just went out to get—"

"For chrissake," I said, my own voice tight and harsh. "You should have expected something like this. Going outside alone, at night. What the hell were you thinking about?"

Nothing like blaming the victim.

"They're gonna keep me at least overnight," he said, ignoring my attack as though criticism and blame like that were just part of the everyday air he breathed. "I was unconscious for a while. I guess I lost a lotta blood." His words came as a dull monotone, and it was impossible to tell if he was looking at me or not. "But I'm okay," he added.

Not that I'd bothered to ask.

"Has your sister—"

"I told 'em I don't have any relatives. They kept asking for a name. Finally I gave 'em yours." He paused. "I'm sorry."

"Yeah. Well, I suppose I'm glad you did. I . . . I'm glad you're okay, too." My anger was dropping down from boil to simmer. "What happened? You were gonna stay inside. Keep the doors locked."

"There was hardly nothing to eat at home. So I was goin' to the White Hen for some milk and stuff and—"

"Why didn't you call me?"

"You didn't tell me I could. You said you'd be calling me. But then you didn't, and I thought—"

"Okay, okay. You're right. I forgot to call. But didn't you think someone might try to hurt you? I mean, after that dog and all?"

"Yeah. I was scared. About goin' outside. But I was hungry and . . ." His voice trailed off.

"And what?" I asked.

He took a breath. "And I decided you weren't gonna help me after all 'cause you didn't call and I was on my own and I hadda just go out whether I was scared or—"

"Jesus Christ."

"I'm sorry." His voice cracked like an adolescent's.

"Stop saying that. I'm not mad. Not at you, anyway." Moving closer, I picked up a glass of water from the bedside and held the bent straw to his lips. "Here. Have a drink. Then tell me what happened."

A HALF HOUR LATER I rode down the elevator with a dour-faced young Latino whose dark blue lab coat said "Transport" above the breast pocket and who was pushing an empty wheelchair. The car stopped once before ground level and when the doors slid open there were two beefy, hard-breathing Chicago cops standing there, with a short, thin man in handcuffs propped up between them. The prisoner wore a khaki-colored cloth over-coat that ended below his knees, a baseball cap turned back-ward, and lots of bright red blood all over his face. When the cops saw us one of them just shook his head in disgust and the other vaguely waved us on with a shotgun he was holding by its sawed-off barrels. The doors closed again, leaving the cops there with their gang-banger and the weapon they must have found hidden under his coat.

A sign on the elevator wall said "A Smile and a Cheerful Word Just Might Make Someone's Day!" So I smiled and gave it a try. "Never a dull moment around here, huh?"

He looked up at me. "Fuckin' gangs," he said, his sad expression deepening into a sour frown. "Ask me, they oughta just fuckin' let 'em inside the building, man. Evacuate everybody else and throw in some extra fuckin' ammo. Then they could lock the doors from outside and come back in a goddamn week. Haul the motherfuckers off, man, in fuckin' refrigerator trucks."

Sanitize the language just a bit, and he could have been quoting from any number of election campaign speeches I'd spent the previous autumn trying not to listen to.

I hustled back to my car, planning to drive straight home and call Renata Carroway for another little chat about "witness intimidation." When I got to Belmont, though, there was a blue-and-white squad car double-parked beside the Cavalier, and a cop was sticking a parking ticket on the windshield.

"Hey!" I called, breaking into a trot. "I'm moving it right now."

"Too late," the cop said, heading toward the squad car. "Shouldn't park in a bus stop. Shows a disregard for the common good."

"Yeah, I know. But what about the Cadillac?" I pointed to the shiny black Fleetwood that took up most of the rest of the bus stop. It looked freshly washed, not yet covered with sprayed salt, and its rear bumper was backed up snug against the front of the Cavalier. "Why not give that guy a ticket, too?"

28

The only response was the slam of the squad car door and the roar of its motor as it left the scene, emergency lights flashing. And as it did, a very large man climbed out of the front passenger seat of the Fleetwood, opened the rear door, and invited me to get into the backseat.

I did.

And so did the other very large man, who'd appeared from somewhere behind me and taken me firmly by the arm.

CHAPTER

6

"CASTRATING A DOG, *Gus*. That's what all this newspaper talk is about. Grabbing my client on the street and throwing him head-first through a window. That's what's bothering me, *Gus*."

The man on my right, the big one with the recently permed long golden hair and the brass knuckles, kept putting new bruises on my rib cage each time I disregarded his earlier admonition: "You should call Mr. Apprezziano by his last name, asshole."

But I figured if the man on my left, the one with the white wavy hair and the thousand-dollar alpaca coat and the long thin fingers, was going to call me Malachy—and mispronounce it as *Malachai,* at that—I'd call the skinny old fart by *his* first name, too.

They'd caught me off-guard, and when I'm embarrassed like that I tend to act even less prudently than usual. "So, *Gus,* lemme tell—"

"Wait, wait, wait, Mr. . . . uh . . . Foley. Let's all just calm down, and I'm sure we'll have a more profitable discussion." Gus Apprezziano had one of those affected, world-weary voices, as though he'd seen it all, and it was all so very tiresome. Maybe he really felt that way. Or maybe he just watched too many movies.

I waited, silently happy to be on a last-name basis.

People I trusted had told me that Gus had the moral sense of a crawling swamp creature, but was a man of his word—like it or not. He was upper management—not at the top, but still up there a ways—and along with a bunch of other Outfit types was taking a lot of high hard ones just then in a *Chicago Tribune* series called "Uncovering the New Untouchables." I was guessing he didn't like his name surfacing in the papers, especially when the reporters kept hinting that the Feds were closing in. That's why, at Melba's, I'd thought mentioning the newspapers would catch his ear.

And that's why there were three of us shoulder to shoulder in the backseat of his car, staring at the backs of two more heads in the front, and waiting to calm down and have a "more profitable discussion."

In fact, quite a long time passed, while no one said anything. A CTA bus rumbled up beside us. Three passengers, a heavy-set young woman and two small children, stepped off into a deep pool of salty slush ten feet from the curb because the bus stop was occupied—by us. When the bus roared away a squad car followed it, then turned the corner to the right. If the cops happened to notice five men in a black Fleetwood in the bus stop with its motor running, they certainly didn't let on.

Finally the game got too boring even for me. "Okay, Mr. Apprezziano. I'll go first." I'd already shown him I was dumb enough to disobey orders even at the risk of a punctured lung. I didn't have to prove that I was patient as well. "I have a client named Lambert Fleming."

"Yes," Apprezziano said, "the creep who attacked—"

"Hold it. First, it's doubtful that Fleming sexually assaulted that little girl. Second, even if he did, that doesn't give Stevie Boy the right to threaten to cut off his balls, or to throw him through a window."

"You might have doubts, Mr. Foley, but Steve Connolly is convinced that this Fleming person is the guilty one. And so am I. On the other hand, I have Steve's word that he had nothing to do with either of those incidents."

"Third," I continued, "Steve Connolly's word is worth about as

31

much to me as yours is. Which is to say I wouldn't bet the cost of a cold fart on it."

Just what that meant even I couldn't have explained, but it did earn me another love tap from Goldilocks, and a sad sigh from an increasingly gloomy Gus. The thing is, you have to keep these people's attention if you want them to remember you.

"Maybe, though," I added, once I'd regained my breath, "maybe that's because we haven't really gotten to know each other yet."

"Steve would not lie to me. He is well known in his community, a precinct captain. He has friends, neighbors, people he has helped. Little people, if you will, people who cannot tolerate the abuse of an innocent child by a cowardly pervert."

"*Little* people who want to score points with Steve Connolly because he's got one foot in City Hall and one on your side of the street. People who don't give a damn whether Lammy did it or not."

"Lammy? Ah, Lambert Fleming."

"Yeah, Lambert Fleming for chrissake. Did you forget him? That's what this is about, remember? It's about getting Steve Connolly to lay off him. The court'll decide whether he messed with that little girl, and what should be done about it if he did. That's why I'm sitting here talking to you, for God's sake."

"No. You're sitting here because I put you here." The world-weary tone had dropped away, and Apprezziano's voice was cold and harsh. "You made a threat today, a foolish threat. Connolly did not order, or even suggest, that anyone harm that animal you call your client."

"You have only Steve's word—"

"That's enough for me. What's enough for you is what I tell you now. I've made it known that I disapprove of these incidents with your client. Eventually he will be found guilty and sent to prison. I'm confident he'll receive punishment enough there, even for his unspeakable behavior."

"Oh? And what if he didn't do it? What if he's found not guilty?"

"That's absurd." He paused. "But I won't be responsible for anything that happens if he's cut loose. In the meantime, though, until the trial's over, no one will bother this animal. I promise that. I guarantee it."

Bingo! How foolish could my threat have been, after all.

Apprezziano must have seen the satisfied look on my face. "Don't bother to congratulate yourself, Malachai." He still didn't get it right. "You are entirely disposable. You know that."

As though on a prearranged signal, Goldilocks opened the car door and climbed out.

"We're all disposable, Gus," I said, not moving. "In the end we all slide down the same cold chute."

He stared straight ahead. "The difference," he said, "is that I have the power to choose the time for you to slide, and the place. But no matter, just believe what I said. No more threats or harm to your client. And in the meantime . . ." He hesitated, seemed to switch gears. "Now get out of the car, I'm through with you."

I got out of the car, digging into my pocket for my own car keys while Goldilocks took my place. He slammed the door without even a good-bye.

The Caddy's motor roared and its rear tires whined, spinning in the slush. Then it was gone, coating me from head to foot with a spray of cold, salt-gray water. And with all the noise, they probably didn't even hear the squealing scrape as I dug my key into the shiny black paint and held it there, letting the moving car draw its own long gash into its side.

Stepping off the curb, I waded to my own car and sat behind the wheel for a minute. I believed Gus Apprezziano when he said Lammy would be let alone. So why didn't I believe him when he said he was through with me?

CHAPTER

7

THE FOLLOWING MORNING I went to church.

The last time I'd been to church was over a year ago, when I'd sat through Mass twice in one day, a Sunday, in the heart of the city's west side ghetto. The priest that time, Kevin Cunningham, had two mothers and both of them had hired me, for different reasons. Dealing with his demons—both internal and external—grew into a full-time job for both of us. It was a job he hadn't given up on, either, the last I heard.

But this time was different. This was Our Lady of Ravenna, just a few blocks from Lammy's place, at seven o'clock on a Wednesday morning. Ten after seven, actually. I was late, but that was intentional. The sun wasn't up yet, and it was very cold. A wide expanse of concrete steps, swept clean of snow, led up from the sidewalk to three sets of double doors.

The bruised ribs from my encounter with Gus Apprezziano and his golden-haired lackey had been more than enough to keep me awake to worry about whether Gus had something else in store for me. Then, about two in the morning, not long after the pills had finally shut down the pain and I'd fallen asleep, a woman had called. She gave lots of instructions and one of them was that only the set of church doors on the left would be unlocked. I tried the others first. She'd been right.

Inside, a dimly lit vestibule ran almost the width of the church, and there were three more sets of double doors—tall, dark-stained oak doors that swung both in and out and had brass kickplates near the floor and windows with crosses etched into the glass about head-high.

I peered through the window of the left door of the center set. Row upon row of dark wooden pews marched precisely down either side of a wide center aisle, and there were narrower aisles along the side walls. The only brightly lighted area was up around the altar, about fifty yards away, where a white-robed priest stood off to the side of the altar at a reading stand. As I watched, he raised a large book high in the air in a ceremonial gesture, set it back on the stand, then turned and walked toward the altar.

Once he wasn't looking directly my way, I pushed open the door, the one I'd been told didn't squeak, and stepped silently inside. None of the dozen or so worshipers, all huddled up near the altar, turned to look.

Above my head was a twelve-foot-high ceiling that extended out only a few paces and kept the area just inside the doors in deep shadow. Beyond that, the ceiling arched up from the side walls to a center peak that must have been fifty feet high. Down the side aisle on my right, built into the wall just barely beyond the shadow of the lower ceiling, was what I was looking for— a small booth with two doorways, each one covered by a purple velvet drape.

The far-off priest, facing his little congregation across the altar, droned on in a voice barely audible despite the stillness of the huge church. He gave no sign that he saw me as I walked across to my right and stood against the wall in the shadows. I inhaled the ancient aromas of burning tapers, dust, and furniture polish—and suddenly thought of the vulgar jokes we used to make whenever the principal at Saint Robert's would speak of the "odor of sanctity." In a few minutes, all but one of the people in the pews stood and walked up toward the altar to take communion.

Now or never.

Stepping forward out of the shadows, I moved quickly along the wall to the booth, and ducked behind the heavy curtain of the first doorway. It was pitch-dark inside, but using my hands I found a built-in cushioned bench seat. I sat down, facing the curtain I'd just slipped through, and ordered my breath to slow down. I hoped the woman would know I was there.

I hoped even more that no one else saw me go inside that booth, because I was in no mood to hear anyone's actual confession.

Once my eyes adjusted to the dark, I opened the little sliding door next to my right ear and sat there waiting. When the Mass ended, I heard what must have been the heels of the priest clicking across the marble floor into the distance. A far-off door closed. I heard people walking down the center aisle, then heard them push through the doors on their way out of the church. Meanwhile, from up in front came the sound of several voices mumbling in unison. The rosary had begun, just as the woman on the phone had said it would.

I strained my ears, but that's all I heard.

Suddenly I felt a presence, very close by. Only a feeling, not a sound, and I decided it was my imagination. That's why I jumped so high at the sibilant whisper just inches from my right ear. "This is Rosa," she hissed, identifying herself as had been agreed.

"Malachy."

"I must be gone before the rosary is over. I must not be seen."

"Me too."

"I am trusting you." Her words were precise, her accent first-generation Italian. "You have sworn you will never speak of this conversation."

Actually, I hadn't sworn anything at all. "What is it?" I asked. "What do you have to say?"

"I wish to avoid a great injustice."

"What do you mean?"

"This boy, this Lambert. I know him for many years. And his

mother. They are . . . backward, perhaps. But this evil thing. I do not believe he did it."

"Then why did Trish—"

"My grandchild was afraid. They asked her so many questions. I was there, but I could do nothing. She did not mean to say what she said."

"She told you she was lying?"

"She will not speak to me of what happened. But I have taken care of this child almost from the day she was born. I know her. She wishes to tell the truth, but cannot. She is too afraid."

"Then it's you who'll have to come forward. Tell the judge."

"I will not." She paused, and I heard her soft breathing, scented with toothpaste and garlic. "Because I am afraid, too. Not for myself. I am old enough to be familiar with suffering, ready even to die. But I am afraid for Trish. My son-in-law, he loves her in his way, but—" She stopped. "Steven Connolly is . . . he is not a man prepared to be a father. With her mother gone to God already, the child needs me. If something happens to me I fear for her."

"Let me talk to Trish, then. I need to find out who it was."

"No."

"Jesus, Rosa, you—"

"This is a holy place." A new, harsh tone, threatening to rise above a whisper. "Do not take the sacred name in vain."

"Sorry."

"There is no need to ask Trish." Her voice dropped again. Barely audible. "I know who it was who attacked the child."

"You just said she won't talk to you about it. How do you know who did it?"

"I know it in my heart. Trish was fine when I left her at her Uncle Dominic's on my way to bingo. Later, when I found her at home, she was crying. Steven, my son-in-law, was to pick her up and bring her home. Trish said her cousin went to her room to talk on the phone and when her father was late she was bored and decided to walk home. But she would never do such a thing. She is very bright, and a good child. She would not have left her uncle's house without a reason."

"Are you telling me . . ."

"In my heart I know it was not this Lambert. It was . . . it must have been Dominic who did this. The child's uncle. The husband of my other daughter, Tina."

"You've got to tell Steve."

"Steven and Dominic have become close over the years. Even so, he would kill Dominic if he knew the truth. But if I even hint that it was not this Lambert, Steven becomes enraged. His mind is made up. He cannot accept something different. He is a man unable to look deeply into anything. He has filled his soul with hatred for that boy, and his mind will never change now, no matter what. This man, Steven, I warned my poor daughter not to marry him. He drank too much even then. He is a man of cruelty and violence, which gets worse as he gets older. He is Irish—not one of us—but he is so much like Dominic, it is as though they were brothers—brothers in evil."

"But if you won't speak out, why are you telling me all this?"

"I must protect my grandchild. But I do not wish to be responsible, before God, that something terrible happens to an innocent one. So, as I must protect Trish, you must protect this Lambert."

"But that means he has to beat the charge. You know that. If he goes to jail, they'll kill him in there, or worse."

"I understand. But even to win the case will not be enough. Steven is nearly insane with anger at this Lambert. I have learned that my brother Gustavo will prevent him from acting until—"

"Gustavo? Your brother? You mean—"

"Gustavo Apprezziano. He brings me shame, but he is my brother. He will hold Steven back until the court case is over. But then . . ."

"Then what?"

"Then, if this Lambert is not convicted, Steven Connolly will kill him—or worse, as you say."

"Jesus Christ, I—"

"Quiet!"

"Sorry, it's a holy—"

"No. Listen." She paused. "The rosary is almost over. I must go now or my friends will see me."

"Wait. There's something else I need to know." But she was gone.

A moment later, the praying from the front of the church had stopped. I could hear people moving down the center aisle, pushing through the doors. Footsteps were even coming down the side aisle. As soon as I was sure they were all gone, I'd—

The rustle of clothing—soft, but unmistakably coming through the grate beside my ear. Then harsh, labored breathing.

My own breath froze in my chest.

"Benedite mi, Padre." The voice of another woman, probably older than Rosa.

"Please, I . . ."

"Padre, parli Italiano?"

"Uh . . . *Si, si,"* I lied, hoping to keep her where she was.

"Ah, buono. Ho peccato, Padre."

I stood up, still not daring to breathe.

"Sono passati due mesi dalla mia ultima confes—"

I slipped silently through the curtain and out of Our Lady of Ravenna.

Driving away, I passed four women in black, headed home from Mass. Women walking carefully, avoiding the slippery spots, gesturing, shaking their heads. One of them may have been Rosa. There was no way to tell.

Too bad, because there was a question remaining, something I needed to know. Who had told Rosa who I was, and that I was helping Lammy? If I was guessing right, it was the woman who'd called during the night and set up my meeting with Rosa, a woman whose voice had a hard veneer of bitterness and cynicism that couldn't cover up its underlying soft southern drawl.

And, while I was at it, I'd guess that the woman—whoever she was—had a fondness for black leather boots and crossword puzzles.

CHAPTER

8

I DROVE AWAY FROM the neighborhood, learning yet again why I hate being out on the streets at that time of the morning. For one thing, whether you're headed into or out of the city, rush hour is there, both ways. Worse than that, though, I usually end up comparing myself with all those other drivers—people who have real jobs. Chastising myself, consoling myself, finally questioning my choices . . . again.

Who do you think you are, I ask, with no paycheck, no health benefits, no retirement plan?

True, I answer, but also no mortgage payments, no tuition bills, no—

Uh-huh, sure. And no family life, either. And no routine to keep you sane.

So I headed for Western Avenue, recalling the times I've had regular employment. There's a lot to be said for not having to think, every day, about what time to get up, when to leave home, where to go. At Western, I slowed when the light turned yellow, then gunned into a left turn just after it went red. Horns blared. The sun was barely up and people seemed mad as hell already, as though they couldn't wait to get to their real jobs and complain about the traffic.

One block north on Western, I threw a hard right and fishtailed on a patch of ice onto a residential street. It hadn't been plowed, but it was one-way and previous cars had dug ruts in the snow, which was now frozen firm. I pounded hard on the accelerator. The Cavalier's rear tires wanted to slither side to side, but couldn't because of the ruts, so they finally grabbed hold and sent me forward. One more block and another hard right. A few more blocks, a few more turns, another questionable lurch through an intersection, and pretty soon I was on Ashland Avenue, headed north again.

Yes, there's something comfortable about routine. But there's consolation, too, in knowing you can still shake off a car that's tailing you, without making it obvious you even know it's there. On the other hand, maybe those two goons in the dark blue Ford that wasn't behind me any more just weren't that good. Or maybe they weren't trying all that hard by the time I'd spotted them, which was a couple of blocks from the church. After all, I hadn't noticed any blue Ford when I left the coach house an hour and a half earlier.

And certainly the coach house must have been where they started to follow me. Because no one could have known I'd be at Our Lady of Ravenna for seven o'clock Mass. Could they?

I DON'T KNOW WHERE Dr. Sato lives, but at eight-thirty in the morning he was there at his dojo, smoking a cigarette in his glass-walled office in the corner, on the second floor over the cleaners on Central Street in Evanston. A few of his other students were there, too. After I bowed and stepped onto the mat that nearly covered the entire floor of the huge, bare room, I waited for Dr. Sato to stab out his cigarette and walk barefoot across the mat to me.

"Good morning, *sensei*," I said.

"Good morning, Malachy." Another one who never got the last syllable wrong.

After a ritual exchange of greetings, I told him about my bruised ribs, courtesy of Goldilocks and his brass knuckles.

I could swear Dr. Sato stifled a grin then, but maybe he was just trying to look sympathetic. He always smiled a lot, anyway. "Ah, well then," he said, "let me watch you stretch out."

I did the best I could, but it hurt like hell to move.

In a moment he said, "You are fine. No problem."

"Thank you, *sensei.*" No problem that he could feel.

"So," he said, "prepare yourself. Ten minutes for the mind. Ten minutes for the body. Then we will begin, and I and the others will take it easy with you."

The hour and a half session was the usual whirlwind of throws, rolling falls, kicks, and punches, with Dr. Sato demonstrating good technique on me when one of us didn't get things right. If anyone took it easy on anyone, it went undetected by me. When the time was up, he went back to his office and lit another cigarette, while we students swept the mat and then placed the old-fashioned straw brooms carefully in their stand.

Dr. Sato approached. If he was as tired as I was—and he sure should have been, since he had more than twenty years on me—he didn't look it. "And the pain, Malachy?" he asked.

"Still there," I said. "Worse than before."

"Good."

"Pain is good?"

"Everything is good."

Since this was turning into one of the longer verbal exchanges of our relationship, I decided to go ahead and ask him. *"Sensei,* why do you keep smoking those cigarettes?"

"You do not approve?"

"Well, it's just that . . ."

"My wife does not approve, either." His eyes turned sad. "Ah, well, I enjoy them, don't I." It wasn't a question, and he sounded sad, too. But then he smiled, and held out a small white paper bag. "Here. Japanese tea. Try this."

"Will it help ease the pain?"

"Maybe. Maybe not. But it is good, anyway."

I trotted down the stairs from the dojo, stunned. Not at his gift of the tea, which was loose in the bag and smelled awful. But amazed that Dr. Sato might feel sad. And he had a wife, too. Imagine that. Just like some ordinary human being. He probably slept, ate food. Maybe he even had children. Wouldn't that be something? Little Sato kids, throwing each other around the living room.

When I got to the Cavalier, there were no blue Fords in sight, and no black Cadillacs. I drove home and called Barney Green and asked him to get me a quick reading on a few license plates. Barney can do things like that.

Meanwhile, I fried up some lean bacon I'd brought home with me and ate it with two English muffins spread with the Lady's homemade strawberry jam, along with some of the Japanese tea. The tea actually tasted better than it smelled.

Barney called back. The Ford van at Melba's was registered to Steve Connolly; the Cadillac to someone in River Forest who sounded very much like he might be related to Gus Apprezziano. But there was no information available on the Ford sedan that was following me.

"No information?" I said. "What does that mean?"

"Maybe it's a computer screwup," he said.

"And maybe it's not."

"Right. Anyway, gotta go." Barney's always on the run. He makes a lot of money.

As soon as I hung up, the phone rang. I let the machine answer.

"Hey," the voice said, "it's Casey. Pick up the damn phone if you're there, will you?"

Casey's real name is Father Casimir Casielewiecz, or Caseliewicz or something. The only time I asked him he claimed even he'd given up trying to spell it right. He was still the pastor of Saint Ludella's, the church where I'd watched Kevin Cunningham say those two Masses awhile ago. Casey's claim that he couldn't spell his own name wasn't true, of course, but it was the sort of thing he liked to say.

I picked up. "Casey, how are ya?"

"Goin' nuts, as usual. But the parish is great. Had confirma-

44

tion last week. Seventeen eighth-graders and five adults. Great day. Had a guy playing trumpet in the choir loft. And the Cardinal himself was here. Surprised the hell outta me." Casey couldn't help himself. He loved to talk about Saint Ludella's, whether anyone was interested or not. "Then we got the church's seventy-fifth anniversary coming up in March. My idea was a pot-luck supper, but the people wanna make a big deal about it. Between you and me, it's not gonna be worth it. No point in a big anniversary party unless you can rake in some big bucks. Shoot, if we invite three thousand former parishioners we'll be lucky if fifty show up. The rest are either dead or afraid to come back into this neighbor—"

"Casey?"

"What? Oh, talking too much. But what the hell, that's 'cause I'm havin' a great time." He paused. "So, we still on for the game Saturday?"

"I'll do my best. I'm working on something, but Jason's playing, so I don't want to miss this one."

"Working on something? You mean you actually got a paying client?"

"Well . . . a client, anyway."

"Damn, you're as bad as I am. Anyway, if you can't make it, could you leave my ticket at the gate? I'm supposed to be on vacation and—" He stopped, and somehow I knew an idea had just flown into his mind. "Say, maybe I could give you a hand," he said, "with whatever you're doing."

"Uh-uh. I don't think so. Last time I dragged you along you were lucky to survive."

"You didn't drag me, and what happened wasn't your fault. If I hadn't been so overweight I coulda run faster. Hell, I lost fifty pounds in the hospital, anyway, which I'd have never done on a diet. Besides," his voice took on a more serious tone, "I, uh, got a kind of a problem of my own."

"Problem?"

"Yeah. Like I said, instead of the other bishop that was scheduled, the damn Cardinal himself showed up for our confirmation last week. 'A pastoral visit,' he called it. Nice guy, y'know, but he's kinda mad that I haven't taken any time off. Claims that was the deal when they let me come back here after I got hurt and all. Says I oughta go to Florida or some damn place. Jesus, Florida. Anyway, he said if I don't get out of here for two weeks he's gonna move me to another parish. Some place 'less stressful,' he said. I told him forget that stress crap and just let me be happy, right here on the job, for chrissake."

That's the way Casey would have said it, too, to a cardinal or anybody. He never sounded like my idea of how a priest should talk—however that was.

"Just go stay with one of your sisters for a couple weeks, Casey."

"Are you kidding? They'll drive me nuts. I mean, they're nice, but they always make a big fuss over me. Besides, they're too . . . pious, or something."

We argued a while. He wasn't kidding. He really needed something to do. And, in fact, I thought of something that would get him away from Saint Ludella's for awhile. And there wouldn't be any danger. Not that he cared. His parish included some of the scariest public housing projects in the Western Hemisphere, and he wandered around them night or day. The only time he ever got shot at was sixty miles out in the country, when he was safely with me.

We arranged to meet at two o'clock, at a restaurant a few blocks from Lammy's apartment. Casey said he had to take the el because his car wasn't running right. The car was a brown Dodge Aries, about four years old, and it would have worked just fine if he'd ever remember to change the oil or get an occasional tune-up.

Meanwhile, I showered and shaved and washed the dishes, then took the garbage down the back steps and left the bag by the door, but inside, because pickup wasn't until Friday. There was still plenty of time, so I went back upstairs and took apart both my phones. I backtracked the wiring all the way down to the box in the garage, even looked at the lines outside.

The fact that I found nothing wasn't entirely satisfying. Someone could have been bugging the place by satellite, for all I knew. But the hell with them. I took a mug of Dr. Sato's tea to the battered old Steinway upright in the room beyond my bedroom and banged away for almost an hour. If there were any listeners, they got a real good dose of the turnaround from "Angel Eyes," the same eight bars about a hundred times.

Finally, I took my mail with me and sorted it while I drove to meet Casey. There wasn't much to sort. The few throwaways I threw away, into a box in the backseat. What was left was a fat envelope from Renata Carroway. Copies of the police reports from Lammy's arrest. There were maybe ten pages, some handwritten, some typed, plus another packet of typed transcripts of statements taken from Trish. I couldn't read it all and drive, too, so they'd have to wait.

Lammy's street had been plowed, and the alley, too. It was, after all, the precinct captain's block. But I knew there'd be no place to park, which there wasn't, and which was why I was meeting Casey at a restaurant with a parking lot.

We left the Cavalier there and walked. I had Lammy's keys and we went down the alley and into the backyard. Casey's only luggage was a duffle bag the size of Rhode Island, but it looked small with him carrying it. He's taller, broader, and a whole lot meaner-looking than I am, even though his disposition is five times more pleasant. He may have the vocabulary of a sailor's parrot, but he's seldom sarcastic and never insulting.

At the bottom of the enclosed back stairs, he set the lumpy bag down, obviously meaning to switch hands before climbing the stairs.

"It shouldn't be more than a week," I said. "What have you got in there?"

"See if you can guess. Pick it up."

So I did.

But not for long. "Bricks," I said, dropping the bag back onto the concrete. "I told you we've been guaranteed no trouble, at least till after the trial. You won't have to wall yourselves in."

He laughed. "Not bricks." He lifted the duffle bag again and followed me up the stairs. "Books. I'm way behind in my reading. Plus some clothes, a one-ounce bottle of wine and my chalice in case I wanna say Mass, a few boxes of fig bars, and a couple of six-packs of Pepsi."

"All the basics."

We let ourselves in the back door. The apartment had a kitchen, a living room, one bathroom, and three small bedrooms. One bedroom was obviously Lammy's, one his mother's, and the third was made into a TV room. Even in a second-floor walkup, no one ever lives in the living room.

Casey tossed his duffle bag onto the sofa in the TV room. Maybe it was a test, because when the sofa didn't collapse he announced, "This is my campsite," and moved the bag to the floor.

Out in the kitchen, we popped open two Pepsis and sat at a white wooden table.

"So," I said, "they're discharging Lammy tomorrow. I'll pick him up and bring him here. Like I said, I got a guarantee I'm sure is genuine. No trouble. You guys can go to the store, whatever. But don't let him out of your sight. One hint of anything, one nasty phone call, you call me and you're both outta here."

"Fine. But didn't you say Lammy has a job?"

"I'm on my way there. See if I can get them to give him sick days or a vacation or something. No way he could work, even if he wasn't all beat up." I drained my Pepsi and stood up. "You don't mind? Helping out an accused child molester? I mean, I don't think he did it, but—"

He held up his hand and I stopped talking. "Look at me, Mal." I did. His voice had a serious, almost angry tone. "You're looking at a bona fide, goddamn drunk. Sober as the Pope, these days. Trying to be a good priest, too. But a goddamn alcoholic all the same. And I could turn back into the same disgusting, stinking lout I was any day of the week. All I gotta do is fall one time." He crushed the can in his hand. It wasn't empty and Pepsi spurted all over the table. "Sure. I hope this guy didn't do it. On the other hand, whether he did it or not I'm gonna do what I can to see he gets a fair shake. Not 'cause I think he's innocent or not. I mean, who *is* innocent, for chrissake? But 'cause he's a goddamn human being." All of a sudden he stopped, looked embarrassed, then grinned. "And that, dear congregation, is the end of today's sermon."

The refrigerator was pretty bare and Casey said he'd make a list and then go to the grocery store. "Maybe I'll fix my famous meat loaf for supper tonight," he said.

I went downstairs and walked back to the restaurant. It was snowing by the time I drove out of the parking lot and headed for the City-North Canine Shelter. I drove carefully, partly because the streets were slick and partly because I had no interest in shaking off the blue Ford for the second time in one day.

It had been there since I left the coach house for my meeting with Casey. Of course I had Gus Apprezziano's word. But that guaranteed Lammy's safety, not mine. Besides, who said the two men in the Ford were friends of Gus?

CHAPTER

9

THE MANAGER WASN'T THERE, but three employees of the City-North Canine Shelter all claimed they used to like Lammy. He'd been a maintenance worker there for years and none of them knew anything about his family, whether he had friends, or what else he did with his life. He was "real quiet" and "kinda backward," but "not stupid." He was especially smart about dogs, "like he has a gift for it." In fact, it seemed as though he liked dogs more than people, and—even if it wasn't part of his job—he could always calm them down when they barked or even growled at visiting children when they screeched and squealed too much and made the dogs nervous and aggressive.

Lammy was polite, did his work, and hardly ever talked to anyone. Yes, they used to like Lammy, sort of. But not any longer.

They'd hardly believed it when they saw it in the papers and on TV. But then the investigators from the state's attorney's office arrived, and they were shocked to find out it was all true. This guy who flushed the crap out of the dogs' cages and mopped the floors was in fact a pervert, a sexual deviate who preyed on little girls. They'd been urged to search their memories for times when he'd acted strange, "you know, like connected with sex." They hadn't come up with anything, except that time when this little runt of a terrier that had supposedly been neutered kept trying to hump all the female dogs, no matter how big they were, and Lammy had thought that was funny. Of course, everyone else thought so, too. But . . .

At first no one recalled ever seeing Lammy touch any child.

But when the investigators kept pressing, someone thought of the time this little black girl had come to pick up her dog that had run away and it turned out not to be her dog at all. She cried and cried and Lammy was there and she grabbed at him and he hugged her, and he seemed to have "a kind of a weird look on his face."

They figured they should have suspected something, but their surprise soon turned to anger. In fact, they were infuriated. How could someone they knew do such a terrible thing?

"Maybe," I suggested, "he didn't do it after all."

"Yeah, sure," one of them said, and all three suddenly stared at me as though I were from an alien galaxy. "And maybe the police just arrested him 'cause it was a slow day, huh?"

"And why'd the prosecutor charge him if there wasn't evidence?" another said. "Where there's smoke there's fire."

"You gotta be a little sick yourself, you think a little girl's gonna lie about something like that."

Three decent people. Not mean, or evil. Their working days were spent sheltering strays. And they all agreed. They sure didn't want creeps like Lammy working around them, by God.

And they didn't care much for me, either, if I thought vicious animals didn't belong in cages. Besides, the state's attorney's people said they didn't have to talk to Lammy's lawyer, or anyone working for his lawyer, if they didn't want to.

"I understand that," I said. "And thanks for your time." I'd overstayed my welcome. A habit of mine.

"It's those darn lawyers, you know. They're the problem. And people like you, who work for lawyers. You'll all do anything for money."

"And don't forget the judges, too, who just keep letting these sickos back out on the streets, no matter what they do. Victims got rights, too, you know?"

I decided not to wait around and ask the manager to give Lammy a paid leave of absence.

No state's attorney's investigators had shown up at the branch library in Lammy's neighborhood, according to the kindly, silver-haired woman I spoke to. But if they had, they'd have learned that Lammy was a painfully shy patron who came in once every few weeks. Sometimes he'd browse for a while among the shelves at the small facility.

"But he never *loitered*," she said, frowning at the mere mention of the word, as though loitering were an especially vexing problem. "Most often, he just comes straight to the desk and asks us to order books from downtown for him."

"What sort of books does he read?" I asked, and immediately, nearly as visible as if it were made of concrete blocks and not of librarians' ethics, a wall rose up between us.

"I'm afraid, sir, we don't keep records of what our patrons read."

"Yes, but if he so frequently asks you to order books, you must remember—"

"If I did remember, I surely wouldn't tell you. The library is here to serve its patrons. We respect people's rights to read whatever they choose. It's not our business to care what patrons read, nor to keep track of it, nor to inform others about it."

"I couldn't agree more," I said. "It's right there in Article Three of the American Library Association Code of Ethics." That seemed to make a favorable impression, and I was glad I'd looked it up. "So, anything else? Was he ever any problem at all? Like, I don't know, staring at people, bothering kids, anything like that?"

"Nothing. Not one hint of anything." Her manner eased a bit. "I wish I could be of more help, but . . ."

"Thanks for your time." I turned to go, then turned back. "As a matter of principle, you know, I'm happy you won't tell me what library patrons read. On the other hand, though, I don't think Lambert Fleming did this awful thing he's charged with."

52

Her face softened even more. "But he told me what he likes to read, and I really need to verify things he's told me, so I can know that he's being truthful, that I'm not kidding myself."

"I understand," she said, "but—" Just then the door burst open and a gaggle of chattering eight-year-olds burst in. "Oh, the Cub Scouts are here. I really have to go . . ." She closed her eyes momentarily, as though thinking, then reached down and, from somewhere below the counter, brought out two large books. She set them on the counter, then abruptly turned and marched off toward the noisy newcomers.

I thought of all the ingenious lies I've told to get information from people who've refused it, rightly or wrongly. This time I'd told the flat-out truth, and still got exactly what I was looking for. Was this an effective new technique, or just a fluke?

Anyway, stuck under a thick rubber band that held the two books together, there was a yellow slip of paper. The handwriting on the paper said "Hold: Fleming, L." I twisted my head to read the titles on the book spines: *Twenty Centuries of Armed Conflict* and *The Seven Greatest Battles of WWII*.

Near the door, the librarian was bent over, struggling to get a snow-drenched hooded coat removed from a hyperactive little boy who was grabbing at a book in another boy's clutches, a book with Michael Jordan flying across the cover. "Patience, Corey," she said, laughing. "This is a library. There are lots of other sports books."

"So that's what he's interested in?" I asked.

"Oh!" I'd startled her and she stood upright suddenly, which left her holding a miniature parka in her hands, as its former occupant shot across the room toward a display of sports magazines. She smiled at the little boy, and then at me. "Yes. Very limited interests. But," she added, "he's a good boy. I'd bet on that."

We both knew she wasn't talking about little Corey.

We exchanged good-byes and I started for the door, thinking

maybe I should call it a day and go sample some of Casey's meat loaf. But there was one thing irritating me.

So far that day I'd been to church, to Dr. Sato's, and back home to the coach house. From there it was on to the restaurant to meet Casey, then to Lammy's place, to the animal shelter, and finally to the library. And, with the exception of Dr. Sato's dojo, I'd had a tail everywhere I went. It was getting dark outside, and snowing again, and the two men in the blue Ford were getting on my nerves.

Ah, well, maybe it was time I got on theirs.

CHAPTER

10

THERE HAD TO BE a rear exit from the library, and I found it.

Given the lousy weather, it was likely my baby-sitters wouldn't be sitting more than about a block behind the Cavalier, facing the same direction—east. I went into the alley behind the library and headed west. A block and a half later, I left the alley and turned right, then right again at the liquor store on the corner, and came out half a block behind the Ford.

I used a pay phone inside the liquor store.

"Body shop," the man answered.

"Put Caesar on. Tell him it's Mal Foley and it's an emergency."

Caesar Scallopino's an ex-client who'd been finishing up the MBA program at Northwestern's Kellogg School of Management, and getting recruited like crazy, when his dad died at the age of fifty and left a business with eight employees. His mom thought Caesar should take it over for a while so all those people wouldn't be suddenly out of work. That was fifteen years ago. These days, Caesar invents industry-specific financial management software for small businesses, still runs the family body shop near Western and Touhy, and manages to be one of the happiest human beings on the planet.

Plus, he hardly ever asks me why I do the goofy things I do.

So . . . Caesar would call a nearby towing service and a truck would be along to pick up the Cavalier within ten minutes and tow it to his body shop. Meanwhile, I kept my face turned away from the clerk in the liquor store, and kept my eyes on the street outside. When the tow truck went by I made sure it was stopping at the Cavalier. Then I punched out 911 on the phone and cranked up my Tennessee twang, to tell how two thugs had just jumped out of their car and kidnapped an elderly man.

"A Ford it was. Or maybe a Merc'ry? Anyway, a big ol' blue four-door sumbitch, with a 'X' and a 'A' in the plate number. Them boys just grabbed him. Fancy dressed, he was. Kinda rich lookin'. Happened so fast ain't nobody seen it but me, I guess. Shut that ol' boy up in the trunk and climbed back in the front seat. Still sittin' there, big as life. Like they's Mafia or somethin'."

"Just wait there, sir, and—"

"Shoot no. Like to scairt me t'death. I'm gittin' my tail outta here."

But not too far out. I caught a cab headed west and then had the driver wait just down the street until the cops came along. By that time, one of the men from the Ford had gone to see about the Cavalier being towed and whether I was still in the library. He came back and the Ford was just nosing out from the curb when the squad car cut it off.

That's when I left the scene. Because it wouldn't take the men in the Ford forty-five seconds to prove there'd been a mistake, and the cops would start looking around for the guy that called in the false alarm. They'd find out what phone the call was made from, and somebody might guess who made it, too.

I just hoped they weren't able to prove it with a voiceprint or something. Technology threatens to take all the fun out of life.

LAMMY POKED A SPOON at a bowl of orange Jell-O, he was struggling to hold still with his bandaged left hand. Increasingly gaudy shades of yellow and purple were developing around his eyes. He was up in a chair by his hospital bed, and may have been more alert than the night before, but with Lammy it was hard to tell.

"They're discharging you tomorrow, and I'll pick you up," I said. "Don't leave with anyone else, unless I call and say I'm sending someone. Don't even talk to anyone on the phone unless you're sure you recognize their voice."

"My sister called," he said, still not looking at me. "She read about me in the paper. I told her not to tell my ma. She won't."

"She say she's coming to see you?"

"Uh-uh. She just said she's mad I'm causing all this trouble."

"Jesus. I thought *my* family was bad."

"Huh?"

"I mean, you—" But why try to explain? Most of us get only one family. So what else do we know? "Anyway, did you hear what I said about picking you up?"

"Yeah. Sorry I'm so much trouble."

"I told you last night to stop saying you're sorry."

"Okay, I'm sor— Oops." He lowered his head, but not quite quickly enough.

I stared at him. "Hey! Lammy!"

"What?"

"You started to grin, didn't you?" He shook his head, but I knew better. "Oh yes you did, you sonov—" I stopped because he'd have thought I was angry.

But I wasn't. The poor lonely guy had caught himself saying something funny, and he'd actually let his guard down far enough so that he smiled—or started to, anyway—right out in front of someone, whether he wanted to admit it or not.

Maybe I was smiling, too, as I rode back to Evanston on the el. That could explain why nobody bothered me. Maybe I was smiling and the muggers and panhandlers all thought I was crazy.

It had stopped snowing, and I walked home from the el station by what I call the "back way," down some alleys and through some yards, going in by my rear door so someone watching the gated entrance to the Lady's drive wouldn't see me arrive home. Inside, on the floor at the bottom of my back steps, was a fat envelope with a note in the Lady's handwriting saying someone left the envelope with her and she'd used her key to put it inside.

In the envelope were the police reports I hadn't read yet and had forgotten I left in the Cavalier, along with a note from Caesar Scallopino telling me he'd have to do some actual work on the car because someone might contact him to see why he'd towed it. God knows, there were plenty of dents and rust spots he could deal with. Climbing the stairs, I realized my rib cage was aching again, so I made some more of Dr. Sato's tea and took some aspirins before I settled in to read the police reports.

The first thing that caught my attention was the catalogue of "evidence" taken from Lammy's apartment. What had sounded in the media like a substantial cache of pornographic materials turned out to be a couple of *Playboy*s and a *Hustler*. Not on everyone's list of recommended reading, certainly, but not reliable indicia of a maniacal rapist, either.

The report said that Steve Connolly called the police because he'd found Trish in Rosa's arms, crying uncontrollably, when he got home. Rosa told the officers she hadn't been feeling well, and came home early from church bingo. She was surprised to find Trish at home without Steve being there, because the child was to wait at her cousin's for Steve to pick her up. Trish started to cry and Rosa saw bruises around her mouth and cheeks, but Trish wouldn't tell her what happened. Ten or fifteen minutes later, when Steve came in, Trish still wouldn't say anything except that someone had tried to hurt her.

Most interesting, though, were the reports of the interviews of Trish Connolly. If various things she said weren't flat-out inconsistent, that was because—or so it seemed to me, at least—her interrogators took pains to avoid that.

She was only a child, of course, and traumatized, and one would expect she'd have had some difficulty expressing what happened. But all she told the beat officers who arrived first was that someone hit her and pushed her down and did "bad things," and she didn't know who it was or where it happened. Then she just cried and wouldn't say anything else.

It was an hour later, to a female police officer at the district station with a court reporter present, that Trish said she was at her cousin's and her father was late so she walked home through the alley. Someone grabbed her from behind, she said, and he dragged her somewhere. He pulled her pants down, she said, but she couldn't see who he was, because it was dark. When asked why she kept saying "he" if she couldn't see him, at first she didn't know. Later she said "it seemed like a man," and still later said she could see enough to know it was a man. She said the man pushed her down on the floor, but when asked what floor she said she didn't mean "floor," but "ground." Why weren't her clothes and hair all soaked from slush and snow when she got home? She didn't know. Did he pull her inside someplace, like a garage? "No, nothing happened in the garage." Where, then? She just didn't know, but nothing happened in the garage. All told, she repeated that same phrase, "nothing happened in the garage," three times, before finally saying she hadn't been in any garage.

They terminated the court-reported statement, and took her back to the alley, starting from her house and retracing her steps back to her cousin's, looking for where it happened. The first backyard without a garage was Lammy's. "Maybe that's the place," she'd said, when they pointed out the enclosed porches. While they were there, Lammy came outside and stood there, watching. Was that the man? She didn't know, but it might have been him. Lammy had his coat on and Trish said yes, the man had a coat on, and it could have been a coat like that one.

At that point Lammy became the only suspect the cops were interested in.

Trish was taken to the hospital and examined in the emergency room, and later interviewed again, this third time by a female state's attorney, again with a court reporter present. She was asked what she meant when she said the man did "bad things." She said she meant he hit her. The state's attorney reminded her that earlier she said the man hit her and pulled down her pants and did bad things. That's when Trish said that he opened up his pants and "took out his thing." His penis? "Yes," she said. The man pushed her down, then, and she couldn't remember anything else.

According to the reports, when the officers tried to talk to Lammy in his backyard he turned and ran into the house. Since Trish had "identified the suspect" and he was "fleeing," they chased him into the house. The "sexually explicit photographs and reading materials" were in plain sight when they followed him into his bedroom and they confiscated them. They took him to the station and read him his rights and he said he'd answer their questions. He said he was home in his room all evening and denied seeing Trish or talking to her, or even going outside until he went into the kitchen and saw the police and went outside to see what was going on. He repeated that story several times, until finally he talked to a public defender. After that, he refused to answer any more questions.

Lammy's mother told the police she'd gone to bed after supper and had fallen asleep. They had awakened her when they came in the apartment after Lammy. When they told her why they were there she started to scream and cry and that was the end of that interview.

There were more pages to go through, but I stopped and called Renata Carroway.

"You know," she said, "I have an office. You could call me during the day."

"Thank you. I'm reading the police reports. What the hell's this business of taking court-reported statements from the victim?"

"Hard to believe, isn't it? It's someone's idea of an experiment in sex cases with kids. The idea is that they may be more open right away, and get scared and clam up later. There's a statute that lets the state use the statement without the usual hearsay problems."

"Jesus, the prosecution's far better off with a police report that's as vague and general as possible, not tying themselves into a set of specific facts."

"Sure. That's why the state's gonna drop this experiment in a hurry."

"Certainly helps Lammy in this case. In fact, in my opinion, the greenest first-year public defender in Cook County couldn't lose this one."

"Easy for you to say. Did you ever defend a sex abuse case?"

"Once. But the circumstances were far different."

"With a little girl victim to try to cross-examine?"

"I told you—"

"And a defendant that the whole neighborhood thinks is a 'loner' and a 'weirdo'? A defendant who has opportunity, motive, and no alibi?"

"Motive?"

"Gratification, ladies and gentlemen of the jury. Picture this defendant, sitting alone in his room, paging through his pornographic magazines, working himself into a sexual frenzy. He stands up, prowls around the darkened apartment, ever more excited, ever more frustrated."

"Come on, Renata."

"He peers out through his steamy windows into the darkness. Slips into his coat. The coat, by the way, that poor little Trish later identifies. He creeps out the door, the back door. Is he hoping to cool his rising passions? Or is he seeking a victim? But wait . . . there she is! Helpless. Innocent. Available. She could have been anyone's little girl, ladies and gentlemen." Renata finally stopped. "Anyway, Mal," speaking matter-of-factly now, "that's how it'll sound. These cases aren't always won or lost simply on the facts."

"Even if you get as far as a trial, I wouldn't think you'd demand a jury."

"No. Although the judge we drew isn't as strong as I'd like. And he'll be reading the newspapers." She paused. "But I've won a helluva lot tougher cases in my time. And I'm going to win this one. State's attorney Cletus Heffernan won't know what hit him, the creep." Her voice rose. "Lots of emotion and sympathy, ladies and gentlemen, but where's the evid—"

I stopped her before she could get any further into her own closing argument, and told her about some of my interviews that day, and how Casey would be staying at Lammy's place with him. I didn't tell her about Gus Apprezziano's promise, or Rosa's belief that the attacker was Trish's uncle. Nor did I tell her I didn't know who else, if anyone, might be on the line with us as we spoke.

When we hung up, I was still confident of a "not guilty."

The problem, though, wasn't just winning Lammy's case in the courtroom. The problem was hoping the case would go on long enough to give me a chance to prove who it was that had really attacked Trish Connolly. The principal person I had to prove it to was Steve Connolly, who Rosa said would never change his mind, and that had to be done before the judge said "not guilty" and Gus's guarantee expired. I had to prove it to Steve Connolly, in other words, before Steve killed Lammy—or worse.

I drank another cup of Dr. Sato's tea and fell asleep trying to think of a plan.

CHAPTER

11

BASKETBALL WAS ALWAYS MY game, but for a few foolish months I played college football. They had me returning kickoffs, and although the playbook listed seven different plays, the coach routinely ignored them all. His strategy was to keep it simple: "First thing is, you gotta catch the goddamn ball. After that, you fake right, fake left, then charge straight up the middle and hope something breaks."

Needless to say, one cold Saturday afternoon in late November, something broke.

I never played football again, but I still found myself turning to that strategy whenever the ball fell into my hands and nothing better turned up. Like now. I'd awakened without the slightest hint of a bright idea, then spent the morning practicing the piano, working out, and talking on the telephone.

At two o'clock I was to pick up Lammy at the hospital and take him to his place, where Casey was waiting. For what to do until then, no really creative strategy arose. So I picked up a rental car, faked right and faked left all over the north side until I knew no one was tailing me, then turned around and headed straight up the middle.

It was a dismally gray Thursday afternoon, temperature in the low twenties, and I was on the sidewalk leading to Dominic Fontana's front door. He lived about a block and a half from Steve, with Lammy's place in between. The police report said Dominic was unemployed and "on disability." I'd asked around and learned he was a few years older than Steve and, if he looked younger, it was because he was a workout junkie and obsessed with his appearance.

He had a wife named Tina, Rosa's other daughter, who was a hostess at The Captain's Choice, a seafood restaurant on Sheridan Road near Loyola University, and a daughter named Lisa, in junior high. They'd had to do without Dominic, though, for fifteen months, while he did time at the federal prison in Oxford, Wisconsin. He'd pled guilty to a pretty minor gambling charge, but got hard time anyway when the government informed the judge Dominic had "failed to cooperate" and even "obstructed justice," which probably meant he wouldn't flip on somebody—somebody like Gus Apprezziano, maybe.

When he'd been released a few months ago, Dominic moved back home, which was a little surprising because his wife had filed for divorce while he was gone. On my way, I stopped and called The Captain's Choice. Tina was on the job, and I hung up before she made it to the phone. So, with the daughter almost certainly at school, Dominic might be home alone. Of course, even if he was, why he'd open the door and let me in, and exactly what I'd say if he did, I couldn't imagine.

The house was a brick bungalow similar to Steve's. It had a room with leaded glass windows that jutted out in the front and, to the right of that, the concrete stoop had wrought iron railings painted white with brown rust stains bleeding through. One railing was loose and leaning to the side. The snow was a foot deep on the steps.

The plastic doorbell button on the door frame was missing one of its screws. I pushed it, though, and heard the far-off sound of a two-tone door chime. Otherwise, nothing. A cheap aluminum screen door hung slightly ajar and behind that was a very solid-looking front door, closed and windowless. I pushed the button a second time. Again, no response but the distant door chime—unless you counted a slight disturbance of curtains behind one of the leaded glass windows to my left. I waited, then pushed the button again.

Third time's a charm, they say, and they may be right.

It was a man who opened the door, and I recognized him as one of Steve Connolly's companions at Melba's. If he was disabled, it sure didn't look like a physical problem. He was about my height and had on a pair of those bikini-type briefs that apparently appeal to some people, but must be inconvenient when you're taking a leak in a public washroom. Besides the underwear, he wore a deep bronze tan on his muscular body, and—unless that long wavy hair was a toupee—nothing else removable. He could have been a black-haired Conan the Barbarian.

"What are you doing here?" He had a tenor voice that was tight and strained, like a man haunted by a host of evil spirits.

Past his shoulder I could see part of the living room and, beyond that, a dining area with table and chairs. Heat poured out through the screen door toward me. "You know," I said, "you oughta have a storm door put on here. Save a lot on heat."

An ordinary person would have shut the door in my face. He just stood there. Which certainly meant something or other.

"My name is Foley, and—"

"Who is it, Dominic?" It was a woman's voice, calling from somewhere behind him.

He turned his head a little to the side and called back, "Shut up, will ya? It's nobody." Then, to me, "I already know who you are. What I said was what do you want?"

In fact, that hadn't been his original question. But this was an easier one, so I answered it. "I want to come inside and talk."

He didn't move. "Why would I wanna talk to you?"

"Maybe because I'm a great conversationalist," I said, trying to appear focused on him, and not on the long-legged woman in dark tights and a man's shirt who had moved into view back by the dining-room table, looked out at me, and then disappeared again. "Or maybe because I know your secret."

"My secret?"

"Afraid so," I said. "The one you can't afford to have anyone else know."

Dominic stood there, his dark eyes void of expression. Maybe he was thinking. Finally he pushed open the screen door. "C'mon in, then, and tell me the secret," he said, and something about his voice told me that wouldn't be a wise thing to do.

But wisdom's never been my strongest suit. I stepped inside and let the screen door fall closed against my back. It must have been ninety degrees in the house.

"Maybe you should come in farther and close the front door, huh?" Dominic said. "Cold air's coming in." As he spoke, his right hand was moving toward a little table that sat just to the side of the front door.

I grabbed the edge of the open door to my right. "And maybe you should put some clothes on." I paused, then added, "And get rid of the weaponry."

"This?" he asked. He raised the barrel of the nickel-plated revolver he'd pulled from the drawer in the table, until it was pointed at my belly. "If I get rid of this, what'll I use if I wanna blow you away after I hear your big fucking secret?"

I really couldn't think of an answer to that.

"I mean, you pushed your way in here," he went on, "and you might even be armed." He had that part right, anyway.

I moved my hand from the edge of the door to the doorknob, and pulled it toward me a little.

"Forget closing the goddamn door, stupid," he said. "Get in here and tell me your fucking secret." He jerked the gun up toward my face and, whether the flame in his eyes was chemically fanned or came from a more permanent madness, I could see he was wacko enough to shoot me.

"I suppose I better go," I finally managed to say.

"Sorry, asshole." He stepped toward me, the gun almost brushing my face. "You shouldn't have started this if—"

Glass shattered somewhere behind him. "Help! Oh my God! Help!" A woman was screaming hysterically. "Help me!" She burst into the room. "My milk glass. A goddamn roach in my—"

Dominic twisted his head and leaned back just slightly, and when he did I stepped backward into the screen door and yanked the heavy front door toward me—hard and fast. The sharp edge of the door slammed into Dominic's right arm. He tried to jerk it back out of the way, but didn't quite make it and his thick muscular wrist was pinned between the door and the door frame. I thought for sure he'd drop the revolver then, but he didn't. His hand was twisted in such a way that the barrel of the gun pointed up and to my right. He was struggling to swivel it around toward me, but so far he couldn't do it.

With both hands on the knob, I held the door closed against his wrist. Blood started oozing from where the edge of the door was breaking through the brown flesh of his wrist. Still, he wouldn't let go of the revolver. I pulled even harder.

"Jesus, Dominic," I yelled, "just drop the goddamn gun and I'll let go."

He didn't say anything, but the woman inside was hollering again. "Kill him, Dominic!" she screamed. "Blow his fucking brains out!"

Dominic, though, wasn't wasting any energy on speech. He'd grabbed the edge of the door with his left hand and was trying to pull it open, while I strained to hold it closed against his right wrist. It was a standoff. He couldn't open the door. I couldn't close it. And if I eased up even a little—and his hand still worked—he'd shoot me.

Meanwhile, the woman kept screaming. "Shoot the sonovabitch! Kill him!"

The instinct to survive was driving me, but he was too powerful a man, with pain and rage adding to his strength. On top of that, maybe he felt I'd shamed him in front of the woman. Anyway, it soon became clear that Dominic was about to prevail in this tug of war. I couldn't hold on much longer.

So I took a breath, then slammed my body forward into the door. It flew inward a few inches and collided with something solid, like bone, but whether it was his forehead or his chin, or what, I didn't wait to find out.

I didn't wait to listen to his curses, either, or to hear whether the woman would complain about the cockroach in her milk or berate him for not shooting me. I was half a block away before I turned my head to verify my hope that even an enraged Dominic Fontana wouldn't go chasing after me through the snow in his bare feet and red silk bikini briefs, waving a revolver.

I made it to the car, with the shouts of the woman still echoing in my brain: *Shoot the sonovabitch! Kill him!*

Dominic's wife was at work, so who was his screaming lady friend?

The question might not have seemed so important, except that I'd seen that woman before, wearing high-heeled leather boots and working a crossword puzzle at Melba's. Her voice was familiar, too, with those frenetic, inflammatory shouts not quite hiding that same southern drawl I'd heard when she called to set up my meeting with Rosa. Whoever she was, one day the woman's helping Rosa tell me Dominic's the bad guy, and the next—after Dominic's reaction pretty much confirms Rosa's charge—the same woman is screaming at Dominic to blow my brains out.

So much for charging up the middle. Now seemed like a good time to go back and study the playbook.

CHAPTER
12

I DROVE TO THE hospital, wondering how soon I'd be hearing from Dominic again. He had to be worried about how much I knew and how I knew it. Actually, if you looked at things from Dominic's insane point of view, killing me—or anyone likely to finger him as Trish's attacker—was a pretty sensible thing to do.

Even so, there were more immediate problems than Dominic. He'd hesitate to go after me on his own out in the open field, and he certainly couldn't tell Gus Apprezziano, or anyone else, why he wanted me out of the way.

Meanwhile, there was Lammy. The clothes he'd been wearing when they took him to the emergency room were torn and bloody, so I stopped at Sears and bought him new things—socks, underwear, extra-wide-cut jeans, a plaid flannel shirt, a bulky, dark blue ski jacket, and even a warm cap with earflaps. It was fun, actually, and I got everything but shoes, figuring shoe size I wouldn't be able to guess.

When I got to the hospital, he was sitting in his chair, still wearing just a hospital gown. "Sorry I'm not dressed," he said.

"I thought you were going to stop telling me you're sorry all the time."

"Oh, I forgot." He was looking everywhere but at me. "Uh, the nurse said you were bringing some different clothes."

"And I did. Here, see if they fit." I dumped all the packages on the bed and started opening them. It was the first time I'd ever bought an entire outfit for anyone, and I thought I'd done a pretty good job.

Lammy didn't even stand up, just sat there staring at the bed. "Those aren't my clothes."

"They are now," I said. "Come on. They already let you stay way beyond discharge time. They'll be charging for another day if we don't get moving."

"I . . . I don't have money for expensive stuff like that."

"Hey, these are from Sears, not Nordstrom or something. But they're nice. See?" I held up the plaid flannel shirt, a great mixture of brown and blue. I was especially proud of that.

He just sat there. "You gotta take 'em back. I can't pay—"

"Be quiet." I was suddenly angry. Selfishly, stupidly angry. "Look," I said, "I spent time as well as money getting those goddamn clothes. I thought you'd be happy about it. Jesus, you think I care if you pay me back or not?" I walked over to the open door. "I'll be back in five minutes, damn it. Put those clothes on and let's get the hell outta here."

I went out in the hall and there was a nurse standing there. "He's such a dear, isn't he?" she said, nodding toward Lammy's room.

"Uh, yeah, I guess so."

"He hasn't had one single visitor except you." That's what her words were, but the look in her eyes seemed to be saying much more than that.

"You, uh, overheard our conversation, didn't you?" I asked.

"Yes. But don't worry, people don't always act appropriately when they're treated in ways they don't expect. I try never to be too hard on them."

"You're right. Lammy doesn't know any better."

"Oh," she said, smiling kindly, "I wasn't talking about Mr. Fleming. I was talking about you." She started to walk away, then turned back. "He's going to have some trouble getting those clothes on. That dressing on his hand and wrist, remember?"

I'd never thought of that.

Back in his room, Lammy had his new jeans on and was struggling with the shirt. It was plenty big, and we were able to get it on over the fat bandage that left only the tips of his left fingers exposed. I had to button it for him, and then I went to the closet to find his shoes. When I turned back he was standing in front of the bathroom mirror, admiring his new shirt. He caught me watching him and his face glowed red between the purple and yellow bruises. He turned around and mumbled something.

"What did you say?" I asked, trying to sound nonthreatening.

"I said . . . thank you."

"Oh," I said. "You're welcome." There were tears in the corners of his eyes and I looked the other way. "Sorry I yelled at you."

Neither of us said another word as we fumbled with his socks and shoes. I tied the laces. Finally, riding down on the elevator, I had to say something to break the silence. "So . . . did your sister call?"

"No, nobody called." He paused. "Oh, except for Miss Carroway. She called."

"Oh?"

"Or at least her secretary. Asked where I'd be going when I left here, because Miss Carroway might need to reach me. I told her you were taking me to my place. But that was it. I didn't expect my sister to call."

"No," I said. "Of course not."

THERE WAS AN OPEN spot on the street near Lammy's place, so we parked and used the front door. Lammy went ahead of me up the steps and it wasn't until he was unlocking the door on the second-floor landing that I remembered I hadn't told him he'd be having company. He pushed open the door and then stopped, because both of us heard the same strange noises, like metal scraping across metal, over and over.

I pushed Lammy aside and yelled through the open door. "Casey, is that you?"

"Course it is," the call came back. "I'm in the kitchen."

He was down on his hands and knees, with his head stuck inside the oven. The oven door was off and was sitting on the other side of the room, leaning against the cabinet under the sink. Casey extracted his head from the oven and hauled himself clumsily to a standing position.

Lammy stared up at the huge man.

I didn't know what to say anymore than Lammy did. Casey was wearing black pants, a white collarless shirt, and bright yellow rubber gloves that were covered with swirls of greasy slime. He held what looked like a putty knife in his massive hand, and a red, white, and blue stocking cap on his head. There was more greasy gunk smeared on his shirt, and even some on the cap.

"You must be Lambert Fleming," he said, then looked down at his yellow gloves. "I'd shake hands except this chemical crap would burn holes in your skin." He waved at the stove. "Damn thing looks like it hasn't been cleaned in about twenty years. Had a helluva time getting the door off."

"Lammy," I said, "this is Casey, a friend of mine. He's been ordered out of his own home for a while, and I asked him to stay with you." I stopped, then added, "I have to run, so I'll leave you two to get acquainted."

"C'mon back for supper if you can," Casey said. "I decided to wait and make the meat loaf tonight. At least, I will if I can get that damn oven door back on."

Lammy shrugged off his new coat and hung it on one of the kitchen chairs. Then he just stood there looking embarrassed, like a kid who might be ordered out of the room any minute, so the grownups could go on with their work.

"I could use some help here, Lammy," Casey said. "But you

72

better change your clothes." He leaned forward. "Hey, that's a really nice shirt you got there. It's new, isn't it?"

"Yeah," Lammy said, staring down at the floor. "It's new. I better go change." He fled from the kitchen.

"He's all yours," I said.

"Yeah," Casey said. "Doesn't look like much of a sex maniac to me. Course, don't know that I ever met one before."

I left by the back door because it was the quickest way out. It was Casey's turn to help Lammy struggle with his clothes.

WALKING DOWN THE ALLEY toward Steve Connolly's garage, I wondered if he was home. I don't know why I wondered, and I don't know why I thought I'd be able to tell, since I'd have had to go into his backyard to look through his garage window, and that would only tell me whether his van was there, not whether he was home.

Thinking about garages, though, reminded me of something. According to the police reports, Trish had said at first that she didn't know where she was attacked. Later she said the man pushed her down on the floor, then changed "floor" to "ground," then said her clothes were dry because the man had dragged her inside somewhere. It seemed clear to me she was making things up—maybe not the attack, but how it happened.

It was Trish's insistent repetition of the statement that "nothing happened in the garage"—before she corrected herself and said she wasn't in any garage—that most intrigued me. I turned around and walked the other way down the alley, past Lammy's backyard and into the next block, where Dominic lived. And yes, Dominic had a garage.

It nearly filled the width of his lot, a brick, two-car garage. Its wide overhead door opened onto the alley, and could have used a couple of coats of paint. I'd had enough of Dominic for one day, so I kept on walking, even though I really wanted to see what the floor looked like in there, and whether that might help prove that Dominic's garage was the garage nothing had happened in.

I KEPT TO THE alley for a half mile farther. I knew it was a half mile, because in Chicago eight blocks make a mile—most of the time. It was already dark, and my lower right ribs were beginning to ache again. Whoever had called Lammy, claiming to be Renata Carroway's secretary, had learned I was driving him home, and must have identified my rental car by now. So it would stay right there on Lammy's block until somebody could pick it up and return it.

A cab took me east, all the way to the el station at Wilson Avenue, and I called Barney Green's secretary from a pay phone to make arrangements for a new rental car, a process more complicated than it sounds, since I have no credit cards. Maintaining this absence of plastic gets harder by the hour. But Barney, my ex-partner, helps out. We both see it as part of an experiment in liquidity. In other words, if one has no credit, no bank account, no real estate, minimal personal property, virtually nothing but cash—in unpredictably fluctuating amounts, unfortunately—can one function as we enter the third millenium? One thing for sure, one seldom has to check one's mailbox.

Then I made two more calls. Casey would save me some of his meat loaf for a sandwich. The Lady would be busy that evening, but we agreed we'd get together the next day. She seemed to think I needed cheering up.

I took the el to Central Street in Evanston. My recollection being that my pantry was still pretty bare, I stopped for a couple of cheeseburgers with lots of greasy French fries. Then I walked the "back way" to my place, carried another package from the Lady up the rear stairs, and went inside and listened to my two phone messages.

The first message was brief. "The person you talked to the other day about sliding down chutes wants to talk to you again."

He left no number, but said he'd be in touch. Maybe it was about the paint job on the Fleetwood. The other call was more unexpected, but the message was similar. Someone else wanted to meet with me, too. This someone left a name, Dan Maguire, and a time and a place as well. Said he wanted to confer with me about a certain Dominic Fontana.

I swallowed a few aspirins and thought seriously about shining my shoes, what with all these conferences coming up. Instead, I poured myself an inch of scotch over one ice cube and sat down at the kitchen table with the book the Lady had left in my back hall, *A Christmas Carol,* by Charles Dickens. A few years back, when domestic affairs had been going better, Cass and I had taken the Lady to see the staged version at the Goodman Theatre. Cass, ever the English lit professor, claimed it was the world's most popular ghost story. I told her I thought *Casper* had greater name recognition. Anyway, the Lady must have decided there was a lesson in the Dickens tale somewhere for me, or she wouldn't have dropped it at my door. My best guess was she wanted to remind me that even a cynical, miserable Scrooge of a person might wake up some morning transformed into an optimistic and happy old coot—and discover that "the Spirits had done it all in one night."

I caught myself nodding before I got much beyond the part right near the beginning about Jacob Marley's ghost appearing to Scrooge, but that wasn't Dickens' fault. I got up and set the timer on the coffeemaker before I went to bed. One musn't oversleep when one's been invited to a morning audience with the great Daniel O'Laughlin Maguire, Grand Poobah of Bauer & Barklind, a Partnership of Professional Legal Corporations.

Well, possibly *invited* wasn't exactly the right way to describe that second message on my machine. *Summoned,* that was more like it.

Gosh, maybe I really should have polished my shoes.

CHAPTER

13

THE LAW FIRM OF Bauer & Barklind occupied floors thirty-two through thirty-seven of a prestigious marble-clad building west of State Street, on Wacker Drive, across from the Chicago River. On floor thirty-five, I was barely out of the elevator when a young woman with a Miss America smile and a brushed silk suit, teal blue, strode forward to greet me and show me where to hang my hooded parka.

"I'll keep the coat," I said, taking a good look around. "This looks like the kinda place, you know, you don't keep your eye on things, they disappear."

If she had any visible reaction at all, it was on the right side of her upper lip, maybe. "This way, sir," she said. "Would you care for a cup of coffee, or—"

"You got any strawberry soda?" The time might come when I'd want her to remember the day Malachy Foley came in. "Oh," she'd say, "you mean that rather odd man?"

She left me sinking into one of three identical sofas that were drawn up to three sides of a low, square table—and was back in thirty seconds flat with a cold can of Cherry Coke. "Closest I could come," she chirped. She was enjoying herself.

After that I was abandoned for a while. Oddly enough, there wasn't a piece of reading material in sight, presumably so one could sit undistracted and contemplate one's surroundings and be put in the proper mood for one's encounter with power.

Stated succinctly, Bauer & Barklind had a pretty classy-looking suite of offices. The reception area was spacious and bright, with parquet flooring that would have sneered if you breathed the word *oak,* or any other tree any of us has ever actually run into. Straight ahead, I looked into the wide space between two banks of elevators. To my left were broad circular staircases leading to the floors above and below, suspended by thin cables that stretched up and out of sight.

To my right, and just beyond earshot, Miss America sat at a reception desk and answered an apparently ceaseless flow of telephone calls. She kept an eye on the elevators, though, and whenever the need arose, she abandoned her phone without hesitation, helping people stow their coats, steering them in the right directions.

She never steered anyone my way.

I killed time first by wondering if she had a way of instantly forwarding calls elsewhere, or if she were just faking all those conversations.

Then I thought about Dan Maguire, and how the hell he could be involved in this mess. The patriarch now of a family in its third generation of power in Chicago, he had followed a father and grandfather who—with blood-kin and in-laws hanging on tight—had built and maintained an empire on patronage and clout, and a noticeable lack of scruples. Dan Maguire had inherited all the power that money and connections can buy, but managed to shake off the shady reputation of his forbears. He never ran for office, but nearly everybody who did consulted with him. If the Illinois Supreme Court wasn't asking him to chair committees to dream up ways to improve the state judiciary, the United States Congress was naming him special prosecutor in some heavy investigation. He'd been a member once of the Chicago Crime Commission and, more recently, been appointed to a presidential committee to study the effects of organized crime on international trade. He'd been counsel to politicians and corporate presidents, and was on more boards of directors—nonprofit and Fortune 500 alike—than most people could have kept straight. Everybody had heard about Dan Maguire, and nobody I'd spoken to said anything negative.

I was getting the feeling, though, that I wasn't going to like him. It wasn't just that he'd called and obviously assumed I'd show up on one day's notice. It's that he was giving me all this time to sit there and reflect on how being ignored is just about my most unfavorite thing in the world.

There must be people besides me who notice how often it happens that someone who ought to be paying attention to them . . . isn't. Oh, I don't mean times when I'm struggling at the piano in some bar, and can't seem to catch the ear of a single soul who isn't drunk or depressed, or both. That I can take pretty well. In fact, that seems to be one of the rules of that game. But when I'm busting my ass trying to figure out how to keep a guy *(a)* out of jail, and *(b)* out of worse than jail, and some Mr. Wonderful calls and says he has a suggestion and I should show up at eleven o'clock sharp, and—even though I'm pretty sure I won't like his suggestion—I *do* show up at eleven o'clock . . .

Anyway, I have this thing about being ignored.

At fifteen minutes after eleven, I stood up, tucked my coat under my left arm, and started toward the elevators.

"Oh, Mr. Foley," Miss America called, "you're not leaving us, are you?" Her heels *tap-tap-tap*ped across the floor after me. "I *know* Mr. Maguire wants to see you. He must—"

When I whirled around she almost fell over backward. "Great," I said. "His office is that way, isn't it?" Pointing to my left.

"Well, actually, no. It's that way and around the—" She caught herself, but too late. She was already pointing to my right.

"Thank you." I went back for my can of Cherry Coke, then strolled slowly down the wide corridor toward the office of

Daniel O'Laughlin Maguire. With a sip of the sweet cold drink to lubricate my own pipes, I was ready.

"Oh, Danny Boy," I sang, loud and lilting, my brogue turning *boy* almost into *bye*. "The pipes, the pipes are call-all-ling. From glen to glen . . ."

My range is a good five tones below a true Irish tenor, but it has a fine carry to it all the same, don't y'know. Anyway, heads poked out of open doors up and down the hallway.

". . . and down the mountainside."

People who looked like lawyers were attached to the heads sticking out from the doors. Most wore dark pants and long-sleeved white shirts with ties and multicolored suspenders, and the rest opted for dark skirts and tailored white blouses, adorned with various bright accessories. All the haircuts looked expensive; and all the faces a bit worried. And why not? Seems like once a year some disgruntled client shows up in the Loop and opens fire on his or her lawyer, or an opponent's lawyer. Which is bad enough, but the shooters are usually deranged and frightened, and tend to shoot at everyone in sight—often including themselves.

"The summer's gone, and—"

"Is that you, Mr. Foley?" A man's voice—clear and loud and strong. Heads retracted back into their offices. Doors closed.

"In the flesh," I said.

Up ahead, where the corridor made a right-angle turn, were two men. The one I didn't recognize had a pinched, mean face and a widow's peak, wore gray pants, a white shirt, and a thin blue tie that hung down and draped over a potbelly the size of a volleyball. The other man was Dan Maguire, looking like he was headed for the plane to his place in Palm Springs, in cordovan loafers, dark blue slacks, and a light blue short-sleeved golf shirt. He was over fifty years old, maybe over sixty, but trim and lean and lightly tanned. Not tall—about five-nine—with curly graying hair that was receding back from his forehead. The closer I got to him, the more he looked like a pleasant, intelligent, self-assured man—a take-charge guy, but someone you could trust.

As far as I knew, he really was everything he looked like. But then, there's a lot I don't know. At any rate, I was determined to dislike and distrust him, no matter how difficult he made it.

"Glad to meet you, Mr. Maguire," I said, sticking my hand out toward the potbellied man.

"Very funny," the man said. "You know—"

"Relax, Paul," Maguire said, and then, to me, "I'm Dan Maguire, Mr. Foley. Pleased to meet you. This is Paul Anders."

"Hold this a second, Paul," I said, shoving the Coke can at Anders. He actually took it, too, freeing up my right hand. Maguire and I shook hands. Anders just stood there. I didn't know him and I didn't like him, and the look on his face didn't make that hard at all.

"Sorry to keep you waiting," Maguire said. "Long-distance call and I couldn't—"

"I'm sorry you did, too." I took the can back from Anders. "Where shall we talk?"

"I've reserved a conference room," Maguire said, leading Anders and me around the corner and, just a few steps down the hall, into a room with a long table and ten chairs, all in a dark, polished wood. One wall of the room was a panorama of the city, looking north from downtown through blue-tinted glass.

We settled in, with Maguire seated at the end, naturally, and Anders and I facing each other across the wide table. There was a brief pause, during which nobody offered anybody coffee or wished anybody well.

"I understand," Maguire finally began, "that you represent Lambert Flem—"

"Wait a minute," I said. "You mean you aren't going to tell me exactly who your buddy Anders here is?"

Anders didn't move, just stared at me. Maguire said, "Why sure, Paul's assisting me in this case, and what we—"

"Oh, well," I said, "that explains everything. But as I recall, you said something on the phone about a suggestion."

"Yes," Maguire said. "You see—"

"Incidentally," I said, "I don't *represent* Lambert Fleming. I'm doing some work for him, or more accurately, for his lawyer. Anyway, what's the suggestion?"

If Maguire was insulted that I'd interrupted him in three out of his first three sentences since we sat down, he didn't show it. "For now, Mr. Foley, let's call it a request. I'd like you to cease all contact with Dominic Fontana—immediately."

"Dominic Fontana? The brother-in-law of Steve Connolly? The Dominic who's married to the niece of Gus Apprezziano? *That* Dominic Fontana?"

"Yes."

"My, my, Counselor. How long you been feeding from that trough?"

Maguire's eyes looked suddenly sad. "Mr. Fontana is a citizen, Mr. Foley. With the same rights you and I enjoy."

"Right," I said. "The inalienable ones."

"Including the right to enjoy his home in peace."

"Uh-huh. That's the request? Stay away from Dominic?"

"That's it."

"Well, sir, suppose, with all due respect and as a matter of principle, I deny your request. Then what?"

"Then, regrettably, the request would become a demand. Dominic has directed me to file an emergency action against you seeking a protective order, a permanent injunction, and monetary damages."

"That's hard to believe," I said, happy that no one was talking about breaking fingers or crushing kneecaps, not yet. "I mean, did Dominic use all those big words?"

"The suit is being drafted as we speak. As a courtesy, I'll give

81

you a copy of our proposed complaint against you as soon as it's completed. You have already caused bodily injury to Dominic." He paused and took a deep breath.

But it was Anders who spoke next. "Think over your position quite seriously, friend. Because if we sue you, we'll take everything you own, and everything you ever will own for the rest of your life."

Ah, one of those times that the struggle for total liquidity is so rewarding. I placed both hands on the table in front of me, palms down, and stared straight across at Anders.

"Listen up. First, I'm not your friend. Second, you and Danny boy here can file your suit against me and I doubt I'll even file an answer. You could take a fifty million dollar judgment against me by default and it wouldn't bother me one bit."

"You'll be a ruined man," Anders said.

"Maguire," I said, turning to look at him, "do you have any idea what I'm worth?"

"We're working on that, also."

"I wouldn't spend much time or money on it. I own my clothes. Like these nifty leather boots I'm wearing, these khaki pants, this handsome WFMT Chicago Symphony Orchestra Radiothon sweatshirt, and a closetful of stuff pretty much like them. I rent a furnished apartment, up over a garage. Oh, I do own a piano, which I don't play very well. But then, it's not a very good piano, either." That last part wasn't exactly true.

"You live well," Anders said, "without regular employment. That suggests substantial assets."

I'd maneuvered them into playing my game. "No real estate, no investments, one bank account—and that's owned by a trust, not me, and seldom has much in it. Check it out. Take a look at my tax returns." Something that passed through Anders' otherwise expressionless eyes suggested they'd already done that. I turned back to Maguire. "If I live well, which is debatable, it's because I spend what little comes in as fast as I can. Like the Buddha once said, 'If you ain't got much, they can't take much.' Or words to that effect."

"Mr. Foley," Maguire said, "I'm afraid you—"

"Something else." Anders broke in. "If you continue to harass Mr. Fontana, you'll face criminal charges, and lose whatever assets you have or don't have stashed somewhere. Plus, there's your private detective's license. That can be taken away."

"So what's this? Round two?" I looked back at the man across the table from me. "First, you won't convict me, or even get my license, not on the testimony of a lowlife hood like Dominic Fontana. Second, I've been locked up before, and it didn't change my behavior much. Third, I hope I never have—"

"Mr. Foley," Maguire was talking again, and getting to his feet. "We've talked long enough, and I believe we've made our position clear. Now what about it? Do you plan to stay away from Dominic Fontana, or not?"

"That was my third point, Danny boy. My only goal is to see that Lambert Fleming doesn't go down for a nasty crime he didn't commit. Period. I'll be ecstatic if I can do that without getting one more whiff of Dominic Fontana. People rut around the pen with a hog, y'know, the stench rubs off on 'em." I drained the last of my Cherry Coke. "I mean, consider the two of you."

CHAPTER

===

14

ONCE IT DEGENERATED TO barnyard talk, my meeting with Maguire and Anders went to hell in a hurry, so it wasn't long past noon that I was on Lake Shore Drive, headed north in my latest rental car, a white Dodge Intrepid.

I might hold them off for a while by my claim that I wasn't really interested in Dominic. But if they knew what I knew—or if they had reason to suspect it—they'd have to figure my best option for getting Lammy off the sexual assault hook was to skewer Dominic firmly on it.

It didn't seem likely they'd file a lawsuit against me, though. They'd soon discover it was true that I had little of monetary value to lose. If they brought criminal charges I'd be entitled to a jury, and even with Dan Maguire's help no state's attorney would want to try to make Dominic Fontana look truthful to any group of human beings who managed to stay awake.

I took the Drive to Hollywood Avenue, then Hollywood to Ridge, and on up into Evanston. I'd already called and asked Barney Green's secretary to check *Sullivan's,* the directory of lawyers. There was no Paul Anders listed at Bauer & Barklind, or anywhere else in the state. On the other hand, he didn't seem much like a mob associate of Dominic, either.

I'd had the clear impression throughout our conversation that Maguire was wishing he were somewhere else, that he was doing a job someone else wanted him to do. And the more I rolled that around in my mind, the more I wondered what the hell was going on.

At Green Bay Road and Central Street I noticed I was hungry

and turned east. A few minutes later I parked in the shadow of Northwestern's Ryan Field and walked back to pick up some lunch at Mustard's Last Stand. By the time I left, with a couple of root beers and two jumbo hot dogs to go—no fries today—I was wondering whether I should be mad at Maguire, or feel sorry for him.

Back in the car I continued east, then north. Just past one o'clock, I twisted the old-fashioned bell at the Lady's mansion and she opened the door herself. She already had her coat on.

Walking her to the Intrepid, I asked, "You want to drive?" It wasn't an offer lightly made. The Lady's one of the few people I feel truly comfortable riding with. She handles a car like a good cop on the beat—smooth and steady, eyes everywhere, never missing a thing.

"Not today," she said. "I'll simply sit and enjoy everything."

Everything? That had to include the sky—a dismal, dark blanket that drooped about three stories above ground level—and a temperature that had risen a few degrees above freezing, so that sprays of salty slush thrown up by passing cars merged with the gray mist that already hung in the air and kept everyone's lights on and windshield wipers working hard.

I headed south. The Lady accepted one of the root beers, but left her hot dog for me. The idea was I'd take her to pick up my Cavalier from the body shop. She'd use it the rest of the day to visit her shelters and then leave it in the garage under the coach house for me.

"You always do, don't you," I said.

"Um . . . I'm afraid I missed something, Malachy."

"Enjoy everything, I mean."

"Oh. Yes, usually. Occasionally I lapse, drift off into old habits."

"Even you?"

"Even I." Her British accent and proper grammar were inseparable. "At any rate," she continued, "how is your ghost?"

"My ghost? You mean Lammy? Well, they beat the . . . beat him up pretty badly, but he's home now. Casey's staying with him." I glanced across at her, but she was looking out the window, enjoying the damnable weather. "I . . . uh . . . I kinda thought he'd stay out of my dreams now, y'know? But he was back last night, up to his knees in the river again." I thought for a minute. "Maybe it was all those French fried potatoes I had with the cheeseburgers that brought him back."

"You said nearly the identical thing once before, Malachy. Only it was *mashed* potatoes that time." When I looked over and caught her smiling at me, she turned her head as though to look out the rear window. "In fact, it was the potatoes that made me think of—"

"Ah, so *that's* why you sent me that book," I said. "Scrooge. When Marley's ghost appeared, Scrooge figured his senses were deceiving him, that undigested potatoes were giving him bad dreams and the ghost wasn't real. Right?"

"As I recall, he mentioned a fragment of an *underdone* potato."

"Right," I said. "That was it, or a bit of undigested beef. And Marley's ghost was transparent, or hollow, just like—"

"Yes. Anyway, rereading *A Christmas Carol* made me think of you and your ghost." She paused and leaned forward, apparently trying to look into the outside mirror on her side of the car. "I'm not really surprised, though, that the boy in the river is still making his appearances."

"I am. I thought once I started helping the *real* Lammy, the one in my dreams would go away. But apparently that'll happen only after I get him out of this mess he's gotten himself into."

A moment passed and then she said, "That's really quite extraordinary."

"What?"

"The way you phrased that. From what I've heard, your friend hardly seems to have been personally responsible for his predicament."

"Well, I just——"

"And you apparently take for granted that you'll succeed in extricating him."

"That's what——"

"Then there's your belief—or hope, anyway—that the boy reaching out for help will disappear from your dreams."

"Damn it, Helene." The traffic signal just ahead turned yellow. I accelerated, then slowed, then accelerated again through the intersection, and just missed being broadsided by a UPS truck. "Sometimes you can be so——"

"Malachy?"

"What now?"

"Didn't you want to turn west there, on Howard Street?"

"Ha! Gotcha! You think because I was mad at you I wasn't paying attention to my driving." I threw a hard right and hit the accelerator. "That's a very long light there, at Howard. And I may just have gotten rid of that car that's been following us."

"Oh," she said, "you mean that dark-colored Ford. I wasn't certain you'd noticed it."

"I hardly have to notice. They're almost always there. When they lose me, they just go back to the coach house and wait for me again."

We drove around haphazardly for awhile, while I told the Lady everything that had been happening. Sometimes she has helpful ideas; sometimes she doesn't. But she always listens, remembers everything, questions each detail, tries to keep things straight.

Sometimes that helps me keep things straight.

Eventually we arrived at Caesar Scallopino's and I drove around to the rear entrance. When the overhead door lifted, I pulled inside and cut the ignition. My Cavalier was sitting in one of the bays, looking better than it had in years. We sat and talked for a few minutes more. No one bothered us, and by now I'd left Lammy behind and was complaining about Cass and how much I missed her and just wasn't able to chase those depressing nostalgic thoughts from my mind, no matter how hard I tried.

Her response—something to do with not trying so hard—sounded simple but wasn't, I was certain. She ended up with, "Why not just feel sad when you feel sad, and let it be?"

"But I don't *like* feeling that way. You don't understand, because you never have those sad feelings." When she didn't answer, I looked across and caught her smiling, more to herself than to me, and something suddenly clicked. "At least, I never thought you did. But you *do,* don't you? I mean get down sometimes. Sad, depressed, whatever."

"Certainly I do. And it doesn't surprise me, and it doesn't bowl me over."

"What is it that—"

"That woman sounds interesting."

"What?"

"That woman," the Lady said. "She's the one I find most intriguing."

"Oh?" I said, still not sure which woman she meant.

"Yes. First, she's there at the coffee shop. Then, she's the one trusted by Rosa to call you. Finally, she urges Dominic to kill you."

"He didn't need much encouragement. But I swear her screaming pumped him up even more."

"But only after she interceded and saved your life."

"Right." So the Lady didn't believe the woman's hysteria over a cockroach in her milk was coincidental any more than I did.

"There's an ambivalence about her that makes her interesting, and—oh my." She was looking at her watch. "I really must be going now." She opened her door, then turned back and laid her hand on my arm. "Be careful, Malachy."

The keys were in the Cavalier, and she backed it smoothly out the door into the alley and was gone. I paid Caesar in cash and he gave me a receipt that detailed every bit of the body work, and the tow. Caesar's extremely careful to keep proper records—as am I.

When I pulled into the alley I really didn't know which way to turn. I agreed with the Lady, though. That crossword puzzle woman was intriguing.

CHAPTER

15

I DROVE TO THE animal hospital, where Doctor Lynette Daniels told me Lammy was right about one thing—the dog by his back door had been dead before it was mutilated. "The minimal bleeding shows it couldn't have been alive at that point," she said, "although it wasn't hit by a car." Stripped of the chemical jargon, she told me the cause of death was the "ingestion of a toxic substance."

"You mean the dog ate poison."

"Well, sort of," she said. "An overdose of chocolate."

"Chocolate? Like a Hershey bar?"

"Probably baking chocolate. It wouldn't take many ounces of that to be fatal to a dog that size. Especially as malnourished as this one was."

"So the dog could have eaten some chocolate accidentally, and become a handy prop for somebody's sick joke?"

"Possible," she said, "but not likely. He was cut so soon after death that it was probably a deliberate poisoning. It's common knowledge that chocolate is dangerous to small animals. There was an article in the *Tribune* just a couple of weeks ago about it. Not a very pleasant way to die, either. There'd be convulsions and . . . well . . ."

"So Lammy was right," I said. "You know, Lynette, you mentioned he was good with dogs, and his co-workers at the shelter told me the same thing. Like, he can calm them down when they're frightened and aggressive. He has a gift, one of them said."

"I haven't seen him do that, but I know he's comfortable

around dogs, and they around him. There's talk in the literature about how some people relate better with animals than others. Many of the studies are with dogs. Some people . . . well, we know dogs don't think, that they're instinctual. But some people seem to have a sort of intuition into how dogs react. It's all a little beyond me, Mal, I admit."

I'd have liked to spend more time talking with Lynette Daniels, about instinct and intuition—or anything else. She was easy to look at, and we'd slipped comfortably into a first-name basis.

But I paid for the autopsy and the disposal of the remains, then went back out into a rain that fell in thick drops that were just this side of real snow. A huge blue city truck rumbled by, spraying ever more salt into the slush. Which reminded me . . .

I went back inside and Lynette let me use her phone.

"D'par'men'AviationO'HareSnowR'moval."

"Y'all got a Steve Connolly there?" I asked.

"Yeah. Who's callin'?"

"Tell him it be LeRoy."

"Hol' on." A minute passed before he came back on the line. "Gonna be awhile. Wanna leave a nummer?"

"I'll call back. How long he be there?"

"Startin' to freeze up out here. Could be all night."

"I best try a different day."

"Good idea." He hung up.

It was past three o'clock by the time I got to Melba's and again the sign said "CLOSED." I circled the block and drove by once more, slowly, peering through the gray rain. The lights were on inside and the big-breasted woman with the hair on her upper lip was sitting beside the cash register, probably counting the day's take. I couldn't see Gus Apprezziano. But I knew he must be there, because Goldilocks was sitting with another man at the first table by the front door.

I drove around and into the alley, and locked the Beretta in the trunk. An exhaust fan was rattling away just above Melba's back entrance. The door was unlocked and I stepped inside and closed it again quickly. There was nobody in the kitchen. From where I stood I couldn't see through the service window into the dining room, but over the sound of the fan I could make out the sound of a man's voice.

I stood with my back against the the alley door, feet spread wide, and flipped the switch that shut off the exhaust fan. It was suddenly very quiet.

"Hey, Gus!" I yelled, and clasped my hands on top of my head. "Whaddaya want on that burger?"

There was no answer, although I heard quick, padding footsteps and a chair scraping softly on the floor. Then the door across the room from me burst open.

It was Goldilocks, holding a large black semiautomatic pistol pointed at my face. When he saw who it was he grinned, but not very cheerfully. I just hoped he wouldn't come over and punch me in the side again.

"For chrissake, tell me who's out there, asshole." That was Gus Apprezziano, sounding awfully tough from behind his bodyguard.

"It's that dumbnuts Foley," the man answered.

Gus pushed his way into the kitchen.

"You said you wanted to talk," I said, leaving my hands on my head, "and the door was open, so—"

"Shut up."

So I did, and—once I was patted down and seated, and the cashier was sent home, and Gus's two goons were sent to wait outside the front and back doors, and Gus had gotten rid of whomever it was he'd been talking to on the telephone, and we both had full coffee mugs—we talked.

"You oughta stop trying to prove how brave you are, Foley. You coulda been killed."

"You wouldn't shoot an unarmed man, would you?" We both knew the answer to that one, so I added, "At least, not a man you called and said you wanted to see, and who probably told people he was coming here."

"For sure no one could trace any telephone call from me to you, and almost for sure no one knows where the hell you are. I doubt you know yourself where you're gonna be, one minute to the next."

"Anyway—"

"Anyway, I'm not talking about you coulda been killed by me. I'm talking about Dominic. I was you, I'd stay away from Dominic."

"Right. And if I were you, I'd retire to New Guinea or someplace even farther away from Chicago. But then, neither of us is very good at taking advice." I tried the coffee. It was dark and bitter from sitting too long on the hot plate. "So, is that what you wanted to talk about? To warn me to stay away from Dominic like you warned me to stay away from Steve?"

"The way I remember it, I didn't warn you anything. You're the one warned me Steve should stay away from that pervert friend of yours."

"Hold on. I never said he was a friend. Not all my clients are friends."

"And I promised nothing would happen to the fucking creep, at least till they lock him up with the rest of the animals and he gets what's coming to him." He drank some of his coffee and smacked his lips with apparent satisfaction. Tastes vary. "I don't need to warn you to stay away from Steve or Dominic. They're both big boys. They can take care of themselves." He took another gulp of coffee. "Course, they *are* family, you know. Even the mick, at least by marriage."

"Yeah, I know." I stood up. "See you around."

"Sit down," he said. And when I did, he added, "I wanna talk to you. Besides, you haven't finished your coffee yet."

"They serve better coffee in County Jail, for chrissake." I paused. "By the way, who's this guy Paul Anders?"

"Huh?" Gus's face showed nothing. "Paul Andrews?"

"Anders. I . . . uh . . . got a call from someone named Paul Anders. No message, except he'd be in touch about something. Thought maybe he was one of your people."

"I got no fucking *people*. And I never heard of any Paul Anders."

"Well, I suppose he'll call back."

"Yeah. I suppose." He drank the rest of his coffee and stared down into the thick white mug.

"Say, Gus, I'm parked in the alley, you know? I might get a ticket. So, unless there's something else you wanted—"

He raised his head. "I got a job for you."

"Don't be silly."

"A background check. Simple."

"I know you said you got no *people*. But if you did, why couldn't one of them handle it?"

"Because this is confidential, asshole. I wouldn't want my people, if I had any, to know about it. Fact is, I—" He stopped. "Anyway, I want *you* to do it. And you know what?" He stared across at me. Nothing changed except the look in his eyes, but I felt a sudden chill, and got an idea of why people were afraid of Gus Apprezziano. "You know what?" he repeated, pointing a thin finger in my face. "You're gonna do it."

"Gus," I said, once he'd dropped his hand back on the table, "the answer is no."

"Like I said, it's a background check."

"Like I said . . . no."

"It's a broad. I wanna know who she is."

"I told you—"

"It's Dominic's new lady friend."

"Maybe you didn't—" I caught my breath. "Dominic's lady friend?"

"You probably seen her," he was saying. "I wanna know who she is, where she came from, everything. And . . ." He poked his bony finger at me again. "You, my friend, are the one that's—"

"Okay," I said.

"Good." Gus smiled, thinking he'd frightened me into agreeing.

"But why don't you just ask Dominic?" I asked. "You don't trust him?"

"Dominic I trust like a son. He's proved himself. But he's not the brightest kid on the block, you know? He picked the broad up in a bar in Louisville during Kentucky Derby weekend. So you're gonna find out who this tough-ass little Kentucky filly is for me. It's confidential, and the pay is good."

"How much?" I couldn't believe I was negotiating with this creep.

"First off, I'm keeping Steve, and anybody else, away from that fucking pervert client of yours. That oughta be enough. But you gotta live, too. I know how it is. So I'm adding ten thousand bucks, cash."

"No. It's gotta be—"

"Fifteen, then. Don't push me."

"Ten is fine. But payment's gotta be by check."

"Cash."

"I have to report who it's from, anyway, Gus. That's the law for a cash transaction that big."

"Jesus Christ." He closed his eyes for a few seconds. "It's cash. Call it from Osceola Nursery and Landscape Company. For an employment background check." He drew an envelope from his jacket pocket and slid it across the table. "Here's the first five. I'm in a hurry."

I put the cash in my pocket and slid the envelope back at him. "Two installments," I said. "Maybe I don't have to report it, after all. I'll ask my—"

"Jesus, that's your problem, not mine."

"Dominic's not gonna like me poking around."

He shrugged, as though Dominic's likes and dislikes were my problem, too, not his.

"How do I get in touch with you?" I asked.

"You don't. I get in touch with you." He stared at me. "I want an answer. I'm protecting your boy, and I'm paying cash. I've hired you, Foley, and I want an answer."

I stood up. "This just proves what I said earlier."

"What's that?"

"That not all my clients are friends, you know?"

Gus stood up, too. "Nobody knows about this but us. Understand?"

"Got it. You're not . . . uh . . . wearing a wire or anything, are you?"

He led me through the kitchen and opened the alley door. "Get your ass outta here."

Goldilocks was standing beside the Intrepid in his shirt-sleeves, sopping wet and shielding his cigarette from the half-rain half-snow mess the wind sent slanting down between the buildings. He waded in our direction, and as he and I passed on my way to the car he didn't even look at me. But he did throw an elbow—hard—into my right ribs.

My response was a savage backhand, a chop that caught him from behind, just above his belt. No way I missed his kidney, but he never broke stride and I didn't, either. I guess we'd reached a mutual understanding.

Once the back door to Melba's was closed, I went to the trunk of the Intrepid and retrieved the Beretta before I drove out of the alley. It was clear that when he'd told Gus about our encounter, Dominic hadn't mentioned there was anyone else he was telling. So Gus was in the dark about Dan Maguire and Paul Anders. I'd have bet my life on it.

In fact, I was going to.

CHAPTER

16

"NEVER BEEN TO A basketball game before," Lammy said, and for once it wasn't a mumble. Casey had taken him to a psychologist's office for some testing Renata arranged for him. Now, at supper, there was even a hint of enthusiasm in his voice, and he looked straight at me for almost an entire second. Casey was good for him.

"Sure you have," I said. "Remember? Back in high school when you—" The despair that fell over his face stopped me cold.

"Anyway," Casey broke in, "it'll be great. Wisconsin at Northwestern. Badgers and Wildcats. Jeez, I wonder if either one of 'em's any good." He pushed a large, nearly empty platter to my side of Lammy's mother's kitchen table. "Hey, Mal, you take this last chunk o' catfish. You get two. Lammy and me're only having one each, 'cause we're both too fat already. Right, Lammy?"

"Yes, Father," Lammy said.

Casey lifted his eyebrows and tilted his head, and I knew he'd have loved to tell Lammy to "knock off the 'father' crap," But instead, he pointed his fork at me. "I thought you only had two tickets, though."

"Thanks," I said, sliding the broiled fillet onto my plate. "This stuff's great. I don't eat a lot of fish." I reached for the tartar sauce and the ketchup. "Two tickets are enough. One for you and one for Lammy. I'll be working."

"Hell, no," Casey said. "You and Lammy go. I got reading to do. Truth is, I didn't really wanna go in the first place." I'd seldom heard a more genuine—and less successful—effort at sounding sincere.

"Uh-uh," Lammy said, "I don't wanna go with Mr.—" He swallowed. "I mean, I don't wanna go to any basketball game."

At least Lammy's statement was only half a lie.

"So it's settled, then," I said. "You guys go to the game. Afterward, go to the dressing room and find Jason. He'll be expecting us. I'll get there by then and we'll all go out for burgers or something."

"Is that a friend of—" Lammy started. He didn't finish his question, but just stared down at his plate.

"You mean Jason?" I asked.

"Uh-huh," he mumbled.

"Yeah," I said, "he's a friend who started out as a client. Like you, I guess. I mean you're a client, not a fr—" I stopped. "I mean you're not like him. That is—"

"Hey, Mal," Casey said, and I knew he was dying to laugh out loud. "Why don't you just explain who Jason is and stop stepping on your tongue?"

So I skipped comparisons with Lammy and explained how Jason Cooper was a basketball player whom I'd come to know when his sister hired me to find him before he got grabbed by some very nasty people with their own reasons for wanting him.

"I've met him," Casey chipped in. "He's a great guy. Of course, he's an *athlete,* you know? So it helps if you talk about sports. Especially about basketball. Especially about his own exploits and—"

"I don't know very much about sports," Lammy said. Funny how he could talk to Casey in complete sentences.

"Yeah, well, I s'pose Jason doesn't know very much about the First World War, either," Casey said. "So we'll widen his horizons a little, huh? Anyway, I bought a chocolate pie for dessert. Nothing goes with catfish like chocolate pie."

I gave Casey the extra key for the Intrepid so he and Lammy could use it. After the dishes were washed and dried they drove me to the el.

A FRIDAY NIGHT RIDE on the CTA from, say, Fullerton on the near north side to Howard Street, the city limits, could launch a sociologist's doctoral dissertation. The statistically infrequent, though certainly possible, mugging is only one of a rider's worries. Raucous shouting and hilarious laughter and whatever passes for music—not always recorded—all batter your eardrums. Panhandlers and preachers demand your attention. You pick your way cautiously, lest you slip on the remnants of somebody's chicken-wing dinner. And through it all you wonder what sort of death-dealing microbes are lacing that stale air you're breathing.

Although the car that night was half empty, I ignored the vacant seats and stood with my back against the door to the next car. Everyone probably thought I was a cop—which can have its own disadvantages, of course, but does offer the best view. I decided long ago that when I no longer enjoy riding the el, I'll know it's time to look for a new line of work.

It was nine-thirty when I got off at Loyola University, several stops before Howard Street. A storm front that had held on to its snow was passing through to the east, leaving starry skies and falling temperatures in its wake. With time to kill, I walked across the campus toward the lake. Loyola keeps adding more buildings, of course, so the open space on the lakefront keeps shrinking. But I could still get right up to the edge of the water, alongside the chapel of the Madonna della Strada.

The night was far too cold for anyone with any sense to stand there and stare at the lake, so I had the scene to myself. To the east, far out over the dark water, the rear flank of the cloud cover moved away, its uneven edges catching white light from the half moon hanging low in the south. I was counting on the cold air and the clear view to help me plot out a strategy.

Fat chance.

All I did was stand there and remember it was Friday night,

and that Cass was probably somewhere within a five-mile radius, maybe talking, maybe laughing, maybe sharing a meal. Maybe sharing somebody else's life.

They moved in over me again, those heavy, sad longings for days gone by, and I instinctively tried to push them out of my mind, as though I could send them out over the water to catch up with the clouds and fall with the wet snow on somebody else, across the lake in Michigan. But my feelings could fall wherever they wanted and no one would ever feel them but me, anyway. So I finally stopped pushing and let them hang out with me, beside the empty chapel in the dark, recalling some of what the Lady had said: how the feelings don't win when you let them be, when you just look right back at them. They're as real as the clouds and the wind and the water lapping at the rocks. Just as real, but no more real. You were already there before they swept in, and you watch them swirl and mass. Then, when they roll on out again you're still there to see them go and to wonder how soon they'll be back. And you don't die from them, the Lady says.

And I didn't die, either, but I got awfully cold while all that was going on, and I still had no strategy plotted out.

I turned away from the lake and walked several blocks to The Captain's Choice. Inside, only a few tables were still occupied. The hostess was olive-skinned, petite, and—unconsciously, it seemed—seductive. She smiled up at me and said the kitchen was closed for the evening. I frowned, as though I didn't know that already.

"But it's Friday, so the bar's open till midnight," she added, nodding toward my left.

"That's great," I said. "Maybe you'll join me, Mrs. Fontana?"

She shrank back then, like a frightened cat crouching into an attack stance. "Outta my face, creep," she said, her eyes narrow slits, her voice a snarl, barely audible. This Tina Fontana was a tough lady all right. A battle-scarred combat veteran. ". . . your

100

ass hauled outta here," she was saying, and her hand hovered over the phone beside her.

"Hey, hold on, will ya?" I held out my business card. "I'm the one put the hurt on good old Dominic yesterday. Do I get any points for that?" Even just how Tina felt about that was worth finding out.

She stared down at the card, holding it with two hands, the phone apparently forgotten. She shoved the card in the pocket of a red-and-black plaid vest she was wearing over a white blouse. "Wait here," she said.

She walked across to a waiter who'd been filling salt shakers at the empty tables and spoke with him briefly, nodding my way once. When she came back, she put a sign on the hostess's table that said "Dining Room Closed."

"You'd have got more points," she said, "if you'd have squeezed his *neck* in the door instead of his arm."

"That means you'll talk to me?"

"Just a few minutes. I got stuff to do to close up here, and then I gotta get home."

We sat in a booth with a glass of Diet Coke on her side and a glass of Berghoff draft on mine. The bar was busy, not raucous. Mostly couples.

"So," she said, "you're the guy helping that Fleming kid." She had a nice face. A little heavy on the mascara, but a very pretty smile.

"Kid? He's my age, you know. That make me a kid, too?"

"However old he is, he's still a kid." She wrapped both hands around her glass and tilted her head forward so she had to raise her eyebrows to look at me. "But you? No way. Definitely not a kid." She smiled, then lowered her gaze again.

"Jesus," I said. "Are you flirting with me?"

"Yeah." She smiled again, this time looking embarrassed. "I guess I am. But that's all I do. Just flirt. And not much of that either, these days." She paused, as though suddenly remembering where she was. "It's stupid for me to even talk to you. You don't know how stupid it is."

"Maybe not. But—"

"But I got three reasons," she said, and I realized she didn't need any encouragement from me just then. "One thing, I'd help out a spider if it bit Dominic. Two, you seem kinda decent and I don't get to talk to anyone these days. No one I feel like talking to, anyway. I got a whole new start coming, you know? But I just wish they'd hurry up and—" She stopped and drank some of her Diet Coke. "And the third reason is I still got a conscience, I guess, and I think the Fleming kid is gonna go down. And I . . . I just don't think he did anything, damn it."

"Why not?"

"Because . . . because it was probably . . ." She was looking down at the table. I stared across at the top of her head, at the soft waves of her smooth black hair, and I wanted to reach out and touch it. That surprised me, but it's how I felt.

"Probably who?" I said.

She didn't answer, but she lifted her face and there were tears rolling down her cheeks.

"It was Dominic," I said. "And it's not the first time. He did it before, didn't he?"

"No, he— I mean . . ." She looked surprised, and afraid.

"I looked for your divorce file," I said, "at the courthouse. It isn't there. It's been impounded. The judges don't do that very often anymore, order files kept secret like that. What was the reason, Tina?"

"I . . . I can't say."

"I think the reason is that Dominic's done this before. Maybe not to Trish. But maybe to your daughter. That's in the papers you filed in your divorce case, isn't it?"

"You don't understand." She reached down beside her for her purse. "I have to go now. Really, I—"

"Wait. You've still got a conscience, remember? Just a little longer."

She nodded, saying nothing.

"You were going to divorce him while he was away, in jail. Because of what he'd done. But then something, or someone, stopped you. You didn't go through with it. And when he got out you took him back into your home, back in with your daughter. Why would any mother do that?"

She opened her mouth, then closed it.

"You don't have to tell me. I'll tell you. You took him back because someone wanted you to. Maybe threatened you, maybe forced you. Who was it, Tina?"

She looked at me and shook her head, not crying any more. Nothing in her eyes at all but hopelessness. "I shouldn't even be talking to you. I promised."

"There's a man," I said. "A mean-looking man, with slick black hair that comes to a point over his forehead and—" I stopped then, because I could see that I was right.

"I had to do it," she said. "Let him back in, I mean. But . . . but my daughter is safe."

"How do you know that?"

"I just know. Now I gotta go." When she started to stand, I reached across the table and grabbed her wrist. She sat down again and I released my grip and let my fingers rest on the back of her hand. Her skin felt smooth and soft and warm.

"One more thing," I said. "The woman. The one I saw with Dominic at your house. Who is she?"

"Karen Colter? She's . . . she's how I know. Karen's watching . . ." She slid her hand out from under mine. "You don't understand . . . about Trish, you know?" She stood up, keeping her hands close to her, as though afraid I'd reach for her again. "Honest, I gotta go now. If anyone finds out I was talking to you—" She spun around and left.

103

I watched her walk away. She was very afraid, but that wasn't all. She seemed ashamed of herself, probably for letting Dominic back in the house, close to her daughter. Maybe guilty, too, about Lammy taking the blame for what happened to Trish. She had a conscience, all right. Maybe I should have told her to let the shame and the guilt come and just feel them. But I really wasn't sure yet whether that worked very well.

What I did know was that Tina Fontana had a surprisingly deep effect on me. I couldn't help noticing the way she walked. I threw some money on the table and hurried after her, amazed at the thoughts and feelings that surged and flooded through me. All the way out the door I fought to chase it all out of my mind—about wanting to stroke the back of her hand and touch her hair, and liking the way she walked. I didn't want those feelings. They weren't going to help Lammy, or me—and certainly not her. Tina's "whole new start" sure didn't include me.

So out on the sidewalk I stopped in my tracks and watched her drive off and ordered my rising feelings to fall away again. Then I walked back to the Loyola el station and went home to dream about the boy in the river—the one who still kept reaching out to me.

CHAPTER
17

I DIDN'T KNOW DAN Maguire well, but I was guessing that, first, if he were in town he'd be in his office by nine-thirty on a Saturday morning in February, and second, if he agreed to see me at all, it would have to be somewhere out-of-the-way. I was only half right. He was there when I called, and he invited me right down to his office.

At noon, he met me in the empty reception area and walked me back to the same conference room we'd used the day before. There were lots of lawyers in khakis and expensive-looking sweaters in the offices along the way. What was missing from my previous visit was the support staff. Secretaries and clerks probably wore cheaper clothes on the weekends, and got to stay home with their families.

"I don't suppose," Maguire said, once we'd poured our own cups of coffee from a plastic carafe and were seated on opposite sides of the table, "you're here to tell me you've changed your mind."

"You're right. But how about you? You're not afraid to be seen talking to me?"

"Not at all. You see, with the obvious exception for privileged meetings with clients, I never engage in business conversations that couldn't be taped and shown on the evening news."

"Even our little chat about Dominic Fontana?"

"Some calls are closer than others, I admit." He smiled, not unpleasantly. "I've had disagreeable clients before, though. I could represent Dominic if I chose to."

"And do you?"

"You called me," he said. "What's on your mind?"

"Paul Anders," I said. "Who is he? Justice Department?"

"Why do you assume I'd answer that, or any other question you might have?"

"I don't assume anything. I just ask questions. It's what I do." I tried the coffee and discovered it was very good. "Sometimes people give answers. Occasionally, true answers. So, FBI, maybe?"

"Why not tell me what *you* think?"

"I think he's with the government. Let's say FBI. I think he doesn't want any boats rocked. And I think he'd let Lambert Fleming go down for a terrible crime, just to protect whatever scheme he's got going."

"They tell me Mr. Fleming has an excellent attorney."

"Good lawyers lose cases. Innocent people sit on death row. Guilty people walk. The point is, for the sake of whatever he's up to, Anders is willing to sacrifice Fleming." I sipped some more coffee. "And, apparently, so are you. Would hearing that on the evening news bother you?"

"Sometimes," Maguire said, "one must make difficult choices." He glanced down at the table for a moment, then looked straight across at me again. "Sometimes there is a significant goal to be attained, and one must walk a disagreeable path to—"

"That's horse shit. We're not talking *disagreeable* here. Anders has something going, and it involves Dominic and his relationship with a woman. To keep it going Anders is willing to let an innocent man's life be ruined. And you're helping him. You know Lambert Fleming didn't go after that girl, and you know Dominic did."

"I don't *know* what happened that night. I wasn't there. I have no reason to believe Dom—" He stopped. "Let me put it this way. I know of no evidence suggesting Dominic attacked Trish that night. Whether Lambert Fleming did, or not, will be decided by someone other than me."

"And meanwhile, you push me around and try to make sure I don't get at the truth."

"Wrong. I don't expect to have any further involvement." He must have seen the surprise on my face. "Frankly, it's my opinion that suing you on Dominic's behalf would be unlikely to have any effect on how you proceed."

"And what else?"

"Pardon me?"

"Besides the chance to tell me I'm not being sued, why else did you agree to meet with me?"

"Oh. Nothing." He poked at his coffee with a red plastic stirrer. "I might add, though, a word of caution."

"You mean somebody's told you to scare me off."

"Not at all. I mean a word of caution from me, personally. And one you would be wise to remember."

Damn. Wisdom again. But I kept quiet.

"There are certain concerns about your interfering," Maguire continued. "You are being watched."

"Tell me about it. I can hardly get into a washroom stall without a chaperone."

"There are others you may be putting in jeopardy, people who—"

"People like Dominic?"

"Possibly. But also those who have . . . relationships with him and who don't need attention drawn to them."

"Are you saying—"

"Also, there are people who may appear to be helping you interfere."

"People like you, maybe?"

"Me? I'm not helping you interfere. If I were, would I meet with you so openly?" He stood up. "I have another appointment. I understand your concern about Lambert Fleming. But I urge you to be concerned about others, too."

"You're saying the FBI would retaliate against someone for talking to me?"

"Any organization can act only through its agents and employees, who in turn act only according to their best judgment—however flawed you might think that judgment is. There are ways of skinning a cat, you know, without taking the knife in your own hands."

I stared at him, trying unsuccessfully to get a grasp on the shifting implications of what he was saying. "What are you talking about? Who—"

"As I said, I have another appointment." He walked me back to the elevators and shook my hand. His expression was difficult to read, but he seemed more sad than anything else. "Good luck," he said. "I think you're going to need it."

Those two ideas, at least, were clear, and I'd have sworn he meant both of them.

CHAPTER
18

DAN MAGUIRE WAS JUST the sort of very important person I'd been ready—even anxious—to dislike, and our first meeting hadn't done a lot to change my attitude. But this time he'd told me, at least by implication, that Paul Anders—if that was his name—was FBI and was using Karen Colter, through her relationship with Dominic, to gather information about Gus Apprezziano. Anders didn't want a gap in his pipeline to Gus, and he was willing to let Lammy take a fall to keep Dominic in place.

Walking back to the parking garage, I saw how clear it was that Maguire had wanted to be sure I knew something, whether I asked or not. He wanted me to know it wasn't just Lammy who was expendable, and that my "interfering" might have a ripple effect.

How far would Anders go?

I could avoid finding out. I could walk away from the delicate hand he was dealing and just let Renata Carroway do her job for Lammy. She'd almost certainly get him a "not guilty." Even if she did, though, they weren't likely to take him back at the dog shelter. Of course, maybe I could get him a better job somewhere else. Maybe even send him back to school and . . .

Right. And I could relocate him to Bangladesh, too, and maybe Steve Connolly wouldn't find him and tear off his arms and legs—and whatever else he could grab hold of—before he sent Lammy screaming into the next world. "Interfering" might mean putting more people in jeopardy. But "not interfering" certainly meant walking away from Lammy, and that wasn't a viable alternative. Not if I wanted to get that ghost of a boy out of the river in my dreams.

Of course, who's to say somebody else's ghost might not wade in to replace him? How the hell was I going to throw a protective shield over Rosa and Trish and Tina—and others I might not even know about? Besides, now that I unwillingly had Gus Apprezziano for a client, too, I couldn't depart the scene entirely. If I told Gus my news about Karen Colter, she was dead. If I didn't, and he ever discovered I'd held out on him, my own longevity was suspect.

I had time to make the end of the basketball game, and far too much to think about, as I wove through Saturday afternoon traffic up the Outer Drive to Sheridan Road, and on to Northwestern's McGaw Hall. The roaring crowd told me the game was still close. Using a pay phone in the lobby, I retrieved two messages from my answering machine. One was Renata Carroway, who said to call her Monday at her office. The other was an Investigator Sanchez, from the Chicago Police Department. He didn't actually ask me to call him back, just left a number and said he wanted to talk to me. I didn't like his tough-guy tone of voice, or the way he used only my first name—and then didn't even pronounce it right. Besides, he's the one who wanted to talk to me. Not vice versa.

So I didn't call him.

UNABLE TO TALK MY way into the game without a ticket even in the closing minutes, I'd missed Wisconsin beating the Wildcats in overtime. Supper was on me, at a place by the el tracks in Evanston called the Noyes Street Café. The food's always great and I usually take home leftovers enough for the next day, too. This time, though, three out of the four of us ate their entrees all the way to the end, and then finished mine as well. Jason had had a great game, so he was on a cloud, and Casey and Lammy and I didn't have to worry about keeping up our ends of the conversation.

Jason had plenty of admirable—if not yet fully developed—qualities, but at that time he was busy becoming a future NBA superstar, and that pretty much exhausted his zone of interest. I knew how that was. I'd never come close to the promise he showed, but I'd had my days. So I could easily cut him some slack. Casey could, too—partly because he'd had a great time at the game, and partly because he's an expert at putting up with difficult people. Me, for instance.

The interesting thing about the evening, though, was Lammy. He wasn't exactly a chatterbox, but he did put some sentences together, and he looked like one of those wide-eyed kids in the TV commercials touting breakfast with Mickey Mouse. He was clearly awestruck, just being in the presence of Jason, who'd been such a dominant factor in the game. He hung on Jason's every word, and Jason loved it and gave Lammy lots of attention.

There was more to it, though. The whole event took place in a world the likes of which Lammy had never participated in. He actually looked alive and interested. "There was a real lot of people there at the game," he said once, when Jason took a break from his personal play-by-play to bite into a hard roll.

"Yeah, well, shoot, man, this was an important game," Jason said, swallowing fast. "Did you see that big dude with the shaved head when I—"

"Hell, Lammy," Casey said, "you want crowds, you an' me'll go to Grant Park next Fourth of July. They jam about a million suburbanites in short pants into—"

"Not really a million," I said. "Not on that one—"

". . . in his face, man," Jason was saying. "Dude won't forget that one, 'specially not after I . . ."

Lammy took it all in. A night out with the boys.

Jason had been excused from taking the team bus back to

Wisconsin, but Casey and Lammy had to drive him up to Madison that night, a five- or six-hour round-trip that Casey insisted was a snap. They were to take me home first.

"Drop me off here," I said, still several blocks from the coach house. "A walk in the fresh air will do me good."

Casey gave me a strange look, but he let me off, made a U-turn, and headed for the expressway.

That there was a car parked down the street from the Lady's drive with two people in it was no surprise. But it wasn't the usual dark blue Ford. This one was two-tone, white and blue, with a bar of emergency lights running across the roof, and red lettering on the side that said "Chicago Police."

For a brief moment I considered heading in the opposite direction, but that seemed hopelessly impractical. So I sauntered past and, when I started up the drive, the squad car pulled slowly in behind me. I turned around, and by that time the cop in the passenger seat was out of the car. She smoothed back her hair and tugged her uniform cap down over her head. "Mister Foley," she said.

"Yes, ma'am . . . I mean officer."

"Get into the patrol car, sir." She was tall and slim, maybe mid-thirties, and looked great, even in her bulky police jacket. But she still talked just like a cop.

"This is Evanston, not Chicago," I said. "I don't know you and I don't get into cars with strange women, not since the early eighties anyway."

Funny thing, my father was a cop. But my instinctive—some say irrational—reaction to police directives certainly wasn't his fault, because he never talked to me like a cop. In fact, he hardly ever talked to me at all, either before or after they kicked him off the force, so—

"I'm Officer Rice." She even gave me her star number. "And my partner is Officer Palka." Palka was out of the car now, too, standing with his blue-shirted beer belly bulging out from his

112

unbuttoned jacket, resting one hand casually on the butt of his service revolver. "Investigator Sanchez wants to talk to you," Rice added.

"Does he? That the same Sanchez as on the Lambert Fleming case?"

"Get in the car sir. Now."

"Your partner gonna shoot me if I refuse?"

Palka spoke for the first time. "God," he said, more to himself than to Rice or me, "just like all the other assholes of the world."

He was right, of course.

"I'm going up to my apartment now," I said, "and you can come back when—"

"You can't go up to your apartment before Investigator Sanchez gets here, with a search warrant. Let's go."

"You two ever hear of the constitu—"

By that time Palka had his revolver in one hand and his radio in the other, but that didn't matter much because an Evanston patrol car pulled into the drive, and an unmarked squad nosed up behind that.

"I guess not," I said, and put my hands on my head.

They didn't cuff me after they patted me down, but they also didn't tell me what was going on, and they didn't let me go into my place when I unlocked the door for them. Sanchez did humor me a little, though, and let me check both front and back doors when I made a fuss about seeing whether someone had been through either of them since I'd been gone.

"Well?" Sanchez asked, when I'd finished inspecting both doors. "Anyone been inside, Mr. Detective?"

"Jeez, I don't know," I lied. "Can't tell."

"Christ. C'mon, amigo."

When we got to Area Three Headquarters they took me to an interrogation room with the usual scarred-up table and chairs. There was the usual one-way picture window, too, to reflect back the table and chairs and the usual suspects.

"If I'm under arrest, what's the charge?" I scowled back at my reflection. "What's going on, for chrissake?"

"No arrest, no charge," Sanchez said. "You're here voluntarily in your capacity as a good citizen, to answer questions. Just relax, and I'll be right back." He locked the door behind him.

He'd probably wait for word from the people tossing my apartment. Whatever they found, it wouldn't have been placed there since I'd left that morning. I was confident no one had been through the doors, even if Sanchez didn't have to know that.

I waited, telling myself over and over that I wasn't there because my "interfering" had put someone "in jeopardy." I suppose some part of my brain thought repetition could make the truth go away.

A half hour later Sanchez came back. He sat down and placed a large manila envelope on the table between us.

"Find anything at my place?" I asked.

"Where were you last night?"

"Where's the phone? I want to call my lawyer."

"Where were you last night from, say, ten o'clock to five this morning?"

"From midnight to five I was home, alone, asleep. Where's the phone?"

"You don't need a lawyer. You're not accused of anything yet. I'm trying to trace the activities of the victim of a crime last night."

"Why don't you just ask him?"

"I'm afraid that's not possible." Which is exactly what I was afraid of, too.

He picked up the envelope and withdrew what looked like a cardboard frame for a photograph, the kind people set on their pianos. But Sanchez held it so I could see only the back. He stared at it for a while, then said, "Know this woman?" and turned the photograph to me.

Tina Fontana smiled out at me from a five-by-seven color print. She was wearing a white dress and a wide straw hat with flowers around it. The dress had a high neckline and ended just above her knees, and it showed off her figure very well. There was a brightly dressed little girl clinging to her right hand. They were standing on a sidewalk somewhere and if I'd had to guess, I'd have said it was Easter, and they were on their way to church.

She looked maybe five years younger than when I saw her at The Captain's Choice. She might have been happier back then, too. Who could say? She was very pretty in the picture, but no prettier than she'd been when she sat across the table from me and grinned and admitted she was flirting.

"I guess you do, huh?" Sanchez said.

"What?" I found myself breathing fast and trying hard to swallow. My mouth was dry and sour.

"I guess you know her," he said.

"Tina Fontana." I forced another swallow. "I met her once. Is she—"

"You met her?"

"Last night."

He took some more photographs from the envelope. "Take a look at these," he said. "And then, amigo, we better talk about calling your lawyer."

CHAPTER

19

THE PHOTOS WERE EIGHT-BY-TEN color glossies, six of them.

One was all it took. A thick, rancid rush filled my mouth and I swallowed, over and over, until the vomit finally slid back to where it had come from and stayed there. Then I paged through the remaining pictures.

Tina's coat was open and the top part of her blouse was ripped away from her neck. It was the same white blouse—with the same plaid vest—she'd been wearing at The Captain's Choice. There were two head close-ups and four full-body shots. She was sprawled on her back on a cement floor, beside a messy table equipped like a workbench. I thought at first it was a basement, but another photo showed it was a garage. There was a car that looked like the car she'd driven when she left the restaurant.

Her mouth was wide open, and so was her right eye. The left eye was half closed, swollen and ringed with bruising. Her nose, upper lip, and chin were all smeared with blood. There were more dark bruises on both of her cheeks, and some on her neck. A thin line of dried blood ran from her left ear.

"I have just read you your rights, amigo," Sanchez said, and he might have, for all I knew. "You wanna talk about it?" he asked.

"You answer a couple questions?"

"That depends."

"I mean, she's been beaten up. But . . . but people don't usually die from that."

"Maybe that's what you wanna talk about, amigo. Maybe it

was an accident. You were just slapping her around a little. Trying to get some information or something, I don't know. Or maybe there was an argument. She's a pretty woman and maybe you wanted . . . Anyway, maybe she slipped and hit her head on something, and then fell down and didn't get up, you know? And you were scared and you just took off and—"

"Let me look a minute," I said, and I paged through the photos again. There was a vise attached to the edge of the cluttered workbench above where she lay, and this time I saw the blood smeared on it—and maybe a clump of hair. "Are there more pictures?" I knew there had to be, including close-ups of the vise.

Sanchez grinned—a treacherous, feline grin. "Just tell me what happened."

I looked again at the photos. The garage seemed quite large, and was a mess. The floor was grimy and oil-stained, and there were half-open cardboard cartons, lawn tools, and miscellaneous junk piled everywhere.

"Is this Dominic's garage? Is that where it happened?"

"You tell me, amigo. That's what I'm here for. You explain what happened, maybe how you didn't really mean to hurt her at all, but she fell. And maybe the doc will agree with you. Maybe it isn't first degree. Of course, you don't cooperate, maybe it is. I dunno. So . . . whaddaya say, amigo?"

I put the pictures facedown on the table and aligned them into a very careful pile, then laid my palms flat, one on each side of the pile, and looked across at Sanchez. He grinned again, looking like a sly cat. It was as though this was about Sanchez and me, not about a sad, pretty woman whose teenage daughter had no mother any more—and still had Dominic Fontana for a father. I knew Sanchez was doing the best job he could, the best way he knew. And I wanted to kick his sly grin straight up his ass.

But I didn't do that. I said, *"Chingase,* amigo. But first, show me the telephone."

CHAPTER
20

RENATA WAS THERE IN less than an hour. I wanted to give a statement, but finally followed her advice and refused to answer any questions. They left me alone in the interrogation room while she met with Sanchez and his partner, and a Lieutenant Lewis she insisted on talking to. When she came back, the lieutenant was with her. He looked very unhappy, and told me I was free to go.

We passed Sanchez on the way out. He looked even more unhappy, and he and I exchanged a few quiet words. "Just enough words," Renata said, once we got outside, "to make absolutely sure there's no possible benefit of the doubt he'll ever give you in this lifetime."

"That's fine with me. I don't want any goddamn favors from that sonovabitch."

"Amazing," she said. "Like two macho twelve-year-olds in a schoolyard. No wonder I never married one of you guys."

That made me smile, which may have been her intention. "You never married one of us guys, Renata," I said, "because then you'd have to get rid of Virginia." Renata and Virginia had been together something like seven years and had recently returned from Korea with an infant girl they'd adopted.

When we reached her BMW, she said, "You don't look so good. I'll take you home."

"No. Take me to Lammy's."

Renata knew Casey was staying with Lammy. "Why wake them up at this time of night?"

"They went to Wisconsin. They're probably not even home yet. I wanna be there when they get back." What I didn't say was I couldn't stand the idea of going home alone and kicking myself around the coach house.

While she drove, Renata told me about her conversation with the cops. "Tina Fontana was killed late last night in her own garage. They've got a witness, a waiter at the restaurant where she worked, who says a man matching your general description came in there last night just before closing. Says Tina was talking to the man and she seemed nervous, like she wanted to get away from him. He grabbed at her. Finally she got up and ran out of the restaurant. The man ran out after her." She paused. "Sanchez says you admit meeting her at the restaurant last night."

"Sanchez is lying. I told him I met her. I didn't say at the restaurant."

"Where was it then?"

"At the restaurant," I said. "Last night."

"What—"

"The waiter's lying, too. Tina left in a hurry, but not running. I walked out after she did. What do the other people at the restaurant say?"

"I haven't gotten that far. I'll have the initial police reports by Monday. How soon after her did you leave?"

"I got out some money and left it on the table. Then I walked out. Tina was driving out of the parking lot when I got to the sidewalk. I took the el home and went to bed."

"So maybe nobody actually saw what you did when you left."

"Right. That's right, counselor. And maybe I jumped into her car and forced her to drive home, to where she lives with this loony-tunes, body-building gorilla of a husband of hers, who's mob connected. And when we got to her garage I thought, Oh, this is a handy location. I'll beat her to death right here where Dominic the maniac can hear what's . . . shit." I stared out the car window, but all I could see was Tina's face, with the bruises and all the blood. "The whole thing's crazy."

Renata pulled up in front of Lammy's. "We'll talk once I've seen the reports."

"They want a suspect," I said, "they ought talk to her psycho of a husband."

"They've talked to Dominic. Says he's got an alibi. A woman, he says, who was with him the whole time, right there at the house. Windows all closed. Garage out back by the alley. Says they didn't hear anything."

"Oh?" I got out of the car and leaned back in. "And it never occurred to them to wonder why Tina didn't come home from work?"

"There are plenty of holes in their theory. That's why you're not a guest of the state already. But they're in an awful hurry to close this with an arrest. Meanwhile, back off, will you? You're not helping Lammy. You're just in the way. You're not helping any—"

I slammed the door—as hard as I could—and set the BMW rocking side to side.

She started slowly away, but I ran beside the car, slapping on the trunk. She stopped and let down the window. "Renata," I said, "I'm sorry. Sometimes I don't—"

"I accept your apology," she said. "And I understand your frustration. I really do."

I watched her drive away and felt exhausted, empty, and entirely alone. It was three in the morning, with high clouds skidding across a starlit sky and a bone-chilling wind whistling down the street out of the north. Every house on the block was dark.

I had two keys, one to the door to the enclosed back porches and one to Lammy's kitchen door. I waded through knee-deep snow that the wind had sent drifting into the gangway between the two buildings and came out behind the two-flat. Key in hand, I turned right . . . and found the door into the porch enclosure just slightly open. Lammy told me they never used to lock that door, and maybe he'd forgotten again. On the other hand, you didn't have to be much of a pro to slip open a lock like that one.

I stood absolutely still, but heard nothing above the roar and whistle of the wind. I pulled the door open slowly and stepped inside. To my left were the steps leading down to the basement and I leaned and peered that way, but saw nothing.

There was just the whisper of a sound, then, to my right and I turned that way. But too late. Someone sprang at me from the darkness, and sent me stumbling off-balance, arms flailing, down the short concrete stairway. I hit the bottom hard, landing on my hands and knees, but was on my feet in a hurry and scrambling back up the stairs.

Whoever it was, he was through the back gate by the time I was out the door and in the backyard. A car door slammed, an engine roared, and by the time I reached the alley there were taillights fishtailing down the hard-packed snow to the north and then turning out onto the street.

I raced back to the house and up the stairs to the second floor. The kitchen door was locked. I opened it and went inside, charging around, turning lights on everywhere. Casey and Lammy weren't there. No one was there. Nothing was disturbed that I could see.

Ending up back in the kitchen, I checked the lock on the door. It would have taken real skill to get through this one, and there was no sign of anyone trying. Was the visitor merely pulling another dead dog–type stunt? I hadn't stumbled across anything in the dark by the basement door, and it hardly seemed worth it to check at that hour. All I really wanted to do was sleep. But if there *was* something, I should get to it before Lammy saw it.

I found the switch to the back-porch lights and went downstairs. There was nothing. The door out to the yard was still open, and I pulled it closed. When the spring lock clicked, I remembered the basement door had the same lock. Anybody who got through one could have gotten through the other. So I used the key and went into the basement. I switched on the light.

It was a cold, bone-dry basement with a seven foot ceiling, and about as clean and tidy as a basement can be. There was a washer and a dryer, and the shelf over the slate-gray double-welled sink was neatly lined with laundry supplies. There wasn't a spider web in sight. The compact gas boiler sat like a dwarf in an alcove that must once have held a huge coal furnace. To the right of that, what might once have been the coal bin was divided into two walk-in storage bins with floor-to-ceiling walls of chicken-wire framed with pine one-by-twos. Both bins had chicken-wire doors about six feet high, padlocked and marked "First Floor" and "Second Floor," as if the two families wouldn't be able to remember otherwise.

Inside the "First Floor" bin, everything was boxed and stacked and labeled with a felt-tipped pen. The other bin—Lammy's and his mother's—was far less neat and organized. A huge old console TV, probably black and white, dominated the floor space, and on top of that a plastic Sportmart shopping bag lay on its side with clothing spilling out. Between the TV and the far wall, cardboard boxes and brown paper bags were haphazardly piled all over each other. There was an ancient child's rocking chair—missing one rocker—and lots of rusting household appliances like toasters and waffle irons.

Most interesting to me, though, were the little lines and marks on the floor outside the bins—some still damp—lines and marks that might have been the remains of dirty snow from someone's shoes. I'm no tracker, but the residue ran in a fairly straight path from the outside door to the second-floor bin—and nowhere else. The padlock was intact, though, and unless some-

122

one had squeezed through the ten or twelve inches between the top of the flimsy door and the basement ceiling—not likely— they'd have had to pick the lock to get inside. It was a cheap lock, but so was the one on the other bin, the bin that would have looked far more promising to any ordinary thief. Besides, why steal something from the Flemings' bin and then replace the lock?

There was another, more likely, alternative. Especially since the Flemings weren't exactly a Sportmart type of family.

Taking hold of the wood frame at the top, I ripped down the door, splintering the flimsy wood around the hinges. The shopping bag was stuffed with old clothes, but not entirely. Near the bottom were three thin paperback books—cheaply printed and bound, but claiming very high purchase prices on their covers. Pamphlets, really, rather than books, and mostly pictures. They were somebody's gift to Lammy, and they sure weren't books about war—other than that age-old profit-driven war against prepubescent little girls and boys. I wrapped them in an old undershirt, and stuffed the other clothes back into the Sportmart bag. Finally, on a whim and just because it might confuse things further, I pushed the bag of clothes through the opening between the ceiling and the top of the door of the first-floor storage bin, and dropped it inside onto the floor.

Dragging myself upstairs, I knew I was far too tired to make smart decisions—like whether to burn the little pornographic books or save them as evidence—so I decided to hide them for now. I'd get them out of the house first thing in the morning, and consult Renata.

Casey's duffle bag was lying open on the floor beside the sofa in the TV room that was his headquarters. Inside the bag, among his books and clothing, was a black leather case—cube-shaped, about nine inches to the side—with a black plastic handle on its hinged top. There was a latch with a tiny keyhole, but the case wasn't locked. Inside, cushioned in purple velvet, was a large goblet-shaped cup made of gold. It was Casey's chalice, and slipped in beside it was a matching gold plate, in a sort of envelope of soft cloth. Substituting the thin pornographic books for the gold plate, I wedged the cloth envelope back into place beside the chalice. That left the plate, so I wrapped it up in the old undershirt and put it, along with the chalice case, in with the clothes in the duffle bag.

"There," I said aloud to no one, "they're within the private property of a guest." Of course, the rules on how far a search warrant extended kept changing, but in the morning I'd get the books out of the apartment entirely, and avoid the whole issue. I collapsed on the sofa and fell asleep with all the lights on.

The next thing I knew, Casey was bellowing at the front door of the apartment. Something like, ". . . upstairs, c'mon, all you guys. We'll tear these suckers limb from limb, damn it, the no-good bums. This way!" Now he was farther inside the apartment, still hollering, "Bring those baseball bats. These guys—"

"Casey!" I called. "It's me."

"Oh." He appeared in the doorway, alone. "Jeez, you look a mess. Me and Lammy saw the lights on and thought—"

"Let's talk about it in the morning," I said, hoisting myself up off the sofa.

"Hell, it's *already* morning, almost six o'clock now. We had a flat tire, and there was no spare in your damn rental car, so we hadda wait—"

"Where's Lammy?"

"I told him to stay by the front door and run like hell if there was trouble." He turned around and shouted. "Hey, Lammy, it's all right. C'mon up!"

There was no answer.

"Damn," Casey said.

But then we both heard pounding on the downstairs front door, and Lammy's voice, louder than I'd ever heard it. "Father Casey! Help!"

Casey ran to the door at the top of the front stairs, with me two steps behind. "Lammy?" Casey called. "Why don't—" He stopped, looking down the stairway, then turned to me and said, "I don't believe this." He shook his huge head. "The police are here."

CHAPTER

21

THERE WERE TWO UNIFORMS with crowbars they were dying to use, and two plainclothes—one named Stevenson, the other my friend Sanchez. He was the one who showed us the search warrant for the second-floor apartment, issued by a night court judge who'd handwritten "plus basement storage for second floor only" right above the typed address.

We gathered in the kitchen. Lammy and I sat at the table, while Casey started making coffee. Sanchez somehow managed to look groggy and wired at the same time. I knew exactly how he felt. "You don't look so hot, investigator," I said. "You oughta get more sleep."

He ignored me and sent the uniformed cops to the basement. "Should be a storage room down there marked second floor." They left, and Sanchez turned and stared straight at Lammy with red-veined eyes. "I'm gonna nail your ass, Fleming, you twisted prick," he finally said. He must have been exhausted, filled with rage he was too tired to hold back any longer. "You might as well give up now, fat boy," he said. Lammy's face turned ashen, and tears filled his eyes.

"Hey, hold on," Stevenson said. "Relax, will you pardner? Jesus. It's just a job, man."

But Sanchez kept on. "I'm nailin' your baby-fat ass, Fleming. Your big brother here's got his own problems now, and he can't do a thing to help. I'm gonna see you go away, fat boy." His mouth curved into an ugly grin. "You like little girls so much? Well, you can *be* a little girl, a fat little girl for some big shine to shove his—"

I was on my feet by then, blind to all but the grin on his face, with his words roaring in my ears. I lunged at Sanchez.

But I couldn't move. I was paralyzed, arms pinned down to my sides. I tried to walk but my feet were off the floor.

"Mal . . . Mal . . . Mal . . ." That was all Casey kept saying, softly, as though to himself, as he carried me kicking out of the kitchen, down the hall to the TV room. He sat me on the sofa like I was three years old, and I let him do it because I knew he was right and I'd been just as out of control as Sanchez was.

Lammy came in, too, and shrank back against the wall, hugging himself, staring down at his shoes. Behind him came Sanchez, with Stevenson nowhere in sight.

"All right, Fleming," Sanchez started, "you can't—"

"Quiet!" Casey roared. "No more!" He stepped close up to Sanchez, looming over the smaller man. "You and I are leaving this room now, officer, and you won't say one word more." His voice was low and soft now, in a way I'd never heard before. "Because if you do . . ." he paused, as though coming to a decision. "If you do, I'll pick you up, too, and I'll carry you the other direction down the hall and out the damn back door."

"You . . . are you threatening a police officer?" Sanchez said.

"Not a threat, no. A promise. From a man who happens to be a priest, don't forget. A priest whose father was a cop who was shot dead in the line of duty. A priest who has a cousin who's watch commander in the Second District and a nephew downtown in Internal Affairs. I'm telling you it's over now. Say anything more to these two, and unless you shoot me—and you're not that crazy—I will certainly carry you outta here, and accept whatever the consequences are."

My shock at what I was hearing must have cleared my mind, and I suddenly remembered something. "Casey," I said, "look at your watch." He looked at me, confused. "You promised to say the six-thirty Mass at Our Lady of Ravenna. You're gonna be late if—"

"Hey, Sanchez!" It was Stevenson, calling from the kitchen.

". . . almost forgot," Casey was saying, still trying to get a handle on things, but playing along. "Let's see now, I—"

"Here's your roman collar," I said, and then dug back into his duffle bag. "And here. Here's your chalice. What else you need?"

"Sanchez!" Stevenson again, banging down the hallway.

"Quiet!" Casey bellowed. He turned to Sanchez, waving his chalice case in the air for emphasis. "I'm taking my friends with me to Mass. You do your search. And close the door on your way out. We'll keep quiet about what's happened here. And you will, too." His voice had returned to the soft, ominous tone of a few moments ago. "Because otherwise you'll have to lie. And if you do, and if I tell the truth . . . which of us do you think will be believed?"

Casey gestured Lammy and me to the door ahead of him and we started down the stairs. From behind, I heard Stevenson's voice: ". . . nothing in there, so the two assholes busted into the other bin and—"

Casey slammed the door behind him and we all went out to the car and I drove us to church.

The wind was still blowing, but no new snow had arrived yet. Our Lady of Ravenna was locked up tight and as dark as a tomb. The sign said the first Mass on Sunday was at eight o'clock.

"We can't go back to Lammy's yet," I said. "Let's just go to my place and get some sleep."

"Good idea," Casey said. He turned to the backseat. "Whadda you think, Lammy?"

Lammy didn't answer. I checked in the rear-view mirror, but he wasn't asleep. He was just sitting there, wrapped up in the coat I'd bought him.

"Lammy?" Casey said. "Shall we go to Mal's, or what?"

"Uh, yeah, I guess so," Lammy said.

"Okay, then we all agree." Casey let a few seconds go by,

then said, " 'Cause like I was telling you before, Lammy, every-body's idea counts, you know? We're all in this together. Okay?"

"Uh . . . yes, Father."

We rode in silence for about ten minutes. "So Casey," I said, "would you really have done it?"

"Done what?"

"Picked him up and carried him outside."

"Jeez, I don't really know. I might have ended up in jail."

"You sounded certain to me."

"Yeah, well, I always got a big part in every play we put on in the seminary. I was the angriest juror in *Twelve Angry Men,* and I was King Henry in *A Man for All Seasons,* and—"

"So you lied to Sanchez."

"Making a promise you might not keep isn't exactly the same as a lie . . . I guess. Anyway, the part I feel bad about is playing up the *priest* business, you know? But then, Sanchez . . . probably raised a Catholic . . ."

"Plus, I knew about your dad getting shot, but I never heard about your cousin and your nephew. Was that all true?"

"Of course it was. I read in the paper about my cousin being made watch commander. Second cousin, actually. Haven't seen the damn guy in thirty-five years. And my sister's youngest kid just got a job in Internal Affairs. He's a clerk-typist or some-thing." Casey banged me on the arm with the chalice case he was still holding. "Anyway, what's this stuff all about? I had my chalice in my bag in case I wanted to say Mass right there at the apartment. If I was gonna say Mass at Ravenna's, I'd just use one of their chalices." He unlatched the case. "By the way, did you ever see my chalice? It's got my mother's diamond—"

"Wait. Don't open that."

"Huh?"

"Here's a White Hen Pantry," I said, as we bounced into the parking lot of the twenty-four-hour store. Casey had his chalice

129

case open. "Gimme that," I said, and snatched the cloth packet from the case. "You don't want to see these," I said.

"Wait," Casey said, obviously offended. "Hold on, Mr. Big Shot. I was just telling Lammy we're all in this together. Now you expect him and me to follow orders while you decide what we wanna see? What the hell kinda attitude is that?"

"Fine," I said. Maybe Casey was a little strung out, just like me, but his Mr. Big Shot remark hit me hard. "Fine," I repeated. "Decide for yourself."

Casey took the kiddy porno books I shoved at him. "My God," he said, and he handed them right back to me. "Get rid of 'em."

"Oh no." I snatched them out of his hand. "Not till *everybody* gets a look. Not just *Mr. Big Shot.*" I thrust the booklets over my shoulder. "Here, Lammy. I found these in your basement storage bin."

"What?" Casey said. "You—"

"No," Lammy said, shoving the books back almost as soon as he'd taken them.

"No, what?" I said.

"Not our bin. I got the only key. I don't wanna look at that kinda stuff."

"Okay, then we all agree. I get rid of this shit."

I went inside the store, bought a large manila envelope and stamps, and mailed the books to Barney Green, marked "Privileged." He'd know by the writing on the envelope that it came from his former partner. He'd know who sent them by the handwritten address. He'd know to throw out the envelope and put the materials in his safe. He'd also know it was a serious federal crime to send child pornography through the mail, and almost as bad to keep it when it arrives. But we were all in this together. The more, the merrier. Who knows? Maybe it would come in handy if there were some identifiable fingerprints on the books—other than all of ours, of course.

We went to the coach house and crashed.

When I woke up it was nearly time for supper. Casey and Lammy had been to afternoon Mass and then to the store, and now they were making an omelet. I sat in the kitchen and saw how Lammy watched Casey with obvious respect, even awe, as the two of them chopped up onions and peppers.

I caught Lammy looking at me once, too. But what showed in his eyes then was more like fear, or suspicion.

CHAPTER

22

RENATA CARROWAY CALLED THE next morning—Monday. "Where's Lammy?"

"He's here," I said. "We had a little trouble after you dropped me off Saturday night."

"I know. I heard about that. Y'know, I asked you to stop interfering, and—"

I hung up the phone. I had to. The alternative was to say what I felt like saying, and Renata didn't deserve that. Besides, I figured she'd call right—

The phone rang and I picked it up. "Anyway," Renata said, "I want to see Lammy. One o'clock in my office. Can he make it?"

"What's up?"

"They're offering a deal," she said.

"What kind of a deal?"

"One o'clock. Can you get him here?"

It was a bitterly cold, brilliantly sunlit day. Lammy's left hand was still in a bandage, but the bruises on his face were fading, and his hair was starting to grow back. We drove along the lakefront toward downtown and I tried to make conversation, but to describe Lammy's responses as monosyllabic would exaggerate their eloquence.

At five after one the receptionist pointed to a tiny closet and Lammy and I were hanging up our coats when Renata came out to her waiting room. "I want to talk to you for a minute first, Mal." We stepped just beyond the door to her inner offices and she closed it behind us. "What have you told him?"

"I told him you wanted to see him. Did I tell him there was

an offer? No. Did I tell him he should plead guilty? No. Or plead not guilty? No. In other words, I haven't told him a goddamn thing. After all, you don't want me to inter—"

"Look," she said, "I can see how heavily you're invested in this. Emotionally, I mean. I don't know why, and I don't need to know. In fact, Lammy's lucky you are. But he's an adult, and this decision has to be his, and his alone."

"Whether you believe it or not, Lammy and I haven't talked about his case at all. I haven't even asked him whether he did it or not. As for making a plea, I agree it's up to him. But I want to be in the room when you explain it to him."

She objected to that momentarily, but couldn't think of a really good argument. So the three of us ended up in her office, a rather odd melange of lawyerlike clutter—papers everywhere, thick file folders and large open books piled in precarious stacks—and decidedly feminine touches. Lammy and I sat on opposite ends of an overstuffed sofa that was loaded with embroidered pillows. Renata slipped her glasses on and leaned back against the front of her desk, legal pad in hand. She peered out through thick round lenses.

"Lammy," she said, "Mr. Foley is helping me. Even with him present, everything we say here is privileged. That means neither he nor I can reveal it without your permission. Do you understand?"

"Yeah, I guess." He sat with one hand resting on each thigh, his head tilted down toward the floor.

"I can ask Mr. Foley to leave if you prefer."

"I . . . that's . . ." He lifted his bandaged left hand and placed it on top of his right hand. But that didn't help. It only made it more obvious that both hands were trembling. He didn't look up, but his head was bobbing in tiny nods.

"I understand," I said. "I'll wait outside. That's okay."

I left the office and went back to the waiting room. But it wasn't okay. I wanted Lammy to want me with him. I was trying to help him. And besides, I can't tolerate sitting in waiting rooms.

But I'd hardly sat down when Renata came out. "He had something he wanted to ask without your being there, Mal." She smiled and I realized she didn't do that nearly often enough. "But now that that's over," she said, "he wants you with him."

I followed her back to her office. Lammy looked up at me. He didn't actually greet me, but he did look at me for a part of a second.

Renata picked her legal pad up from her desk again. "So, let's not waste any more time. Do you know what a plea bargain is, Lammy?" she said.

"Uh, I think so."

"Most cases never go to trial," she began, and while she explained how plea bargaining worked I thought of the defendants I'd represented when I had a license. Too many of them had been dealing with the criminal justice system since childhood, and knew how it worked—for better or for worse—just about as well as I did. ". . . state's attorney called this morning," Renata was saying, "with a proposed plea agreement."

"What's the plea?" I asked. Renata scowled at me. "Oh, sorry. I'll shut up."

"The proposal is, Lammy, that you plead guilty to aggravated criminal sexual abuse. The aggravated criminal sexual *assault* charge will be dismissed and the state will recommend no jail time and a period of probation."

"What's the difference between . . . between those two things you said?" Lammy asked.

"The definitions are very complicated, but *abuse* is a less serious crime than *assault.*"

"And they're both felonies," I added, "so if I were you—"

"Please," Renata said, and I clammed up again.

"So . . . would I just sign something?"

"You sign a written plea agreement," Renata explained. "But

then you appear before the judge and he'll ask you whether you understand the agreement and if you're entering the plea of your own free will. Things like that."

"What if I say I didn't do it, but I signed 'cause I don't wanna go to jail?"

"Then the judge might vacate the plea and set the matter for trial. If you plead guilty, you're admitting you committed the crime."

"So it's still the sex stuff? Just not as bad?"

"That's right. And you won't take a chance on going to jail."

"What about my ma?"

"What?" Renata looked confused.

"My ma. What'll I tell *her?*"

"I don't know," Renata said, "but if you get convicted of the sexual assault, it's not your mother who'll go to the penitentiary."

I thought if his mother's behavior so far was any clue, she wouldn't even visit him. But I kept quiet.

"So," Renata said, "what do you think?"

"I . . . uh . . ." Lammy looked my way, but I wasn't sure he saw me. He dropped his chin down to his chest again. "I guess . . ." His voice drifted off.

"Renata?" When she didn't tell me to shut up, I asked, "What about simple battery? A misdemeanor. Then he can get the record expunged later."

She shook her head. "Not possible. Heffernan says he's gonna have the public and the media all over him as it is. And he's right."

"You know why he's making the offer, don't you. Why don't you tell Lammy? It's because—"

"Wait, Mal," she said. "No one's asked for your opinion, not yet. This is Lammy's decision, and so far he hasn't even asked *me* for an opinion." She turned to Lammy. "Do you have any questions?"

"Well," Lammy plucked at his pant leg with his right hand,

"can you get me off? I mean, if I don't plead guilty and the little girl keeps saying I did it?"

"I don't know if the girl will testify. Even if she doesn't, they could put her previous statement into evidence. But all in all, the state doesn't have a strong case. We have a good chance at a not guilty. But I can't guarantee anything. And . . . there's something else, too, that—"

"Doesn't matter," Lammy said. He was shaking his head from side to side. "Abuse . . . assault. I don't care."

"What do you mean?" Renata asked.

"I mean I don't wanna say I'm guilty. I can't tell my ma and my sister I did that. And not the judge, either. 'Cause I didn't do it."

I let out my breath and didn't realize until then I'd been holding it in. I was proud of Lammy, but scared for him, too. "Wait," I said. "You said there was something else, Renata. What was that?"

"Heffernan told me that if Lammy didn't take the plea, they'd indict him."

"What? They can't do that. He's already charged and out on bond."

"He was charged under an information. They can seek a grand jury indictment, which they'll get. That won't improve their case any, but they can rearrest him on the indictment and—"

"Jail again?" Lammy's voice was strained, high-pitched.

"Rearrest him," she continued, "and ask the judge to set another bond before he can be released again. They can do—"

"I don't wanna go back there," Lammy was mumbling, as though speaking to himself. "It's bad there."

"They can do that," Renata continued, still looking at me as though she hadn't heard Lammy. "I've never heard of it being done, not in Cook County, anyway. But they can. And Heffernan says they will, unless he pleads—"

"Um . . . excuse me." Lammy was standing, rubbing his right hand over the bandage on his left, as though he were washing it. His eyes were wide and he was looking toward the windows. "I gotta go," he said.

"You just got here," Renata said, "and we still have to decide—"

"No. I mean I gotta go to the bathroom." He looked it, too.

"Oh, I'm sorry," Renata said. "It's out in the hall. Get the key from the receptionist."

When he was gone, Renata said, "I agree, Mal. Heffernan wouldn't make an offer if he didn't know he had an uphill battle—one he might well lose. I don't like to lead clients to decisions if I can help it, but I'm glad Lammy's not taking the deal. We're gonna win this goddamn case."

"Yeah, but sending him back to jail. Did you see the panic in his eyes? Jesus."

"I know, but—" Her phone rang and she picked it up. "Hello?" She listened, then looked at me with her hand over the receiver. "It's my daughter's nanny," she said. "It'll just take a minute."

The nanny must have been telling her something especially cute the baby had done. Renata was smiling nonstop now, and said, "Oh, really?" like every other doting mother, about five times. When the call was over, she set the phone down and stared at it for a few seconds.

When she looked up, though, she was all business again. "If that judge has any balls," she said, "he'll rule that the previous bond is sufficient. But if he sets another bond . . . is there any more money?"

"I'm broke," I said, and then remembered Gus. "Except I did just pick up a new client, with an offer I couldn't refuse. Or half an offer, anyway. I only get the other half if I get results."

"I can win this case, you know. Even if Lammy doesn't make a very good witness, I—" Renata suddenly looked around her

137

office as though something were missing. "I wonder what's taking him so long?" she said. "You better go check. He might be sick or something."

I went up front and stopped at the receptionist's desk. "Do you have another key to the men's room?" I asked.

"No-o," she said, and somehow I didn't like the way she dragged out the word and looked mystified. "Just the one. Why?"

"I need to get in there to check on Mr. Fleming. He may be sick."

"Oh, he didn't take the key. Just grabbed his coat and left. He's gone. He was mumbling something about—"

By the time she got to what Lammy said, I was out in the hall, repeatedly punching the button like all those ignorant people who think they can make the elevator hurry up and get there.

The elevator didn't hurry. And when it took me down it stopped about five times, or fifteen times, on the way. Down in the lobby, and out on the street, there was no sign of Lammy in any direction. Running was a dumb thing for him to do, but somehow I found myself even a little more proud of him than I'd been when he announced he wouldn't plead guilty.

A little more proud. But a lot more scared for him, too.

CHAPTER

23

"You're joking," Renata said.

"Nope. He's gone, all right." I offered her one of the Cokes I'd bought at the newsstand in the lobby and taken back up with me to her office.

"No thanks," she said, waving her hand vaguely and walking over to the windows. She stared down as though she'd be able to spot Lammy on the sidewalk—which wasn't even in sight from her floor. "Gone where? Home?"

"Home if we're lucky. But your talk about getting indicted and going back to jail frightened him. Maybe he's running away."

"That's ridiculous."

"Running away when you're scared is a pretty time-honored practice."

"What I mean is he doesn't have . . . well . . . the ambition or something, to run off. Besides, it won't help any—"

"Easy for you to say. You're in his mother's position."

"What are you talking about?"

"You're not facing going to jail, anymore than his mother is." I took a long swig of my Coke. "You don't know, Renata, how bad it is in there for him."

"Oh, I know how bad—"

"You've visited lots of clients in lots of jails, but you've never been a prisoner. You don't know what it's like from the inside. Lammy does, and he's scared to death."

"If he's so afraid, why didn't he jump at the chance to plead guilty?"

"That surprised me, too. Maybe there's something inside Lammy that people don't often see. He's terrified. But you can't be brave if you're not scared in the first place, so he made a very courageous choice." I waited for a long time, but she didn't say anything. "Then, as soon as he makes it, you tell him he'll probably have to go to jail anyway, and he knows he'll *stay* there if he doesn't come up with more bond money—which he doesn't have."

She spun around and glared at me. "Don't blame *me*, for God's sake. He should have spoken up. We could have talked about it." She stopped, then heaved a tired sigh. "I should tell you what he wanted to ask me with you out of the room. He wondered if I knew how he should act around you, to make sure you don't go away."

"Jesus."

"I told him it didn't matter how he acted. I said I didn't know why, but I didn't think you'd leave him alone even if he wanted you to—or even if I asked you to back off." She paused. "Anyway, he's probably on the el right now, headed home. You'll find him there."

"Maybe. Meanwhile, you'll just have to stall Heffernan, tell him Lammy's thinking about the plea agreement. Even if he takes that as a 'no deal,' it'll be a few days before he can get an indictment, if he's not bluffing about that. And, if Lammy really has run, I'll have to find him."

"But there's a status hearing on the case tomorrow, at two o'clock," Renata said. "Lammy has to be in court with me."

"I'll have him there, I hope. Otherwise, you'll have to make an excuse for him, get a new court date."

"Not a chance. You heard the judge when he set the bond. Lammy's to be there every time the case is up. Otherwise, the bond is revoked and he'll be arrested."

Renata took me to a phone in an empty office next to hers. I called the only place I could think of, other than the two-flat, where he might go.

"Hullo?" A female voice, sounding like a teenager, a bored teenager.

"Mrs. Baranowski?"

"Just a minute." There was a bang as she set the phone down. "Hey, ma!" she called. "It's for you."

"Hullo?"

I'd have sworn it was the same bored person, if I hadn't heard the other voice in the background saying, "How do *I* know who it is, ma?"

"Hullo?" she repeated.

"Elaine Baranowski?" I said.

"Yes?"

I gave her my name and said I was an investigator, helping Lammy's lawyer.

"Lammy?" She sounded confused. "Oh. You mean my brother, Lambert?"

"Yes. He . . . uh . . . he's not at home and I'm looking for him. I thought if he shows up at your house and asks to stay there, would you please—"

"Here? You mean Lambert, come by here? Why would he come by *my* house?"

"Well, he's your brother, isn't he?"

"Yeah, sure, I guess so. But he can't stay here. No room here for him. And besides, what'll the neighbors . . ." She paused. "Anyway there's no room here. I told Lambert that already. He won't come by here."

She finally agreed to call me if she saw him, and took down my phone number. But she was convinced—and managed to convince me, too—that Lammy wouldn't even consider asking her for a place to stay.

He couldn't have had much more than carfare on him, so undoubtedly he'd show up back home in time for supper.

Except he didn't.

I'd gotten to the two-flat at two-fifteen and there was a note on the kitchen table from Casey, saying he'd gone for groceries. It was an hour later when he came in the front door, lugging several large bags.

Five minutes into stowing the food in various cabinets and refrigerator compartments, Casey suddenly said, "Hey! Where's Lammy?"

"I think he's run away," I said.

"Oh."

"You don't sound surprised."

"Actually, I wondered if he might try something like that."

"What are you talking about?"

"I was gonna tell you not to let him outta your sight if he got bad news from the lawyer, but I figured you'd know enough to . . ." He caught me glaring at him. "I mean . . . not that I'm criticizing you or—"

"I just wish you'd said something. The thought of him running off never entered my mind."

"He's scared to death, you know?"

"Yeah, but like Renata said, he doesn't seem to have enough ambition or something to actually run off. He's never been anywhere in his life but here."

"And a few days in jail, don't forget." He went back to storing food. "Jesus, that'd sure as hell scare the crap outta me, I tell ya."

"Casey," I said, finally not able to resist, "did anyone ever tell you you don't talk like a priest is supposed to talk."

He laughed. "Lots of people probably think that. Most of 'em don't say it. They just figure I'm a little loony or something.

142

Which is fine with me. I don't care." He bit into one of a half dozen apples he'd dumped out of a small paper sack. "Nobody ever made it explicit, but I'm sure that's what got me transferred out of the first parish I was assigned to, after just a few months. Jeez, I don't know who had the goofy idea to send me into the belly of the posh North Shore. I mean, I liked the people, but I know a lot of 'em thought I'd be a bad influence on their kids. Ha! That's a good one. Those kids didn't need to look as far as *me* to find a bad—" He stopped. "Well, I could go on and on about my illustrious priestly career, but what about Lammy?"

"I called his sister. She'll call if he shows up there, but she doesn't think he will."

"She hopes he doesn't anyway, I bet."

Casey made baked chicken for supper and I spent the time on the telephone. There was a place set at the table for Lammy, but he didn't show. Casey said a blessing before we ate. He always did, and it was never something memorized, but whatever came to him on the spot. This one included prayers for Lammy— "wherever the hell he is, Lord"—and for the people at Saint Ludella's, for Trish Connolly and her family, for Lammy's sister and mother, and for all kinds of other people, including me. He ended with something like, ". . . but anyway, God, we know it's all working out perfectly. So thank you very much for all that . . . and for the food, too. Amen."

I felt a little sorry for everyone in that first parish who'd missed Casey's bad influence. But that didn't mean I had to stick around and help him with the dishes. I had work to do. I'd left the car down the street for my tailing friends to watch, and I was going to leave it there and use the alley.

Grabbing my parka from a hook by the back door, I turned to Casey and asked, "You have bingo at Saint Ludella's?"

He was hunched down over the sink, massive hands and forearms plunged deep into the sudsy water, humming to himself tunelessly. He turned around and wiped his hands on a dish towel. "Nah. I don't like bingo much."

"I'm surprised," I said. His parish was in the heart of the west side, about as poverty-stricken as anywhere in the city. "I hear bingo's a moneymaker."

"Uh-huh."

"So? You don't approve of gambling?"

"It's not that. No one loses too much at church bingo, unless they're addicted to gambling and . . . well, don't get me started on addictions. And bingo does give a lot of people something fun to do." He leaned over the table and swept some crumbs off into one of his palms. "What I never liked about bingo in a parish is it's too big a temptation for some people."

"Except you already said no one loses too much."

"I don't mean a temptation for the players. I mean for the workers. You got bingo, you have to go out and recruit people to work at it. You get mostly men. Good guys, too. Guys that are active and involved. But, you know, week after week they're handling all this money. Looks like a fortune to most of 'em. Sooner or later, unless you got a system that's foolproof—and I never found one—somebody starts dipping in a little. Hell, people just can't resist, what with their bills and all. The other workers kinda catch on, and even if they don't join in they keep quiet, 'cause they're all friends, y'know? Sometimes the priest even suspects what's goin' on. But the money's coming in, and the parish has bills to pay, too. So the priest just kind of—"

"Jesus, is that ever depressing."

"So I never had bingo in my parish. Shoot, when I was drinking and short on cash, I mighta found myself dipping in, too. Jeez," he added, grinning, "I hope you never hear about some of the stuff I pulled in those days."

"Oh, I doubt—" I put a hand in my parka pocket and felt the car key. "Oh, by the way, you still have the extra key to the Intrepid?" He nodded. "Good. Use it whenever you want. I usually park a couple blocks south of here, near where they're tearing down an apartment building."

"I'll find it if I need it," he said. "Anyway, why you asking about bingo?"

"Just because that's where I'm headed right now. To bingo, at Our Lady of Ravenna."

"Oh, yeah. Ravenna's. They're famous around the archdiocese for their bingo. They run it two nights a week."

"I know. Monday and Wednesday. I'm told Trish's grandmother goes both nights. I'm gonna try to talk to her."

"Hope you can find her. They say they get huge crowds there for bingo. Make a ton of money."

"Think their workers are ripping them off?"

"Oh, I don't think so, not at Ravenna's. It might be just a rumor, but they say that's one place that *does* have a foolproof system to keep everybody straight."

"Really?"

"Yeah. That's still pretty much an Italian parish, you know. Story is, nobody'd dare take anything. 'Bout a year ago one of their most faithful bingo card sellers got attacked on his way home from the games. 'Muggers,' is what he told the cops. Thing is, they didn't really beat him up."

"Oh?"

"Nope. They just lopped off both his little fingers. Whammo— one from each hand. 'Puerto Rican punks,' he said. But nobody believed him. People think it was because of the head of the parish bingo committee, the one who runs the whole show."

"You mean this guy was stealing from church bingo so the chairman of the committee had somebody chop off his fingers? Come *on.*"

"Well, it made a great story at the annual priest's retreat, anyway. And who knows? Maybe it's true. Besides, it's not a chair-

man. It's a chair*woman*. This older Italian lady. No one thinks she had anything to do with it personally, of course. They say she's personally like a saint, y'know? Mass every day and all that. But it's her brother. They say her brother's this big-time Mafia guy and, well, you know . . ."

CHAPTER

24

Rosa was my best lead on Karen Colter, Dominic's girlfriend, so I trotted down the steps and out to the alley, thinking I was lucky I'd mentioned bingo to Casey. The pastor at "Ravenna's," as Casey called the parish, was someone he'd known in the seminary, a Monsignor Borelli. Casey had gotten him on the phone, and he verified that it was Rosa Parillo who ran the parish bingo. He also agreed to ask her if she'd meet with me. Since it was Rosa who'd reached out to me in the first place, I was certain she'd talk to me again.

"He claims Rosa's tough as nails," Casey had said, after he hung up. "He's sure she won't wanna talk to a friend of the creep who went after her granddaughter."

"I think she will. I just hope he actually asks her—and keeps quiet about it, too."

"He *said* he would. And if Bobo says—"

"Bobo?"

"Yeah. Bobo Borelli. Funny little guy. He's had two bypass surgeries, so he's not as active as he used to be. But Bobo's tough, too. He does what he says he'll do."

It was a six-block walk to Ravenna's, where a short east-west street, Ravenna Court, cut one rectangular city block into two roughly square halves, with the parish buildings filling the southern square. Seen from a block away, the cluster of buildings loomed up like a massive fortress in the cold, dark gloom, over-shadowing the neighboring buildings, making them appear smaller than the substantial brick bungalows they actually were.

Walking the snow-cleared sidewalks around the perimeter of

Ravenna's, I passed first the church itself, where I'd spoken to Rosa. Facing north, it fronted on Ravenna Court and was directly across the street from a well-lighted, well-filled parking lot. Beyond the church, I turned left and walked past the convent and the parish school, side-by-side and facing west. On the southern boundary was the rectory, and then a large yard behind a high wrought iron fence.

Continuing around the corner and heading back north, I walked along the east side of the fenced-in yard, crossed a paved driveway leading into the interior of the property behind the buildings, and came to a rectangular stone building, easily thirty feet tall, with three sets of double doors that opened directly onto the sidewalk. Etched into the stones across the front, above the doors, were the words: "Our Lady of Ravenna Gymnasium and Community Center."

Pulling open one of the center two doors, I stepped into a tile-floored vestibule. To my right and my left, matching sets of wide stairways led up several steps to landings, one on each end of the vestibule, and on each landing a set of doors. Straight ahead, another set of wide stairs led down to a lower level of the building. The doors on the landing to my left were open, and a voice poured out over a loudspeaker system. *"B . . . three*. That's *beeee . . . thuh-reee."*

I went up those stairs and stood in the open doorway. The bingo hall was a large, high-ceilinged gymnasium, with basketball backboards at each end, and more sets of backboards and baskets on each side wall, making three shorter courts across the main court. All four walls were lined with retractable bleacher seats that were folded up against the walls and out of the way.

The room was jammed with people seated on folding chairs at long lunchroom tables, set end to end in rows running the length of the gym. Rubber mats were spread out everywhere, in a fruitless effort to protect the hardwood floor from maybe five hundred pairs of wet, dirty boots and shoes. The air was warm

148

and humid, heavy with the odors of hot dogs, coffee, and pop-corn, not to mention plenty of good old human sweat.

The huge area was strangely hushed, although filled with the whisperings and rustlings of hundreds of players concentrating on rows of bingo cards laid out on the tables in front of them. Bingo workers, the pockets of the carpenters' aprons around their waists stuffed with bingo cards, stood silently in groups of two or three, stationed around the room.

"*Nnnnnext* number . . . oh . . . seventy-two," the invisible caller announced. "That's oh . . . *sevennnnty-tooooo.*"

"Bingo!"

"Bingo!"

Both shrieks came almost simultaneously, from opposite ends of the gym, and were followed at once by hundreds of soft sighs and murmurs of disappointment.

"I hear *bingo,*" the caller said, managing to sound as though this were an entirely unexpected phenomenon. "But remember, folks, do not—I repeat, do *not*—clear your cards, until the win-ning cards have been verified. This could be a false alarm."

The groans and grumbling that greeted him indicated that no one but he believed in false alarms.

I had a sudden sense that someone was watching me. I swung around, fast, and when I did I smacked right into a solid stone pillar. It felt as if it were wrapped in padding, though, and on the rebound I saw that it wasn't a pillar at all, but a heavy-set, brown-skinned man in navy blue pants and a red nylon warm-up jacket over a light blue dress shirt. The words em-broidered on the jacket said "Our Lady of Ravenna Parish," but they might as well have said "Off-duty cop, and not taking any shit from mopes like you."

He reached around me and pushed the door to the gym closed, shutting out the shouted calling of numbers to verify the winning bingo cards. A young man in a white chef's apron, who'd bounded up from the basement with an open carton of steaming hot dogs, started our way. When he saw us, though, he turned and went across to the stairs at the other end of the vestibule, leaving us alone.

"Excuse me," I said.

"Uh-huh." He folded his arms and looked at me as though he were calculating my body-fat ratio.

"I don't suppose you work here, do you?" I asked. "Security, maybe?"

"You looking for someone?"

"It's that red jacket. A dead giveaway." I paused. When he didn't hit me or pull out a gun, I finally said, "Monsignor Borelli."

"You got a driver's license?"

I dug it out and showed it to him.

"Okay." He seemed slightly disappointed. "The Monsignor said to expect you."

I nodded toward the gym. "He in there somewhere?"

"Nope. The Monsignor never comes to bingo. He's at the priests' house."

He led me down to the basement and through a series of hallways, then back up a few steps to an exit on the opposite side of the gym. Passing through a small, dimly lighted parking area in the center of the parish complex, we came to the back door of the rectory. He pushed the doorbell.

While we waited, he caught me staring at the .357 Magnum he held down beside his right leg. He shrugged. "Just in case some damn fool thinks this is one of the cash runs we make over here during bingo." There was a click from the rectory door, and he said, "Here's the Monsignor now."

A round, smiling face peered out, perfectly framed in a small square window set in the wooden door at about the height of my chest. The door swung inward and the round man standing there fit the round face perfectly. "Hey, hey, hey," he said, each word rising in tone, the voice melodious. He spread his arms as though to embrace us, then brought them down quickly, slapping his hands against his thighs.

"Evening, Monsignor," my escort said, with surprising formality. "This is the Mr. Foley you called over about."

"Thank you so much, Charlie. Thank you." He eyed me up and down with open curiosity. "Malachy. Malachy? Am I pronouncing it right?" When I nodded, he beamed with self-satisfaction. "Well, c'mon in. C'mon in." He moved back to let me in, then looked past my shoulder. "See you later, hey, Charlie?"

"Oh yes, Monsignor," the man said. He was already turning to go. "I'll be back."

The smiling priest led me up four stairs, through two doors, and into a comfortable parlor that was obviously the reception area near the front door of the rectory. The man was round, but not really fat, and somewhere in his sixties. He wore the same outfit Casey so often wore—black shoes, black pants, white dress shirt with no collar. There was something smooth, almost feline, about the way he moved.

"Something to drink?" he said. "Coffee? Soft drink?"

"No thanks, Mon—" I paused, then finished the word. "Monsignor."

"Strange word, huh? Just call me 'Father' if it's easier."

"Actually, I was just noticing how it's easier for me to say 'Monsignor' than it is to call you guys—you priests, I mean—to call you 'Father.' Strange, isn't it?"

"Interesting. Maybe it's got something to do with you and your own . . ." He didn't finish. "But I know you didn't drop by for amateur psychoanalysis. You want to talk to Rosa, right?"

"Yes. Is she—"

"I suppose I should exercise a little caution," he said. "How do I know you're the one Father Caseliewicz said was coming?"

"Casey called you Bobo," I said. "Bobo Borelli. The guy who

got caught organizing the students to flush all the toilets in the seminary simultaneously, at midnight on New Year's Eve."

His smile widened. "I didn't get caught, exactly," he said. "The authorities got wind of it and and warned us off. Good thing, too. With that ancient plumbing, who knows . . ." He spread his arms. "Ah, well. Those were simpler days."

"So," I said, "is she here?"

"Yes." His face turned suddenly serious. "Rosa's a good person. I hope nothing . . . that is, her family . . . well anyway, she said she'd talk to you, which surprised me." He led me into a hallway off the parlor. "Since Rosa took over, I don't have to worry about bingo, thank God." Light spilled out from an open door halfway down the hall. "The guys carry money over here three or four times throughout the evening and she counts it in an office down this way. Here's—" He stopped at the open door and turned back to me. "That's strange. She was here a little while ago. And her granddaughter, too. Rosa's been bringing Trish along, ever since . . . you know."

I squeezed past him into a small office—crowded, but tidy. Against the wall to the right of the door was a gray metal desk, with nothing on it but a telephone. A desk chair on castors was pulled over to a table set against the opposite wall. There was a coin counting machine on the far end of the same table, back in the corner of the room. Ledgers were spread open on the table, and beside them a couple of yellow pencils, and a delicate-looking little blue-and-white teapot with two matching cups and saucers.

"Well," I said, "they've been drinking tea. Probably went to the washroom."

"I don't think so," the priest said. "Both their coats are gone. And besides . . . look at the top of that desk."

"I don't see anything."

"That's the point. It oughta be covered with stacks of money."

CHAPTER

25

A QUICK SEARCH OF the first floor verified it. Rosa and Trish were gone.

"I just talked to her . . . what . . . a half hour ago?" the priest said. "On the intercom line, when she said she'd meet you. Like I said, that really surprised me. And she swore me to secrecy about you, too. But—"

"Was anyone else around?"

"No. The doorbell didn't ring until you got here, and she wouldn't have answered it, anyway. I do that." He paused. "But while I was talking to her, the phone rang. I answered it and it was a man asking for Rosa. I figured it was Trish's dad, although he didn't actually say so. Anyway, I patched it through to Rosa. That was it, until Charlie brought you over."

"Well, I'm sure there's a simple explanation." I struggled to sound matter-of-fact. "Maybe—"

A rasping buzz came from the back door.

"That'll be Charlie and the guys with the last batch of bingo money," the priest said, and looked at his watch. "They're a little early tonight."

"I better be going. Is the front door out through that way?"

"Uh . . . yeah." He was a totally different man than when he'd met me at the door. He looked bewildered and unhappy. Deflated, very pale and very tired. "Rosa couldn't have . . . the money? I guess I should call the police, don't you think?"

"Yes," I said. "Just to be on the safe—"

The buzzer sounded again. Four short, impatient bursts.

His round shoulders sagging, he turned to go to the back

door. I hoped his heart was up to the stress, but I couldn't do much about that. I went out the front way, in a hurry.

The first place the cops would look for Rosa was the Connolly home. I ran, slipping and sliding on dark, icy sidewalks. I hoped I looked like a fitness nut, out jogging despite the cold. When I got there, the house looked deserted, but I rang the bell.

No one answered.

There was no reason for me to hang around there, especially since the cops would be pulling up any minute. I told myself what I'd told Monsignor Borelli, that there had to be a simple explanation. But it was far beyond me and, simple or complex, I didn't think I was going to like it.

I walked down the street a couple of blocks to Dominic's house. There were no lights on there, either. And if there had been, it wasn't likely Rosa would have gone there with Trish.

I walked the streets aimlessly, thinking all I want to do is help Lammy out in his criminal case, but that turns out to be the easy part. The prosecution offers a deal and I'm proud of him for not taking it, convinced Renata can't lose. But then Lammy runs off somewhere, while I end up suspected of murdering the wife of the ex-con who was Trish's real attacker. Meanwhile, another guy—a graying Outfit bum who should have been locked up for the rest of his life the day he was born—has me trying to find out who the ex-con's girlfriend is. So I try, and Rosa, my lead on who the girlfriend is, grabs Trish and the bingo money and runs off somewhere, too.

At least, I was hoping with all my heart that Rosa had run off.

I walked back to Lammy's, surprised to see no cops down the street at Steve's. I had no front door key, so I rang the bell and Casey let me in.

"Lammy here?" I asked.

"Nope. And he didn't call, either."

"Damn." I dropped down onto the couch in front of the TV and picked up the remote.

Casey waved a book at me. "I'll be in the living room," he said.

I surfed until I found the Bulls, playing out in Seattle, but I dozed off before I even heard the score. I needed some rest. Hell, you never know when things might take a turn for the bad.

"Mal! Mal!" The calls came from a ghost of a boy, caught in the river again, his features indiscernible and the water rising. But the voice wasn't a boy's voice. "Hey!" The voice was Casey's. "Come look at this."

"Yeah?" I opened my eyes and they were interviewing Phil Jackson on TV. "What is it?" I called.

"There's two cop cars just pulled up." He paused. "Oops, now it's three. That Sanchez guy just got here. Come and look."

"They're going to Steve Connolly's house," I called back. "They're looking for—"

"Uh-uh. Looks to me like—" The doorbell rang. "That's what I thought." The bell rang again, and this time didn't stop ringing. "Jesus, Mary, and Joseph," Casey yelled. "You better call that lady lawyer. I mean, they're waving pistols around down there like they're ready to take back the Alamo."

I grabbed my coat and raced for the kitchen. "Take your time answering the door," I called. "And don't come back here."

"Why not?"

"How long ago did I come in?"

"Jeez, I don't know. Half hour maybe."

The doorbell kept ringing, as we called softly back and forth down the long hallway, out of each other's sight. "Well, then, you haven't seen me for at least a half hour. Right?"

"Uh, right." He sounded bewildered, but then added, "Yeah, that *is* the truth. I haven't *seen* you." He understood.

Casey would have a hard time with a flat-out lie to the cops, or to anyone, even to help out a friend.

I suppose I knew it was stupid, and I didn't even know what I was running from. But Casey was going to have to answer the door, so I went out the back way and ran down the steps, thinking I'd figure it out later.

CHAPTER

26

It was snowing again, thick heavy flakes swirling down in spiral waves that, higher up, glowed and reflected the amber light that spread from tall poles in the alley. On the ground, visibility was maybe twenty or thirty feet. I was halfway through the backyard when I heard snow-hushed voices moving my way between the buildings. Suddenly, the thin, bright beam of a flashlight stabbed out from the gangway, darting up and down and side to side like a laser cutting through the falling white. If the cop with the light swept the beam across the yard when he stepped out from the gangway, it wasn't likely they'd miss a dark figure moving through the snowfall.

The gate in the fence was open and I was just through it, still far from the safe cover of the neighbor's garage, when the cops did emerge from the gangway. By then, though, I was huddled low to the ground, elbows and arms tucked close, head down. Motionless, I had at least a chance of being missed.

The light swept back and forth across the yard and may have picked out a dark, low blob beyond the fence, or maybe not. But a harsh voice said, "Upstairs, damn it. C'mon." The stabbing light turned then, and bounced its way into the covered back porch stairway. There were two of them, but maybe more to come. Running in a crouch, I made it to the garage to the south and stood inside the narrow shelter of its shadow. Farther down, where the alley opened onto the side street just south of the Connolly home, a squad car blocked the way, its strobe lights sending blue-and-white blurred flashes through the clouds of snow.

I started the opposite way, which meant I'd have to pass behind Lammy's place again, where the sound of a nightstick pounding on the second-floor back door was muffled, but unmistakable. I'd taken just one step, though, when far at the north end of the block a pair of headlights swung into the alley. I shrank back against the garage, sidled along the overhead door and around the corner of the building, away from the car that slid and slithered my way over a quickly building carpet of snow.

Crouching near the ground, I poked my head around the corner of the garage, then pulled back quickly. The approaching vehicle was larger than a car, maybe a police patrol wagon. No more pounding came from Lammy's back door, so I knew those cops would be inside now, soon to discover I wasn't there.

Maybe I had it all wrong, though. Maybe it was Lammy they were looking for. But why? They couldn't know yet that he'd run off. In fact, legally he hadn't fled or violated bail, not until he missed some court date he was required to attend. So they must have come for me. But why in the middle of the night? Was there some new evidence they thought tied me tighter to Tina Fontana's killing?

The headlights grew brighter and then swept past. It wasn't a paddy wagon, but Steve Connolly's Ford van. The falling snow seemed determined to absorb all the sound it could, and the van's motor gave only a low, urgent throb. I creeped forward and watched it slow to a stop near the end of the alley. Light from inside the Connolly garage spread out into the snowfall as the electrically driven garage door rose.

I turned the other way again and my hopes sank as yet another pair of headlights bounced into the alley. But this pair stopped, backed out again, and then the faint, blurred blue-and-white flashing started at that end, too. They had the alley blocked at both ends.

Steve's backup lights went on as he prepared to maneuver the van into his garage within the confines of the narrow alley. Just then, muffled shouts came from the direction of the squad car at his end of the alley, and the bright beam of a spotlight slashed through the swirling snow, swinging from side to side. The backup lights went out again, and Steve swung open the driver's door. The spotlight stopped on him as he half-stood, raising his head above the open van door and waving his left arm.

"I'm Steve Connolly, damn it." The snow muffled his shouted words. "I live here."

A response came, but not loud enough for me to hear the words.

"For chrissake!" That was Steve again. He stepped down and headed toward the police car, pushing backward at the van door to close it. The door didn't catch, but fell open again and Steve ignored it, trudging ahead toward the cops, caught in the steady beam of their spotlight. And as he did, the distant sounds of sirens announced the approach of more police, from two different directions.

I made a choice, then, one of those choices you make when you have to choose, even though you lack the information needed to make your choice intelligently. You're left with a few preliminary decisions that are less than informed, and then you choose a path. Sometimes it works out.

I decided first that the cops were after me, not Lammy. I decided something new must have turned up or taken place and that, whatever it was, it was bad news for me. I decided that with Lammy missing, and with Rosa and Trish missing, and with Dominic Fontana, the maniac that attacked Trish—and certainly must have killed Tina, too—still roaming around, I didn't want to spend even the next twenty-four hours trying to convince anyone I wasn't responsible for any of the bad things that kept happening around me. Ultimately, though, the choice I made was that I wouldn't give myself up, not to that son of a bitch Sanchez, not until I knew what the hell was going on.

They seemed to be flooding the area with cops, and there was scant chance of getting away through snow-filled backyards and over fences, even in the darkness and poor visibility. So, with no good direction to turn, I didn't turn at all. I ran in a crouch straight ahead, to the rear of Steve's van. The motor was still running and the open driver's door was keeping the interior lights on. I tried the handle on the van's rear door. Not locked. I crawled inside, pulled the door closed, set the lock button, and squeezed down into the space behind the rear seat.

In a few moments Steve was back, talking to a cop who had come with him. Steve got into the van and drove it back and forth until he had it parked in his garage. When he cut the engine and got out, he didn't close the overhead garage door, but went back out to the alley, where the cop was waiting for him.

The two of them stood talking, not six feet from where I lay huddled in the van. The cop was trying to convince Steve to come with him and talk to the investigators, without saying what they'd be talking about. I knew, though. They wanted to tell him that Rosa and Trish were missing.

For his part, Steve was plenty loud, almost bombastic, and it was obvious he'd been drinking. "I just got off work, goddamn it. Gotta say g'night to my daughter, for chrissake."

"Well, sir, it's your daughter that . . . anyway, sir, would you come with—"

"The fuck you talkin' about? What about Trish?"

"Can you close the garage door from here, sir? And come with me?"

"Okay, okay. I got a key here somewhere." There was a pause. "But what about Trish? What's happened to her?" The garage door started to close down.

"Probably nothing, sir. But this Foley individual showed up at the church. We aren't sure why. The pastor was there and, well . . . Foley went after him." The overhead door was closing. ". . . our guys got there, he was already dead. Jesus, kill a priest. Who—" The lowering door hit the pavement with a thud.

It was very dark.

CHAPTER

27

AT FIRST AN OCCASIONAL car drove past in the alley, and distant sounds of sirens drifted in through the closed garage door. Strangely, I kept wanting to give up, just get it over with. I had to remind myself that running and hiding wasn't much of a crime if you hadn't done anything to be arrested for in the first place, and if they ever actually charged me with the murder of the priest, whether evading arrest was an aggravating factor or not would be the least of my worries.

Eventually there was an end to the sounds of activity and, after one full hour had passed with nothing happening, I sat up and inspected my hiding place, using the tiny flashlight on my key chain. It was a typical conversion van, with four so-called captain's chairs for the driver and three passengers, and a bench seat in the rear that probably folded out into what the conversion people like to call a "bed"—though you'd have to be less than five feet tall to sleep in one comfortably. The floor was carpeted, and much of the walls and the ceiling as well. There was artificial-looking wood trim everywhere, and fixed to the ceiling above the driver's head, facing the rear seats, a little television set. All in all, like most conversion vans, it must have cost a small fortune, and still managed to look a little tacky.

The interior was neat as a pin, though, and there was a plaid wool blanket draped over the back of the bench seat. That was lucky, because it was getting colder by the minute. I had no idea when Steve would come back, and it wouldn't do to be caught rummaging around the garage for something to wrap up in. Dragging the blanket down with me, I sank again into the

161

cramped space behind the backseat, to ponder how much longer to wait before leaving the seductive safety of the van and venturing out into the neighborhood.

I picked five o'clock as the magic hour, because a few people might be out on the street by then, headed for work, and I wouldn't be so obvious. With my internal alarm clock set, I searched for the least uncomfortable position and tried to fall asleep. Half an hour later, though, the garage door rose again, and someone was climbing back into the driver's seat. I recognized Steve's voice, muttering soft curses to himself, as the van jolted and bucked out of the garage. Then, much too fast to suit my aching joints and muscles, we careened north down the alley.

He slowed just a little at the end of the block, and I braced myself against what was certain to be a too-fast turn onto the street. But, surprisingly, he kept going straight. The van bottomed out, twice, as we left the alley, crossed the street, then bounced into the alley again on the other side. We'd gone maybe another half block when we skidded and fishtailed to a stop.

For a moment there was nothing but the sounds of the idling engine and the wind whistling through the alley. Then muffled voices outside. The passenger door, then the side door, were opened and the vehicle dipped and rose again as two people got in and both doors were pulled shut. At least one of the new passengers had a decidedly feminine taste in cologne.

"The fuck's she doing here?" Steve's voice was strained, anxious.

"She's with me," Dominic said, as though that answered the question.

"I don't want her along." Steve paused. "Who's watching—"

"Hey, that's fine with me." It was Karen Colter's drawling voice, and I heard her open the van's side door. "Christ, Dominic, I told you I should—"

162

"Fuck that," Dominic said. "Close the door and drop your ass back in the seat."

"Gus ain't gonna like us bringing her." This was Steve again, but he slipped the van into gear, the door closed, and we were underway. "Who's watching the kid?"

"Lisa? She got kinda hysterical yesterday, after Tina's funeral, so one of Tina's friends took her to stay with her family for a while," Dominic said. "Anyway, Gus ain't gonna care about Karen. He calls in the middle of the night, what the fuck's he expect? She can wait in the car. Right, Karen? Watch TV or something."

"Oh yeah. Right. Freeze my butt off," Karen said. "Jesus, it's cold in here."

"Whaddaya mean cold?" Steve said. "I got the heater going." The van swung out of the alley and gathered speed.

"Broad's from Kentucky," Dominic explained. "Constantly fuckin' complaining about the cold."

"Yeah, well it's freezing back here," Karen said. "Heat isn't coming back this far."

"There's a blanket," Steve said, "behind you, on the backseat."

I heard her shifting in the seat.

"I don't see any blanket," she said.

"It's there. Should be hanging over the back of the seat."

"I'm telling you, there's no—"

"Probably fell behind the seat," Dominic broke in. "Get off your ass and go back and look. Or else shut the fuck up."

"Okay, okay," Karen said.

Meanwhile, I'd gotten free of the blanket in question and bunched it up on my chest, and now lay on my back and stared up, waiting for her face to appear over the back of the seat. As the van bounced along the icy city streets, I could sense her movement. Then, right beside my head, the cushion of the seat sagged, and I knew she must be kneeling on it.

Her face was suddenly right above mine. She stared straight down.

"Oh my God!" Her cry was too choked to qualify as a scream, because she was gasping for breath at the same time.

"What is it?" Dominic called, and I could hear him twisting around in his seat.

"Um, nothing," Karen said. "Nothing." She had her breath back now, and she could really have screamed if she wanted to. Certainly your average young lady from Kentucky would have, staring down into the barrel of an automatic, six inches off the bridge of her nose. "I just, oh, twisted my knee on the seat here." She was far from average, this particular Kentucky lady, and she looked more shocked than afraid. "You don't have to worry about me." She called the words out, as though to the men up front, but her eyes made it clear she was speaking to me.

I believed her, mostly because my options were pretty limited, and angled the Beretta away from her face.

"What're you talking about?" That was Steve.

"I mean not to *worry* 'cause I'm not hurt, and I found the blanket." She reached over the seat as though having to stretch way down to the floor.

"Who the fuck's worried?" That was Dominic. A real sweetheart.

"Well, anyway," she said, "I got it." She dragged the blanket with her, and disappeared from my view.

Ford vans have double doors opening out the back. I'd have to get them both open quickly to spill myself onto the street if she gave me away. Fortunately, traffic would be light at that time of night and if I didn't break a leg when I hit the pavement I had some chance, at least, of escaping.

But, unless it was in sign language, Karen said nothing about me.

Besides, it was too late to bail out anyway. We were gathering speed, and I knew we were headed down a long sloping entrance ramp onto what had to be the Kennedy Expressway.

Steve and Dominic were talking more softly up front and I strained to hear, but I caught only occasional words. I twisted around in my cramped space, raising my head a little higher, to hear better.

"Hey," Karen said, "how you turn that li'l TV on?"

"There's a remote," Steve answered. "Here it is." And then television voices were added to the mix.

Karen skipped around the channels a while. "Damn, no cable," she complained, and finally settled on an ancient Western movie. She'd killed any chance I had to hear what the two men were saying—and some instinct told me she'd done it deliberately.

I didn't dare lift my head to look out the window, but knew we headed south, and then west, staying on the expressway system. Gus Apprezziano lived somewhere in the far western suburbs, and I figured that's where we must be headed. It wouldn't take long, with no traffic to fight.

It was a bad dream I couldn't wake up from, squeezed into too small a space and hurtling through the cold night with two goons who'd kill me without a second thought—each for a different reason—and a woman who alternated between helping and harming. Talk about living with your choices. Not only was I stuck with the one I'd made a couple of hours ago when I climbed into the van, but another choice—made some twenty-odd years earlier. If I'd helped Lammy then, instead of running home, maybe it wouldn't have changed his life much. But at least he wouldn't have haunted my nights, and then I'd never have learned of his present problems, and I wouldn't be lying here . . .

My mind wandered far with those thoughts, until I suddenly realized we had left the expressway and were back bouncing and sliding along icy streets. I'd lost track of direction as well as time, but we were certainly west of the city somewhere. A little later we were riding more easily on smooth, gently curving roads that might have been rural, except for the frequent street-lights, so it had to be a residential area. I sensed, somehow, that the houses were widely spaced, and very expensive. It soon turned out I was right. Maybe money really does have an odor.

Steve pulled the van into a sudden sharp right turn, went about twenty more yards, and stopped. "Turn off the TV," he said, and Karen obeyed.

We waited a moment and then there was a metallic scraping sound I couldn't place until Dominic said, "It's opening," and I knew it was some sort of electrically driven gate.

We moved forward again, and I pictured the gate sliding closed behind us. A dog barked. Just twice, but loud, deep barks, and not that far away. I was locked inside a compound, not just with a bunch of Outfit people, but their guard dogs as well. At one point we passed over a slight hump in the road, the tires bumping over wooden boards. A few moments later we stopped, and the engine was switched off.

"The broad stays in the car," Steve said.

"We already said that, for chrissake." Dominic didn't seem to like Steve giving orders. "Right, baby?" he said. "You warm enough?"

"Yeah," Karen said, "for now. But how long you gonna be? It'll get cold in here with the motor off."

"How do I know? Half hour, hour. We'll leave the key so you can start it up if it gets cold again."

"Bullshit," Steve said, "I ain't gonna—"

"Just leave the fuckin' key. What, you think she's gonna steal your goddamn van? Jesus, Steve, you—"

"Okay, okay."

They opened their doors and the TV went back on.

"Keep yourself warm, baby," Dominic said, and both doors slammed shut.

166

"Stay down," she said. "The blinds on the side windows are closed, and I'll turn off the TV once they're inside and I don't see anyone else. I was you, though," she added, "I still wouldn't poke my head up."

When the television went off, I sat up. "Thanks," I said. "But I gotta stretch my arms and legs." I climbed over the backseat.

Karen had swiveled her captain's chair to face the rear. She was wrapped up in the blanket, but it was clear she was wearing the same outfit—boots, red pants, leather coat—she'd had on when I first saw her, at Melba's.

She stared at me, but I couldn't read anything in her face at all. "You gotta be as loony as they come," she finally said.

"I suppose, coming from the constant companion of Dominic Fontana, that's the opinion of an expert."

She gave a short laugh. "If there's one thing I know about, it's crazy people. That's for sure."

I separated the thin slats of the miniblinds on one of the windows and peered through. The snow had stopped and the entire area was bathed in floodlights. We were parked at the side of the house, but far enough away to see that it was a mansion in a sort of deco style, part stucco, part white-painted brick, set off nicely with clustered stripes of black. It was all rectangles and squares, with casement windows and no sharp angles or curves. Even without seeing it, I guessed the roof would be flat, and there would be several levels, with upper-floor rooms opening onto rooftop decks enclosed with concrete railings. In addition to the floods, softly colored lights glowed upward from behind low shrubbery along the outer walls. The whole thing looked very Hollywood to me.

"This Gus Apprezziano's place?"

Her chin dipped slightly, in what I took to be a nod. "I don't suppose," she said, "that you really killed that priest."

"Nope. My vote would be Dominic. Or are you gonna give him an alibi for that one, too? Just like for Tina?"

"I feel bad about Tina. But she really shoulda gone away while Dominic was still in the shithouse."

"I was asking whether you'll give him an alibi for the priest's murder."

She pulled the blanket closer around her. "If I was you, I wouldn't hang around here waiting to get myself killed."

"You seemed pretty anxious to have Dominic blow me away, that day at his house."

"I didn't want him blaming me for you getting away."

"So why did you help me?"

"Saved your ass tonight, too. Turned on the TV to cover up the noise of you squirming around back there behind the seat."

"Who are you?" Might as well take a stab at earning my fee from Gus.

"They'll be back any minute." She was an expert at ignoring questions. "How long you think your luck's gonna last?"

"Till it runs out, and I don't guess I'll be around after that to regret it. Anyway, why do you hang out with a demented ape like Dominic?" That got no reaction at all. If she really felt something for him, she sure had great control. "I need to find Rosa," I said, trying a new direction. "You know where she is?"

"I—" She stopped. "You wanna keep that Fleming guy outta jail," she said. "But for what? Steve'll go after him, anyway. Peel off his skin like an orange. Dominic's mean and stupid. Steve? He's mean and smart. That's worse. Plus he's a gun freak, always at the range. What I hear, he could stand Fleming up and shoot his eyes out at twenty yards. Or he might burn the guy alive, maybe. Whatever. Your friend'll be wishing he *did* go to jail."

"Except he didn't attack the girl. I'm gonna prove who really did. Prove it to the cops and Steve and everyone else."

"Fleming's the neighborhood creep. Everyone thinks he did it. Besides, you're making a big mistake messing with these people." She swiveled her chair around and looked out the front window, then spun back again. "Dominic, Steve, Gus. I know the kinda things they do. And they don't care. These are all bad people, deep-down bad."

"Uh-huh. So what does that make you?"

She *did* react to that one. She lowered her head, maybe even shivered a little. "No one's ever accused me," she said, her voice very low, "of bein' a good person."

"And Rosa," I said, trying again, "why did you call me for her that night?"

"Rosa and I talk. She's the only sane person I've met since . . . Anyway, I like her. And she likes me, trusts me. She wanted to meet whoever it was who was helping Fleming. So I helped her. Now she says she trusts you, too."

"She told you why, too, didn't she. Told you what really happened with Trish."

She turned her head to look out the window, but not fast enough. I saw it in her eyes. Rosa had told her.

"And you didn't do anything about it. You were just gonna let Lammy go down."

Karen kept looking out the window. "I called you, didn't I? Maybe she's right. Maybe Dominic . . . But what can I do about it?" She turned back to me. "And now, if I was you, I'd hustle my ass outta here."

I opened the side door of the van. "You'll keep quiet about seeing me, right?" She shrugged, and I stepped down to the ground and closed the door behind me.

Immediately, as though on signal, the menacing sounds began. They came from several directions, but all from the darkness beyond the floodlit area. Deep, throaty rumblings.

They say you're not supposed to let on you're afraid. Dogs sense your fear, they say. But it's hard even to maintain a steady pace when your blood runs so cold you think your limbs will freeze up. Even so, I kept walking, slowly, beside the mounded snow along the edge of the plowed parking area. There was room for half a dozen cars, but the van was the only thing parked there. The low, snarling growls continued, but no dogs appeared.

Turning abruptly, I headed down the roadway we'd driven in on, toward where it plunged suddenly into darkness, maybe thirty yards away. I hadn't taken three steps when the growling changed—not louder, it seemed, but higher in pitch, more anxious. In the shadows off to the left, I thought I saw something moving, low to the ground, heading toward the road to cut me off.

I turned back, to stay in the light, and the growling dropped down again at once. In the parking area, I walked away from the rear of the van, then followed an earlier pair of footprints that had stepped into the snow and circled around to the front of the house. There was more landscaping here, bushes of various sizes, weighed down with new snow, on either side of broad steps that led up to the front door. A flat white lawn sloped away from the front of the house and disappeared into the dark. I followed the footprints up the snow-covered steps. Before I could find any doorbell, though, the door swung open.

I stepped back and looked up at the man. "Well," I said, "it's a small, small world, after all."

CHAPTER
28

GOLDILOCKS SEEMED AT A loss for words, so I jumped right in. "Mr. Apprezziano wants to see me when his meeting is over. Plus . . . he wants to be sure nobody knows I'm here. Got it?" The man seemed to be thinking—a real struggle, from all appearances. "You know who I mean by *nobody?*"

"Nobody means nobody, I know that. But how do I know you're telling me the truth?"

"You don't. So . . . you put me in a room somewhere out of sight. Then, when the two nobodies in question are gone, you take me to Mr. Apprezziano." I stopped, to let his brain catch up. "And then, if I've been lying, he lets you kick the shit out of me. How's that?"

It made sense to Goldilocks, although a dark, overheated three-by-three-foot closet off the kitchen wasn't the sort of room somewhere out of sight I'd had in mind. And I'd handed him the Beretta, so the handcuffs seemed a little excessive.

It wasn't all that long, though, before the door opened again and I was blinking into the bright lights of the kitchen.

"How the hell did you get in here?" It was Gus, looking like an ordinary human being in tan wool pants and a dark green sweater.

"Your stooge locked me—"

"I don't mean in the closet. I mean onto my property, for chrissake. There's a wall, and dogs, and—"

"Ah," I said. "That's why you hired me, isn't it? I have my ways." I twisted around to show him the cuffs. "You have a key?"

He didn't, but he called out and Goldilocks came in, unlocked the cuffs, laid my gun on the kitchen table, and left again.

Gus poured coffee. I hadn't noticed before, in his Cadillac or at Melba's, how tanned he was, as though he'd just returned from two weeks in the sun. I hung my parka over the back of a chair and we sat across from each other, the Beretta between us. Gus picked it up, checked the magazine, and saw there were seven live rounds. Then he handed it back to me and I stuck the pistol back into the sweat-soaked holster below my left armpit.

"Nobody brings a piece onto my property," he said. "Nobody. It's my rule."

"Sorry. Coming here was sort of a last-minute decision." I poured milk from a cardboard container into the dark coffee. "But, speaking of your hiring me, maybe I should give you your money back."

Gus's eyes narrowed, and darkened somehow, and it was suddenly clear again that he wasn't just an ordinary person in a green sweater at all. "Fuck the money." He was almost whispering. "Who is she?"

"I don't know. I'm drawing a blank."

"And . . . you're sure you been trying?"

"I put people on it." He started to say something, but I held up my hand. "Discreet people. Not to worry." I shook my head. "But so far nothing. Seems very strange." What I was saying was all true. I'd put Herb Gatsby on the job. Great Gatsby Investigations was expensive and I might lose money on the deal, but Herb's people were the best.

"You only been at it a few days," Gus said. "Something has to—"

"I know. My people say they need a little more time." That part wasn't true. Gatsby's woman had told me they'd hit a blank wall so far. She'd also told me what the blank wall probably meant, which I'd already guessed. Gus might have guessed, too, which is why I wasn't ready to tell him the search was over.

Gus stared down into his mug, then looked up. "You know Steve and Dominic were here tonight, right?" He'd changed again, seemed more relaxed.

"I, uh . . . I followed them here."

"Where's Rosa? And the kid?"

"I don't know."

He nodded, believing me immediately. "They told me the cops say you killed that priest."

"Is that a question?"

"No. It's what they told me." He drank some coffee. "You're a walking dead man, they say."

"The cops?" I knew better, though.

"Steve and Dominic. They're hoping they get to you first. Figure they can do the cops a favor. Steve especially. He's pissed you're helping that prick that tried to fuck little Trish. But Dominic, too. He's kinda pushing Steve to do something. I guess 'cause he's family. And maybe 'cause he likes . . . excitement."

"What about you? You're part of the family."

"But I'm not young and hotheaded like those two. I'm way past the age to give a shit about goin' after some mope who's just doing a job." He sounded sincere enough. You'd think Gus was beyond the age of bloodletting, if you didn't know better.

"So, did you call off Dominic and Steve? Tell 'em to let this particular mope slide?"

"Call 'em off?" He seemed genuinely surprised. "My promise was I'd keep Steve away from your pervert buddy for now. I made no promise about you. Like I just said, I don't give a shit. Long as they don't mix me up in anything, which they know better than to do." He downed the last of his coffee. "You oughta drop this Fleming thing. Cops think you maybe killed Tina . . . and now the priest. The security guard at bingo ID'd you. Gives Steve an excuse. Him and Dominic get to you first . . . well . . . they're kinda strange, them two. Cops aren't your big worry. You oughta take a trip or something."

173

"Right."

"Except, don't forget." He stood up. "I want some word on that Colter broad. Otherwise, your list of problems keeps growing."

I followed him to the front door, with Goldilocks not far behind.

"You got a car somewhere outside the gate?" Gus asked.

"No. I . . . uh . . . hitched a ride. But that guy's long gone by now."

"Too bad." He opened the door and pointed. "Long as you stay on that road, the dogs won't bother you. Push the button on the post twice when you get there and wait for the gate to open up. After that you're on your own."

The dogs let me be, although they were never far away, moving through the brush on either side of the road. I walked over a wooden bridge that crossed a stream that was frozen, and eventually came to the iron gate. It was bathed in light and set in a high wall that disappeared into the darkness in either direction. I found the metal post and pushed the button twice, waited while the gate slid open, and then walked out.

Gus was right. The gate slid closed behind me, and after that I was very much on my own.

CHAPTER

29

GOING TO MY PLACE, or Lammy's, or anywhere else where someone might be watching for me was out of the question. But then, I had no way to get there, anyway, and only a vague idea where I was.

My guess was in or near Oak Brook, an upscale suburb the old tax code had spawned out of the polo fields and horse farms twenty miles due west of downtown Chicago. Widely spaced homes hid themselves deep behind fences and trees, with here and there a glimpse of a golf course. There were no sidewalks. The roads were all curves and, with the night sky overcast, it was impossible to know which way I was walking. Whenever I heard the occasional car, or saw headlights approaching, I hustled off the cleared pavement and into the snow and the shadows, thinking anyone cruising about at four o'clock in the morning was more likely than not a cop.

Gradually it came to me that, if I paid attention, the distant whine of fast-moving trucks could be heard. That sound had to be coming from I-88, which cuts west across Illinois from suburban Chicago to just short of the Mississippi River, where it merges with I-80 on its way into Iowa and then to the West Coast. With the traffic noise as my compass, I managed to extricate myself from the maze of intertwining, gently wandering streets.

I'd guessed right about being near Oak Brook. With a bag of bagels and a quart of chocolate milk from a twenty-four-hour Mini-Mart, I picked out a motel from a bunch that clustered around an expressway cloverleaf. It was the least expensive, and the rooms opened directly to the outside of the building, so you didn't have to pass by the desk every time you came and went.

My story was ready, about the wife changing the locks on me in the middle of the night and I didn't want to cause a ruckus with the kids and all, so I'd decided to come to my sister's and see if she'd help. But the droopy-eyed clerk seemed unfazed—in fact, barely interested by some worn-out guy named Jackson Pollick from Bettendorf, Iowa, checking in about five o'clock in the morning and paying for two days, with cash.

BY NOON I'D GOTTEN some sleep, made some phone calls, and washed down one too many bagels with my chocolate milk. I went out for a walk and purchased a razor and some deodorant, then showered and shaved and sat by the window of my motel room on the second floor, paging through the *Sun-Times* and the *Tribune* and waiting for a delivery from Barney Green.

Years ago, when Barney and I had been brand-new lawyers together, we worked for Barney's dad, a personal injury lawyer. One of our first cases—and one of my last—was the Lady's lawsuit after her husband went down in a small chartered jet. When Barney's dad died before that case was over, Barney and I ran the office. Barney thrived on the pressure and the battle and just about every other part of the practice, except that he worked too hard and saw too little of his family. What he especially enjoyed, though, was coercing insurance companies and corporations to fork over serious cash to badly injured and disabled people who otherwise didn't have a chance for a decent life. Barney kept at it, and before long he'd become widely respected and financially successful doing a job he loved—not a bad path to travel through life.

It wasn't the path for me, though, so I'd quickly gotten out of the personal injury game and into criminal defense work, and that only off and on. A very large bump popped up in my chosen road, though. I lost my license for keeping my word to a client who was destined to come to a bad end anyway—and later on did, with his throat slashed to ribbons in a one-man cell in a so-called maximum security unit. So now I was far from widely respected or financially successful, but often enough got to do things I enjoyed doing—not a bad path either, when you think about it.

Barney and I saw far too little of each other, but now and then I sent him a client who made him lots of money. So I never felt bad about asking for his help, or accepting it. Like now, at four o'clock on a Tuesday afternoon, as I sat and watched a maroon minivan—a four-year-old Plymouth Voyager—pull into the motel lot right behind a shiny red BMW sedan. The Voyager had out-of-state plates and dark-tinted windows all around, so I didn't get a look at the driver until the minivan slid into a parking slot and a young man got out. With his breath trailing visibly in the cold air, he walked briskly ahead to where the BMW waited. He got in without as much as a look around and the BMW drove off.

Five minutes later I slipped behind the Voyager's wheel and plucked the keys from the spotless ashtray. Twisting around, I saw that the rear seats had been removed. At least one extra layer of thick shag carpeting had been laid out, and on that rested an Eddie Bauer over-the-shoulder traveling bag and another bundle, tightly rolled. On the passenger seat beside me was a tag that must have been attached to the roll when it was purchased. The tag described a "mummy" style sleeping bag, extra-long, expensive, and built to keep a backpacker comfortable down to minus-ten degrees Fahrenheit.

I started the car, saw that I had a full tank of gas, and drove away from the motel. As Gus had said, I was on my own. But now, at least, I had a home.

AT THE INTERSTATE, THE Voyager dearly wanted to head for the Mississippi, and maybe even the West Coast, but I wrestled it onto the east-bound ramp. As foolish as that seemed on its face, it was the only sensible alternative. If I ran I'd be running forever, so I had to head right into the center of the storm to put an end to the flight.

The newspapers were full of how the Right Reverend Monsignor Bonifacio Borelli, pastor of Our Lady of Ravenna parish, had apparently suffered a heart attack when he was slapped around in the parlor of the parish rectory. The perpetrator had fled with the bingo money and, police theorized, had taken a bingo worker, Rosa Parillo, and her granddaughter as hostages. The papers made much of the fact that the granddaughter was little Trish Connolly, recently the victim of a vicious sexual attack, and that the man the police most wanted to question concerning the priest's death was a local private detective who'd been hired by "highly controversial" attorney Renata Carroway to assist her in the defense of the man accused in the sex case. All very confusing, which meant they had to include additional columns laying out the chronology of events, along with pictures of everyone involved.

I was happy that my own photo was an old mug shot, a frontal view taken back when I was sent to Cook County Jail for contempt of court. The shot was taken after I'd been "interrogated" again, this time for about four hours, by a series of understandably angry and frustrated police officers desperately looking for a cop killer. The photo had that chin-up-in-the-air, hair-disheveled, wild-eyed look that corrections facility photographers strive for and—in my optimistic opinion—didn't look enough like my present well-groomed self for the picture to be of much help to the reading public.

Weaving my way through east-bound traffic, I contemplated a growing list of unanswered questions, and finally chose *Where the hell is Lammy?* as my place to begin. He must have missed his court appearance with Renata earlier that afternoon, and the cops would be looking to lock him up, too. It didn't seem possible that he could figure out how to stay hidden even as long as he had.

When I got closer to the city, I pulled off the expressway and looked for a restaurant. I really wanted a couple of beers, but chose a Denny's for supper because they didn't serve alcohol. Once the waitress took my order, I went right to a pay phone.

Renata Carroway's office was closed. I tried her home, but she hadn't gotten there yet. She'd probably just have blamed me for Lammy not showing up in court and complained that now I was making things even worse by getting mixed up in the death of the priest.

I called Casey at Lammy's place.

"Have you talked to Lammy?" was the first thing he said.

"Damn, I was hoping maybe *you* had."

"Nope. But his lawyer called this morning. Wondered if you'd found him. Sounded like it was very important she talk to him today. She seemed very worried."

"He was supposed to appear in court with her this afternoon. The judge probably issued an arrest warrant when he didn't show up. The cops'll be looking for him."

"They didn't come here," he said. "They called, though."

"You tell them you didn't know where Lammy—"

"Hell, they didn't ask about Lammy. They're looking for you. You're a suspect in Bobo Borelli's death. They called twice. Better not tell me where you are, 'cause—"

"I know. You don't wanna lie." I paused. "Any ideas where Lammy might be?"

"Not a clue. He's got no money, although he might have a credit card. I don't think he has any friends. Except maybe somebody at his job?"

"Not a chance," I said. "He's probably the world's most con-

179

scientious employee, and every single one of his co-workers still thinks he oughta be locked up forever. They figure he's been accused, hasn't he? Doesn't that make him guilty?"

"Yeah. Most people do think that way," Casey said.

"Anyway, there's the local librarian, who likes him but who's only slightly more likely to let him hole up in her house than his sister is. Otherwise, I don't know if he even *knows* anyone." Just then an idea crept into my mind. "Except . . ."

"Except who?" he asked.

"The waitress just went by with my supper," I said. "Gotta go."

All the way through my breaded pork tenderloin and into my lemon meringue pie and coffee, I wondered whether Lammy *did* have a credit card, after all. And whether he was up to a little interstate travel.

Back in the Voyager, I rerouted and headed north. It was a clear, dry night, with rush hour winding down and expressway traffic light. Chances were better that even I was wrong, but I'd slept all day and was ready to take some action. And this was the only idea that cropped up.

I thought of calling ahead, but that might just scare him away.

THREE HOURS LATER I signed in at the desk, took the elevator up two floors, and knocked on the door.

"Man, am I glad to see you," Jason whispered. He slipped his tall body through the narrow opening into the hall and closed the door behind him. "Dude's drivin' me crazy, man. I mean, I got no roommate so there's an extra bed for him, but the dude's gotta be almost as old as *you,* man, and he still makes me feel like I'm in *charge* of him or something."

"Why didn't you call me?" I asked.

"Because I promised I wouldn't when he first showed up, which was stupid, but then I couldn't go back on my word. Except I been giving some serious thought to doing that all day. Especially now when I see the Chicago papers and—"

"Just play along with me," I said.

"Huh?"

I reached around him and shoved open the door. "I don't care what you say, Jason," I said, raising my voice louder than necessary. "I looked everywhere else and I wanna see for myself if Lammy's here."

The surprise on Jason's face had already turned to understanding. "I told you, man," he yelled, "the dude ain't here, period. You can't just come bustin' in like this."

He stepped aside as he spoke and I went in. Lammy was already standing, panic in his eyes and ready to run. But there was nowhere to go. Jason came in behind me, pulling on my arm and telling me how I had to leave or he'd call security.

"Sit down, Jason," I said. "And you too, Lammy."

Lammy sat down on the narrow bed beside him, but Jason grabbed his coat from a tiny closet that had no door. He said, "I'm late for practice," and was gone. It was nine o'clock at night. *Very* late for practice.

If Lammy noticed that Jason hadn't called security, and had given up the fight pretty easily, it didn't show in his face. What showed was still fear, but maybe some anger now, which actually made me feel good. "Why don't you leave me alone?" he said. There was just the hint of a real challenge in his voice, and that made me feel good, too.

But as soon as I opened my mouth to answer, his anger went south, and left him only afraid, with tears rolling down his cheeks. He slumped lower onto the bed, then flopped over on his stomach and lay there. Pretty soon he was sobbing, hardly making a sound, his whole rounded body heaving beyond his control. He was trying to say something, too, and when I leaned closer to listen it sounded like, "Just go away. Just go away."

That did it. Suddenly I was angry, so mad I wanted to pick him up off the bed and throw him on the floor. "Damn it, Lammy. What the hell's wrong with you? You oughta be god-

181

damn fucking happy that I—" And then I remembered the nurse in the hall outside Lammy's hospital room, how she'd recognized my stupidity and didn't even blame me for it.

So I shut up and sat there on a hard wooden chair between the two beds and watched the numbers on the digital clock-radio on the desk flip forward for a while. Then I went to the door and opened it and looked out. There was music—or something that passed for music—vibrating down the corridor, and the mixed odors of stale cigarette smoke and beer and marijuana. I turned back and looked at Lammy. He'd stopped sobbing, but now his breaths came in a strange combination of deep sighs and hiccoughing gasps.

I closed the door again and went back and sat down. "Lammy?" His breathing was becoming more regular, but he didn't answer or turn over to look up at me. "I . . . ah . . . I'm really glad I found you. I was worried, you know . . . that something bad might have happened to you."

"What . . . what do you mean?" he said. His voice was muffled because his face was still down in the bedspread.

"I mean," I said, "you might have have had an accident, or—"

"No." He moved, turning onto his side and looking at me, then looking away again. "No," he repeated. "I mean what do you mean by you were *worried?* Why's it make any difference to you?"

"I don't know why. I just care about what happens to you, that's all. I was worried and I came looking for you and I found you. I'm glad I did."

"So then why did you just holler at me?"

"I don't know that, either. There's lots of things I don't know." I paused. "Why don't you sit up?" He did, and he moved to the other chair.

Inside a tiny refrigerator on the floor of the closet, I found two Pepsis, an orange soda, and a wrinkled brown paper bag. Jason wasn't stocking any beer, which made me happy even though I could have used one just then. I took out the bag and it smelled like rotting beef, so I put it on the floor out in the hall and closed the door again.

"You want Pepsi or diet orange?" I asked.

"Jason likes orange. He got the other stuff for me." I took one Pepsi and handed the other to Lammy. He set it on the desk beside him, unopened. "I bet Jason's glad you came. He doesn't want me here. He doesn't like me."

"You're mistaken," I said. "Maybe you make him nervous. But he doesn't put up with things or people he doesn't like. I know Jason. If he really didn't like you, if he wanted you out, you'd be gone."

I was stretching things a bit. But Lammy seemed to accept it, because his eyes filled up with tears again.

I reached over for his Pepsi and popped it open. "Here, drink this," I said. "We need to talk over my plan for what to do next."

We each took a swallow of Pepsi. I looked at Lammy for a while and Lammy looked everywhere but at me. Finally, though, he gave up and looked right into my eyes. "Uh, what's your plan?"

"First, we go get a pizza. After that," and I couldn't help smiling, "what the hell, maybe something'll turn up."

Lammy smiled, too, just briefly.

"Aha!" I said. "That's number *two!*"

He didn't answer, and he didn't look as though he knew I was talking about the smile.

CHAPTER
30

JASON JOINED US. I'D spotted him down the hall when I put the paper bag full of rotten whatever-it-was outside the door, and was surprised and happy to see that he'd taken the bag and disposed of it. We went for pizza and I allowed myself one beer and then switched to coffee. Lammy ordered a beer, too, although he didn't seem to enjoy it much and I wondered if it was a first and if I was starting him down the road to ruin. Jason seemed to have become very health-conscious and washed down his pizza with nothing but bottled water as he regaled Lammy with detailed replays of his own twenty-five or thirty greatest moments in sports. That was fine with me. I had plenty to think about.

When we dropped Jason off at his dorm he made a major point of how welcome Lammy was to come back. "Any time, man," he insisted. "Any time." Jason was so relieved to see us leave that he was able to make it sound as though he really meant it.

Once out on the open road, I showed Lammy how to make the seat recline and he was dead asleep before he had time to close his eyes. I wasn't sure he even knew he was supposed to have been in court earlier that afternoon. I hadn't mentioned it, but told him only that Renata and I would do everything we could to see that he didn't go back to jail. He hadn't asked any more about my plan of action. Maybe he suspected I didn't have one, and didn't want to hear that. My guess, though, was he was as relieved as Jason was that I'd come and gotten him.

"I don't wanna go home," he'd repeated several times, "but I guess I have to." Socially backward he might be, but Lammy had enough sense to know that he couldn't hide out forever.

Two and a half hours after we left Madison, and were approaching Oak Brook, I reached for the phone Barney Green's man had left in the Voyager. It was past midnight and Casey, who was staying on at Lammy's place, would be asleep. Still, he'd want to know I'd found Lammy, so I tapped out the number.

No answer.

I hit the disconnect button and tried again, taking care with the numbers. I counted twenty rings. Then five more.

No answer.

When I set the phone down I caught the speedometer moving quickly toward ninety miles an hour, and forced myself to ease up on the gas. I couldn't keep it below seventy, though. Lucky I didn't get stopped.

When we arrived back at my motel, I dragged a groggy Lammy out of the minivan and walked him to the room. I tried Casey again.

Still no answer.

"Maybe the phone's turned off," Lammy said.

"Yeah, that must be it," I said. "Anyway, I have to go out for a while." I left him a room key and very careful instructions about answering the door and telephone. "The room's paid up until noon. If I'm not back by then, use your credit card and pay for two more days."

"Uh-uh," he said, "I can't. 'Cause how will I pay the bill when—" He saw the look on my face and realized he better shut up.

Then I went to see why Casey didn't answer the phone.

IF THERE WERE COPS, or anyone else, watching Lammy's block and waiting for me to check on Casey, I couldn't spot them. There were a couple of lights on at the Connolly house and, in the

185

next block, lights at Dominic's place as well. That might have been significant, at that hour in the morning. But then, nearly every block in that working-class neighborhood had at least one home showing a light in a window. Someone sitting up with a sick child, maybe, or struggling with insomnia; someone winding down from working a late shift, or gearing up to work an early one.

Lammy's place, the two-flat far from the streetlights at either end of the block, was as bleak and dark as my own suspicions. I'd made a point of reminding Casey to leave the porch lights on all night, front and rear. But they were out. With Lammy away, maybe he thought the lights were unnecessary. Or maybe he forgot. Or maybe some other innocent reason or two. But none of them was convincing, given the splotched remains of about three dozen eggs that had been smashed against the front of the two-flat. Even in the dim light, the splayed, frozen splatters were visible, mostly on and around the second-floor windows.

What about Gus's promise that Lammy would be left alone till the case was over?

I parked a block away to the west and returned on foot through the alley. It was cold. The starless sky was heavy with low clouds that absorbed enough urban glow to turn them a dull gray, but illuminated nothing below. The alley light closest to Lammy's backyard was out. That happens. People support whole families replacing burned-out pole lights around the city, so . . .

Besides, the missing light made it less likely I'd be seen going in through the door—the unlocked door—at the bottom of the enclosed rear porch. Down half a flight the basement door was locked, as was the back door to the first-floor apartment.

I climbed cautiously up the dark stairs, straining for sounds from above, but there was nothing. Lammy's kitchen door was right at the top of the stairs on the second-floor landing. When I got up there I stood perfectly still for a moment, staring. The four-paned window in the door was broken out, mullions and all, just a few shards of glass still hanging in place—and the door to the dark kitchen stood just slightly ajar. I moved forward, bending low to keep my head beneath window level.

With the Beretta in my right hand now, I crouched, left shoulder close to the door. I slipped my left hand through the narrow opening and found the light switch I knew to be just inside. I waited, listening, fingers motionless on the switch. There were the softest of muffled sounds from beyond the door. Short, snuffled breaths, maybe. Or the rustle of clothing.

Or maybe there weren't any sounds at all beyond my own imagination and the pounding in my chest. I could crouch outside that pitch-dark kitchen and wait forever to find out. Or I could withdraw my hand, and turn and creep away.

But I flicked the switch, flooding the room with light, and nudged the door with my shoulder. I pushed harder than I intended, and the door slammed against the countertop behind it and the rest of the window glass broke free and fell on the counter and the floor. By the time the rebound of the door brought it halfway closed again, I'd gotten a glimpse inside. Breathing hard, my back pressed to the brick wall, I stayed out on the porch, out of sight of the wide-eyed man in the kitchen . . . and of anyone else in there that I hadn't seen.

A thousand years of seconds ticked by. Nothing happened.

Still keeping low, I peered around the doorjamb and into the kitchen. There was still nobody in sight but Casey, no noise of anyone rushing down the hall toward the kitchen. I stepped inside. Casey was tied with clothesline to one of the white wooden chairs. His ankles were lashed to the chair legs and there were coils of rope wrapped around his midsection and chest, binding him with his hands behind the chair back. His mouth was covered with duct tape, wrapped completely around his head several times. He was alive, but clearly struggling to breathe through nostrils that must have been partially closed off by blood that had clotted inside, as it had clotted on the tape over his mouth and on the front of his white collarless shirt.

He was far too big to be tied to that ordinary chair, so they'd kept him in place by pushing the back of the chair close to the refrigerator, putting a noose around his neck, and looping the rope around the refrigerator, then knotting it to the handle of the freezer compartment. The skin around his neck was raw, showing old, caked blood, and fresh blood as well, from the rubbing of the rope.

"Is there anyone else here," I asked, my voice a harsh whisper.

He shook his head as well as he could, but that seemed to tighten the noose. His eyes swung crazily in a clear attempt to tell me something I couldn't understand. I dropped the Beretta in my pocket and yanked open drawer after drawer, looking for a sharp knife to cut the rope that dug so deeply into his neck that I thought it might be cutting off his air.

I finally found a scissors and went to work on the rope just beyond the slip knot at the back of his neck. The scissors were dull and Casey was no help, constantly twisting his neck, squirming around and trying to wrestle his arms free. I told him to sit still, but he didn't. His eyes were wild with pain and fear.

"Damn it, Casey!" I finally yelled, my voice too angry, far louder than I wanted, as though he were to blame. "Sit still!"

He stopped struggling abruptly, and there was apology— maybe even humiliation—in his eyes. But still the fear, also. I sawed away with the scissors until the rope finally frayed, then snapped.

Even after I loosened the rope around his neck he struggled, trying to breathe. Maybe what he'd wanted to tell me was to get his mouth free first. Still using the scissors, I went to work on the duct tape, hacking away at the back of his neck; where I was less likely to slash his skin.

When I'd cut it through I set the scissors on the counter and got a firm grip on one end of the tape with my right hand. "Sorry about this," I said, and holding his head still with my left hand, I tore off the tape, bringing hair and tiny bits of skin with it.

He sucked in air hard and fast through his mouth, and blew it out again, over and over—like a boxer between rounds, too winded to talk, staring down at the floor.

"It's okay, Casey. It's okay now." I stood right in front of him, one hand on each of his shoulders, and tried to calm him down. "You'll be fine now."

He lifted his head and the fear was leaving his eyes. I knew he was trying to say thank-you, only the words wouldn't come out.

"Give it some time," I said. "Don't try talking yet. You—"

His head jerked suddenly backward. "Waaash out," he rasped, and a new, hopeless terror sprang up in his eyes.

Then a massive arm locked itself around my neck, squeezed tightly, and pulled the top half of my body backward, against the knee in the small of my back.

For the briefest of instants I may have blacked out—shock maybe—but then rage at my own stupidity snapped my mind alert. In my relief at getting Casey free, I'd absolutely forgotten what I was doing, where I was.

I struggled against being bent backward and clawed at the arm around my neck with my left hand, slamming my right elbow backward, trying to reach the man's gut, but accomplishing nothing. I instinctively reached out for the counter beside me for balance, and my hand landed right on the scissors. I grabbed and held them like a knife and slashed backward, hard, over and over, slicing at anything I could reach. When I finally found flesh, I drove the scissors deeper, twisting and yanking them side to side.

He screamed then, the man behind me, and let go of my neck. He pulled himself away and I lost my grip on the scissors.

189

I turned and faced a man in a ski mask, standing six feet from me. I watched him reach down and pull the scissors out of the flesh of his inner thigh. Blood dripped from them, and he groaned when he saw it. Then he realized the weapon was in his hand now. He looked up at me and took a tiny step my way.

"Hold it," I said, and I held the Beretta aimed at his chest. But the sight of the gun made no difference to him. With the scissors waving wildly back and forth in front of him, he took another step.

He kept coming at me . . . until I shot him.

CHAPTER

31

I was back in control of myself, so it wasn't a killshot. It might not even have stopped him if it hadn't been for the bleeding gash in his thigh. But the slug caught him in his left shoulder and seemed to wake him up, as though he remembered again that he was losing blood, and now had two sources of steadily mounting pain. Whatever the reason, he dropped the scissors on the floor, slumped into one of the kitchen chairs, and stared up at me.

"Fuck you," he said. "You're a walking dead man." The very phrase Gus had quoted.

"Right," I said, "and aren't we all. The difference is, Dominic, I'm still walking."

"You just don't know," he answered. His gaze kept flitting around the room, but try as he might, he couldn't keep it away from the open doorway to my right. "You just don't—"

"Quiet!" I whispered the order because I'd heard the sound, too. Someone had come in the front door of the apartment. Keeping the Beretta trained on Dominic, I stepped closer to the hallway and listened.

No one was coming down the hall. I leaned closer to the doorway, and then heard sounds from the front of the apartment—strange, gurgling, sloshing sounds, as though someone were emptying bottles of water onto the floor. Then the smell hit me. It wasn't water being poured out; it was gasoline.

". . . the sink. Drawer under the sink." Casey was talking, but I hadn't been hearing him. "Knife. Cut me loose."

"There's no time," I said. "We'll be burned." Shoving the gun

191

back in my pocket, I grabbed Casey from behind by his arms, and dragged him—chair and all—across the kitchen toward the porch door.

Dominic sat and watched, but lacked either the strength or the will to try to stop us. I got Casey over the door ledge onto the porch, and right to the top of the stairway. Then I realized I couldn't drag him down the stairs or he'd topple over on me.

"Cut me loose. Please cut me loose." He kept saying that over and over, all the while twisting and wrestling around, panic-stricken at being unable to move his arms and legs.

There was no sign of a fire yet, so I left him backed up to the stairway and returned to the kitchen for a knife. "I'll be right back," I said. "I promise."

Dominic wasn't in the kitchen anymore.

I ran to the open doorway and peered down the dark hall. Dominic was limping badly, but was almost to the other end already. More importantly, there was another man, also wearing a ski mask, coming my way, sloshing gasoline from a huge red can as he came. The fumes were overpowering and a gunshot might have sent us all up and out through the roof.

I turned and ran to the sink and pulled open the drawer. There must have been five sharp-looking knives. I grabbed one and turned to see the man with the gas can burst into the kitchen. He came at me, lifting the can above his head. I swung the knife in a wide arc at his midsection, slicing through nothing but air. The gas can crashed down on the top of my head, and the world went away.

MY NEXT CONSCIOUS MOMENT found me sliding around on my knees, looking desperately for the knife in the dark. Then I realized I was alone in the kitchen, with the light turned off and gasoline everywhere. Still no fire, but there were voices from far away, at the front of the apartment. I struggled to my feet and went to the back door. The wooden door was soaked with gasoline, and it was closed—closed and locked from the inside with a key, and the key wasn't there.

I ran across the kitchen into the hallway, then all the way to the front door. It was open and when I got there I looked down the carpeted front stairway. The stairs took a right angle turn halfway down. I saw no one, but the odor of gas on the stairs was sickening. I made it to the landing hallway down in two jumps and saw the man in the ski mask with his back to me in the door at the bottom of the stairs. When he turned his head around he looked up at me and I stared back, frozen for an instant as he tossed a burning torch of newspaper up onto the stairs.

I dove down the remaining steps even as the flames shot up toward me. I hit the bottom rolling and kept on going, out onto the front porch, down the steps, and into the snow. By the time I got to my feet the front entranceway of the two-flat was ablaze and flames were already showing through the second-floor windows.

I swung around, looking for Dominic and Steve—because the second man was Steve, for sure. They were halfway down the block, just getting into a car, the car Tina had driven. I ran that way, driven by instinct rather than sense, as though I could catch them or get their license plate number, as though that made some difference. Stupidly, I chased the departing car almost to the corner, but they were long gone and I turned back to the two-flat. The wail of fire sirens rose up in the distance. And only then did I remember.

Casey, for God's sake. Casey.

One of the second floor windows exploded above me and flames shot out, as I pounded clumsily through the snow, across the front yard and into the gangway. By the time I got to the back of the building I could hear fire crackling on the upper part of the enclosed wooden porch. Steve must have spread gasoline out there, too, before he locked me in, and the fire had either burned through the kitchen door already, or gone up and through the broken window.

I went through the door into the enclosure and made it up the steps as far as the first-floor apartment. Beyond that it was hopeless. The dry, aged wood made perfect kindling. Pieces of the roof were dropping down around me. I turned and went back down the steps and into the backyard. There was nothing left to do.

Fire engines were arriving out front from the south. I went into the alley and headed north, forcing myself not to run.

I WANDERED AROUND FOR a while, telling myself I was looking for Casey, telling myself he must have gotten out somehow and might be freezing in the snow. And not really believing it. I don't know why I wasn't picked up by the cops, except there were other people on the street now, drawn by the fire and the excitement.

I lost track of where I was, but eventually found myself on the corner diagonally across the intersection from Steve Connolly's house. This was as close as I could safely get, mixed into a softly talking group of men and women, some carrying children on their shoulders, many with pajamas visible beneath their winter coats. It was a crowd that was constantly changing—some people getting cold, or bored, and turning away, but always replaced by others who arrived with the same excited curiosity about what was going on at the pervert's house. I tried to stay within the crowd, and still not engage in any conversation.

It was past three A.M. now, the temperature somewhere in the high twenties and a dark, starless sky threatening snow. But the block in front of me, Lammy's block, was awash in the cold, eerie glow of floodlights, punctuated by competing emergency lights—blue-and-white police strobes flashing frantically against the slower, perhaps more patient, red-and-white bursts from fire department vehicles. A helicopter hovered low in the windless sky, the beam of its spotlight striped and dancing as it pierced through shifting clouds of rising vapor—vehicle exhaust mingled with white smoke and steam from a dying fire.

Lammy's block swarmed with people bustling this way and that in apparent chaos, calling and shouting orders in voices barely audible in the cold night air above the rumbling running engines of more than a dozen fire and police vehicles. Two hook and ladders and a snorkel rig, its long arm folded in upon itself, were clustered closest to the center of the block. Nearby, two huge, boxlike red equipment trucks faced each other, nose to nose, banks of portable floodlights mounted on their roofs. There was a red fire-lieutenant's car and a trauma wagon, with its wide-open rear doors showing activity of some sort within.

Threaded in among the fire equipment were police vehicles of every variety: marked and unmarked squads, patrol wagons, an evidence technician's car, and another large rectangular truck like the fire department's equipment trucks, except this one blue and white, but again with floodlights mounted on its top. Two TV vans were parked just outside the police lines, tall towers rising from their roofs. Even the Red Cross truck was there, with coffee and doughnuts for participants with the proper credentials.

In among the jumble of motor vehicles, helmeted firefighters in knee-length coats of black and reflective yellow climbed carefully in heavy boots over hoses and snow-banked curbs. Uniformed police officers of both sexes in bulky black jackets and fur-lined, ear-flapped hats stood silently—almost casually—at my end of the block, and certainly at the other end as well. Their mere presence was intended, and sufficient, to keep the curious neighbors at bay. Beyond them, in the inner circle, detectives in topcoats and fedoras, and aggressive wool-capped tactical officers in their trademark flak jackets, stood in clusters with their white cardboard cups of coffee, chatting and laughing and shaking their heads, occasionally stamping their feet on the frozen ground . . . and constantly looking around.

Constantly looking around. Pivoting this way and that. Peering at the shifting groups of onlookers around the edges of the scene. Bantering, watching. Gossiping, observing.

I'm told that as hard as any crowd watches any fire, smart cops—especially when they know it's a torch job—watch the crowd right back. Equal opportunity crime notwithstanding, the cops are looking mostly for males, and specifically for some guy shifting his weight rhythmically from foot to foot, or—better yet—a guy with his hand at his crotch. They're looking for the man showing more than ordinary curiosity, the one for whom fire offers a special excitement, a singular, sexual, thrill. The perpetrator—pro and amateur alike, I'm told—is often there on the scene, and quite often ejaculating into his pants.

I wasn't excited in quite that way, but because the smart cops were watching I had to get out of there. I could see that the fire was under control, essentially out. The homes on either side of Lammy's were both still standing, their fronts and sides coated with thick, roped armors of ice. There were no visible flames, and not even much smoke anymore, although firefighters still shot heavy streams of water into what was left of the two-flat, basically the exterior brick walls about as high as the first floor, with the roof, the upper walls, and everything else nothing but a mass of smoldering, steaming ruins that had fallen in on itself.

Lammy wouldn't have to worry about going home anymore. Maybe he'd be better off. Maybe it was all for the best—for Lammy.

I'd left Casey tied to his chair and scared to death. Was he still waiting for me to keep my promise when the flames swept over him?

CHAPTER

32

Leaving the illusory safety of the crowd on the corner, I walked down the sidewalk toward the west. Up ahead, the drivers of two one-man squad cars were conferring through their open windows, facing opposite directions in the entrance to the alley that ran first past Steve Connolly's garage and, farther down, Lammy's backyard. I was headed for the Voyager, but then the squad car facing north drove off down the alley. In the remaining car the interior lights were on and the driver—overweight and on the far side of middle-age—took off his patrolman's cap and dropped it onto the seat beside him.

"Say, officer," I said, hobbling across the street, dragging my left foot in a pronounced limp, "can I ask ya somethin'?"

"Alley's closed, bud, if that's what you want." He shifted a thick toothpick from one side of his mouth to the other.

"Nah, not that." I stopped well away from the car, breathing hard, as though walking were an effort. My gloves were off and I held a small notebook in my left hand, with a ballpoint poised in my right. "Name's Max Bodenheim, officer. I'm a new guy with the *Sun-Times,* and—"

"Yeah? Well, there's a press liaison officer who—"

"Right, I know the drill," I said, talking through his objection, "and I won't quote ya or nothin'. But my damn car broke down and I just got here and I couldn't find the press guy and I was wondering . . . was there anybody inside when that place went up? I need to know that right away 'cause I'm supposed to call in if there was, and I heard the first-floor people were outta town but there mighta been a guy living on the second floor and—"

197

"Jesus, shut up." He sighed, tired of listening to me. "All I can say is they didn't pull anybody out. But the place went up like somethin' in a friggin' Stallone movie. If there *was* anybody inside, you could lose what's left of the poor bastard on the bottom of your toaster." He rolled the toothpick between his plump thumb and forefinger. "Now why don't you——"

But I was already limping away.

Once around the corner I abandoned the limp and hurried to the Voyager. I yanked on the door. But it didn't open, and I remembered I'd locked it so no one would steal my sleeping bag. I dug out the key, but for some reason it wouldn't fit in the lock. I tried the passenger door. No luck. The locks didn't seem frozen. The key just didn't——

The Voyager key was in another pocket. The key I'd been trying was the one to the Intrepid, the car Casey had a key to, also. I U-turned the Voyager, drove two blocks south, then back east again, hoping not to find the white Intrepid where I left it, hoping Casey had gone somewhere in it.

But even before I turned the final corner I could see diagonally across the vacant lot where a building had recently been torn down. The white car was still sitting there in a row of other parked cars, visible in the dim light—and empty.

I didn't make the turn. Why bother? There was nothing to do but go and get some sleep.

In the middle of the intersection I stopped for a moment and stared down the street, past the parked Intrepid, toward the fire scene two blocks north. There seemed to be fewer emergency vehicles down there now, and cops were in the street waving their arms, helping one of the fire trucks back up so it could leave, too. The crowd of onlookers was scattering. The show was almost over. I squeezed my steering wheel hard and cursed at the Intrepid for still sitting there on the street, just another parked car, except . . .

Except now there was exhaust puffing out from the rear of the white car, for God's sake, and—

An angry blast from a monstrous air horn nearly blew me through the windshield. Huge headlights were bearing down fast on my tail and I hit the gas and barely made it off to the side as a long red truck thundered by. Maybe there was another fire somewhere. Or maybe the hook-and-ladder people had cooking duty that week and were hustling back to the station to start breakfast.

I walked over to the Intrepid and yanked open the front passenger door. "Hey," I said, "never sit with your engine idling. What if you fell asleep?"

Casey's head was already up against the ceiling or he'd have banged it there when he jumped. "Thank God almighty!" he said. "I thought you were—"

I got in the car and we congratulated each other on being alive. He had a heavy black cardigan on, over his bloodstained collarless shirt.

"Fact is," Casey said, "I *was* sleeping, laying over on the seat there. But a minute ago I got cold and cranked up the car to get warm."

"But how did you—"

"When you left me tied to that chair I was scared and started throwing myself around, trying to get free, not knowing how close I was to the top of the stairs. Jeez, I flipped over backward down the steps and I thought I was a goner. But when I hit the next landing the chair broke up into pieces and I knew I was gonna get free. So I just kinda kept on rolling, all the way down to the bottom."

"And you went to the car then?"

"Nah. I went back up to help, but by the time I got all the knots untied, and had my breath back, well . . . the kitchen door was locked. I'm wondering if I should try to squeeze through the broken window, when the next thing I know the place is a furnace. And I didn't know if . . . if . . ."

"Right." I interrupted. Neither one of us wanted him to start sobbing. "That's what I thought about you, too. So then what? Where'd you get that sweater, anyway?"

"It was in the car. Thing is, with Lammy and you both gone, and then that lawyer putting the scare in me, I wasn't gonna stick around. I stowed my stuff in here." He jerked his thumb toward the backseat, which was pretty well filled with his lumpy bag. "Then I went back to Lammy's, thinking I'd stay a little longer in case you called. That's when those guys broke in and started asking me where Lammy was."

"Asking? You mean torturing."

"Wasn't all that bad. Thing is, I really didn't know where Lammy was and they wouldn't believe me. I got a bloody nose and a little rope burn. That's all." He grinned.

"John Wayne lives," I said.

"*Was* kind of scary, though, I admit." He paused. "So when the fire started I wanted to stick close by. If you were . . . you know . . . alive, I figured you'd look for the car. I was so tired I laid down on the seat. I knew you'd think of this car. And I knew you wouldn't just drive on by without looking inside, even if you didn't see me."

"Yeah, well . . ."

We drove to an all-night gas station with a little grocery store. I stayed in the car while Casey went inside and washed up a little in the rest room. He came back to the car with two coffees and a plastic-wrapped package of six sweet rolls.

"Probably taste like crap," he said, "but they're loaded with sugar and I haven't eaten since lunch."

I ate one roll and he was right.

He started inhaling the other rolls while he talked. "I almost forgot. That woman lawyer called again. Not that long after you hung up on me. Said you'd tried to call her but she missed you. She was really upset."

"Pissed-off at me, I suppose."

"Well, a little mad, 'cause she thought you'd be calling earlier. But mostly worried. Said she had to get word to you fast. Told me Steve Connolly was . . . well . . . *enraged* was the word I think she used and she was worried him and his brother Dominic might—"

"Brother-in-*law*," I said.

"Yeah. Well, anyway, they're really angry about what happened. I just wish she'd have called me before I talked to you, because—"

"What hap—"

But his words kept rolling out. ". . . because she said I oughta keep an eye out and she hoped Lammy didn't come home and that's what she wanted to tell you, to—"

"What—"

"So she kinda scared the crap outta me and I put my stuff in the car, thinking if everyone was so mad, and wanted to take it out on Lammy, it was a good thing he wasn't here and it might be good if I wasn't—"

"Casey!"

"What?"

"Shut up. Eat that last roll and shut up for a minute and calm down."

"Okay."

"Now just answer one question." I paused to let him finish his coffee, then spoke very slowly. "Did Renata say why Steve and Dominic were so angry?"

"Yes," he said. But that's all he said. He was following instructions.

"Well?"

"Oh. Okay. She told me they were in court this afternoon . . .

I mean yesterday afternoon. Anyway, there was a whole crowd of people there, she said." He was speaking slowly now, too. So slowly I wanted to shake him. "Neighbors, I guess. And other people. And afterward they were all very upset—but Steve the most, I guess—because of what happened."

"Why? Because Lammy didn't show up?"

"No, not that. I didn't understand all of what she said, but basically she said the state dropped all the charges against Lammy. The case got dismissed."

CHAPTER

33

IT WAS TRUE.

Renata was so happy about it she didn't even gripe about my calling her at four o'clock in the morning. But she still had no kind words for the prosecutor.

"I've been telling that damn Heffernan he had no case from the start. He knew it, too, as well as I did, but he was afraid of a hostile reaction from the media."

"Right, and the neighbors, and especially—"

"Whatever. Anyway, when the little girl disappeared, that gave him a perfect excuse to dump the case. He moved to have it S.O.L.'ed, stricken on leave to reinstate. Told the judge—and the press—he'll consider reinstating charges when, and if, his witness is located."

"And will he?"

"Not a chance. Even if the inconsistencies in the girl's statements weren't so obvious, everyone knows that whatever happened couldn't have happened the way she described it, *where* she described it."

I knew exactly what Renata meant. Trish had claimed her pants were pulled down and she was pushed backward onto the ground at the bottom of Lammy's back steps. But the rough, cracking concrete that covered that entire area made the absence of abrasions on her buttocks, or the backs of her legs, simply unexplainable.

Renata obviously hadn't heard about the fire, which happened too late for the ten o'clock news. "I don't suppose," I said, "you have any pictures of—"

"You bet I do. Photos of the back stairs and the whole area, taken the same day Lammy got out on bond. A dozen eight-by-ten color prints, which I showed Heffernan a week ago. Someone may have attacked that child, but not where and how she described it."

"So Heffernan's thrilled to have a reason to dump the case."

"Plus," Renata said, "although I never discussed this with the state, I've received the report on Lammy's psych tests. No sign of a propensity for sexual attraction to, or behavior with, children. Of course, what they *did* find is nothing to write home about, the poor soul, and I hope he never has to read it."

"Hell, I wouldn't want to see my results, either, from tests like that."

"Anyway," she said, "Heffernan gets rid of the case and he doesn't get eaten alive by the press, or the neighbors, or—"

"Or by Steve Connolly."

"Yes. Connolly was in court and he obviously thought Lammy would be there. You know, I can understand the feelings of a father, but this man is unusual. He's overflowing with hostility . . . hatred even. He's supposedly mixed up with the mob, of course, and probably psychopathic. The girl's uncle was there, too."

"Dominic Fontana."

"Right. He's even scarier than Connolly. I'm really frightened for Lammy."

I told her, then, about the fire. Not much, only that I'd heard it was arson, and that Casey was safe.

"Whoever it was must have thought Lammy was home," she said. "You have to find him fast, before they do."

"I already found him. He's fine. Better you don't know where. I've sent Casey to stay with him."

"And what about you?" she asked.

"Me?"

"My advice is to turn yourself in. The longer you hide out, the more it looks like you've gone off the deep end. First with Tina

204

Fontana. And now that priest, and getting rid of the grandmother and the little girl, so she couldn't testify against Lammy."

"You don't think I—"

"The media are certainly playing it that way. The cops seem to think so, too." She paused. "And I must say . . ."

"Jesus Christ, Renata, you can't possibly believe that."

"Of course not. I was only going to say . . . you *do* seem to have screwed things up, and—"

"Screwed things up? I can't believe you said that."

"Okay, I take that back. But you'd still be better off giving yourself up."

"Bullshit. You think the cops are gonna protect me from a couple of maniacs like Connolly and Fontana, for chrissake?"

"Well . . ."

"And that hotshot investigator—Sanchez?—he's gonna see my ass is well-protected, right? Hell, he'll tear off my hide himself if he gets the chance."

"Okay, okay," Renata said. "Calm down. I'm still your lawyer, and I'm doing my legal duty. Cops ask me, I'll say you called. Wouldn't tell me where you were. I suggested you surrender. You're considering it. Everything else is privileged. Now, when will you—"

I hung up on her. She'd taken it back, maybe, but Renata's opinion was that I was screwing things up.

Ah well, it's always nice to have the support of your friends. But when you don't? You push on anyway, with no one to pat you on the back. Maybe I *had* screwed a few things up. But if so, at least the screw-up came from *doing*. The other option—not-doing—was the path I'd chosen when Lammy was in trouble the first time, a path that had led finally into this mess. So I had to push on.

Besides, I was beginning to get an idea or two.

CHAPTER
34

No real plan yet, of course, but a few ideas.

The first thing was to find Rosa. Only I, and the person who'd gone after Monsignor Borelli, knew that Rosa must have run off with Trish on her own. But why? Was it that phone call she'd gotten at the rectory? The caller was a man and the priest said he assumed it was Steve—so he wasn't certain. Was it actually Dominic? Had Dominic learned that Rosa told me he was the one who went after Trish?

Maybe Rosa knew Dominic was coming after them, so she ran away. When Dominic got to the rectory, Monsignor Borelli must have told him he didn't know where Rosa and Trish had gone, but Dominic didn't believe him. He went after the priest to make him reveal where Rosa had taken Trish, and in his anger he went too far. Something similar must have happened with Tina, too. Someone—maybe the waiter at the restaurant, or somebody the waiter told—must have told Dominic that Tina had met with me. He was furious, thinking Tina and I were working against him somehow, or trying to make her tell what we'd been talking about.

If I could find Rosa and Trish, maybe they'd convince Steve that it was Dominic, not Lammy, who deserved his wrath. Who knows what might happen then? Steve might get Dominic off my back—for good. Or Dominic might get Steve off everyone's back—just as permanently. Either way, Lammy could relax.

Of course, all this had to be done in a way that convinced the cops that I wasn't involved in anyone's murder. On top of that, I still had to satisfy Gus Apprezziano's curiosity about Karen Colter. And, since I owed the woman my life, I had to do that without revealing what I'd learned—that she was spying on Gus through Dominic, who was loyal enough to go to jail to protect Gus, but not smart enough to recognize Karen as an FBI informant.

Of course, everything hadn't come together yet. One big thing didn't fit at all.

But I needed some sleep and it was time to put my traveling home to the test, while there were still a couple hours of darkness. I drove a few miles north and west and found a parking place on a quiet residential street on the edge of the city near the forest preserve. With the engine not running, the minivan was going to get cold, so I took off only my shoes, and snuggled into the sleeping bag. The next thing I knew, though, it was way too warm and I was struggling out of my socks and pants, as well. With the tinted windows I told myself I should feel pretty secure. Finally, three hours later—with what seemed like a half-hour's sleep—I was back behind the wheel.

Rosa had taken the bingo money when she and Trish went on the run. She was no thief, so that meant she'd been desperate and had no other money with her when she split. So where had she gone to hide? She probably had family in Italy, but her running that far on short notice seemed unlikely. Plane fares were expensive and, if they didn't want to draw attention to themselves, she and Trish would need at least a little luggage—not to mention passports and picture IDs. Besides, the cops, and anyone else looking for her, would be checking airports, railroad and bus terminals, and car rental agencies—assuming she had a driver's license, which somehow seemed unlikely.

They might already have talked to her friends, too, but I could think of no other leads. I'd be late for seven o'clock Mass again. But with luck I might catch the end of the rosary.

WRONG AGAIN.

Bundled up to ward off a bitterly cold wind—and to avoid

207

recognition even though the street seemed deserted—I climbed the steps of Our Lady of Ravenna and read the announcement taped to the locked door. There was no early-morning Mass that day. Monsignor Borelli's body would be laid out in the church for mourners to view, beginning at eight-thirty. The funeral Mass would be at ten o'clock, followed by a lunch served by the ladies of the Rosary Guild in the church basement, and then a motorcade to Queen of Heaven Cemetery in Hillside.

Monsignor Borelli's funeral was about the last place his suspected murderer ought to show up. So I went to a phone and made other arrangements.

WE HAD DECIDED THAT Casey would take Lammy to his own doctor to look at his hand, and then move Lammy and himself to a different motel, still in a western suburb, but an older, cheaper place, where stays of a week or longer weren't unusual. They'd gotten two adjoining rooms on the first floor, opening onto the parking lot.

I got there about three o'clock that afternoon. The rooms were clean and worn around the edges and smelled like thirty years of cigarette smoke. Casey wasn't back yet, so I'd have some time alone with Lammy. He was sitting on one of the beds, wearing a white V-necked T-shirt and the same dark pants he'd worn to Renata's office the day he ran away. His eyes were still ringed with leftover bruising, but there was a much smaller bandage on his hand. He'd piled some pillows against the headboard and was reading a very large book Casey bought for him. It was somebody's *History of War in the Balkans,* weighed probably five pounds, and had a four-dollar sticker on it from a discount bookstore.

We'd agreed that I'd be the one to tell Lammy about the fire and the dismissal of his case, or at least answer his questions if he'd already heard about them, which Casey said would be unlikely. Lammy wasn't big on watching news on television and, although he did read the papers, Casey would avoid buying them that morning.

I started with the fire. Lammy hadn't heard about it, and I gave him no details. Just that there'd been a fire, and that the two-flat was a total loss.

Lammy thought for a moment in silence. "Good thing my ma wasn't home," he finally said. Then he thought a moment more before adding, "Guess Elaine'll just have to keep ma there with her, in Cicero, and I'll have to find my own place." Maybe there was a hint of hopefulness in his voice, or maybe that was just my imagination.

Lammy's other comments were a concern as to how he'd pay for new clothes and a relief that he'd returned all his library books. He actually spoke more words than I'd ever heard him say before at any one time. One thing struck me—he didn't appear very concerned about where he was going to live from now on.

Nowhere near as concerned as I was.

About that time Casey came in the door, with fried chicken and soft drinks and a half gallon of frozen strawberry yogurt. "You guys probably haven't had lunch," he said. "And I didn't have much, either. Just a couple funny little sandwiches."

The three of us sat at a small round table in one of the motel rooms and ate chicken with slippery fingers and cole slaw with plastic forks out of little paper cups. Having no home to go back to didn't seem to have hurt Lammy's appetite, but it was Casey who divided the food, and when I tried to even out the portions he stopped me with a hard look and it hit me that he had Lammy on something of a diet. By the time we got to the yogurt it was soft enough so Casey could almost pour it out onto the same three paper plates we'd used for the fried chicken. Too soft, actually, for my taste, since I like to pretend it's ice cream.

I waited until then to tell Lammy that the case against him had been dismissed. "S.O.L.'ed," I said. "Their excuse was that the victim, their only witness, is missing. Technically, the case can be reinstated if they find Trish."

"I saw in the paper about her and her grandma being missing," Lammy said. "About Monsignor Borelli, too, and that the police were looking for you." He swirled the yogurt around on his plate with a plastic spoon and, head down, said, "It wasn't . . . I mean . . . you didn't—"

"It wasn't," I said, "and I didn't."

"But they're still looking for Mal," Casey said. "So we have to be very careful. No one's found Trish and her grandmother yet."

"I hope they find them." Lammy had abandoned his spoon, and just sat staring down at his plate. "I mean, I *guess* I hope so, even if it means I have to go back—"

"No," I said. "I'm not letting you go back to jail. But you still have to stay hidden."

"Because of her dad, and the neighbors, right? But if the case got thrown out, maybe nobody still thinks I did it anymore."

"Not a chance," I said. "That fire at your place wasn't an accident. Your house was burned down deliberately."

Lammy's eyes widened. "But—"

"And earlier in the evening," Casey said, "there was about a dozen people outside—yelling and throwing eggs at the windows."

"Well," Lammy said, "I can't go home anyway, 'cause it's burned down. So I guess . . ." His voice trailed off. Then, without looking up, he said, "Why are you guys doing all this? I mean, you don't hardly know me, and I got no money. So why are you helping me?"

When I didn't answer, Casey said, "Well, I'm just helping Mal, and I think Mal's trying to—"

"Maybe we can talk about that later," I said, "when it's all over. Okay?"

"Uh-huh," Lammy nodded.

"Anyway," Casey said, "let's clean up."

We rinsed the yogurt off the paper plates in the bathroom before putting them in the wastebasket.

"I bet you can't guess the one thing I really miss, Father," Lammy said. He and Casey were washing and drying the plastic forks and spoons.

"Nope," Casey said. "Can't guess."

I thought I knew, but Lammy wasn't talking to me, so I kept out of it.

"The shelter," Lammy said. "I really miss taking care of the dogs. Cleaning up and talking to them and all, you know? I like dogs, and they like me, too. I can't wait to get back to the shelter."

"Won't be long," Casey said, "and you'll be back there again. Right, Mal?"

"That's for sure." My guess had been dead right, but I didn't really want to lie about him ever going back there. "Maybe the shelter," I added, "or maybe someplace even better."

It was time to find out what Casey had learned, if anything, at Monsignor Borelli's funeral. On top of that, it was time to decide just how far to let Lammy in on what was happening.

"Well, Casey," I said. "We need to talk."

"Right," Casey said. He pulled a chair back to the round table, while Lammy scooped up his huge book on the Balkan wars and headed for the open door into the adjoining room.

"Hold on, Lammy," I said. "Remember that stuff the other night, about us all being in this together?"

He turned. "Uh-huh."

"So . . . maybe you should sit in on this. I mean, if you want—"

"Yeah," he said. "Sure."

I knew right then, by his tone when he interrupted me, that I'd made the right choice. Of course, I also knew it was a choice, like some others I'd made recently, that I might well regret—at least in the short run.

CHAPTER
35

"PRIESTS' FUNERALS ARE GREAT," Casey said.

"Great?" He'd caught me off-guard. Even Lammy looked a little surprised, and he generally showed no expression at all.

"Yeah. They're great," Casey said. "I love 'em. Definitely upbeat. Lots of talk about rising from the dead, eternal life. That kinda stuff."

"You believe all that?" I asked.

"Hell yes," he said. "Why not? Beats the crap out of the alternative, doesn't it?" He paused. "Anyway, Bobo Borelli got a great send-off. Big crowd. One of the bishops gave the main talk at the Mass, which was okay, you know, kinda bland. But then one of Bobo's priest friends and this other guy—a cousin of Bobo's, or something—got up and they told a few stories about Bobo's life. Some funny episodes, and a couple of real tearjerkers."

"I get the picture," I said. Casey was enjoying himself, and I thought he might even start repeating the stories.

"Then, after the funeral Mass, the ladies of the Rosary Guild served lunch. Not much food, though. And after that, this huge motorcade, with police cars and all, out to the cemetery. I didn't go to the cemetery, of course."

"How come?" Lammy asked, and it seemed significant that he was participating in the conversation.

"Because I stayed after and helped the ladies clean up. Wipe off tables, wash dishes. They loved me."

"Right," I said. "We know. Why don't you get to—"

"Anyway, I'm gabbing with 'em, the ones who speak English, anyway, and I find two pretty good friends of Rosa Parillo, ones who pray the rosary with her after Mass every day. I ask about Rosa and they say they're worried about her and the child being missing, but to me they don't seem all that worried. So I say I heard they were kidnapped and might even be dead, and they say, 'Yes, terrible, terrible.' But they're pretty bad liars, maybe because they're talking to a priest. Tell you the truth, I think maybe Rosa called one of them. They seem to know she's all right."

"But do they know where she's hiding?" I asked.

"Hell, I couldn't just come out and ask them. So I say maybe she escaped and she's hiding with Trish somewhere. They nod their heads and say that's what they're praying for. I ask if she has any relatives or friends where she might have gone." He paused. "I hadda be careful, even though they loved all the attention I was giving 'em, and obviously love to gossip. So it took longer than this, you know, to—"

"Yeah, we know. Get on with it."

"Anyway, the answer's no. I don't think they have any idea where she is."

"No relatives? No—"

"Sounded like her friends are just those ladies, and maybe a couple more like them. And the only living relative they know about—besides her two sons-in-law, who the ladies can barely stand to mention without spitting—is her brother. Guy named Gustavo. I guess he's older than Rosa and treats her like he's her father, even though they say he's a bad man and Rosa's ashamed of him and prays for him all the time. Sounds to me like he might be—"

"Yeah, he is," I said.

"Is what?" Lammy asked.

"Connected with organized crime," I said.

"So," Casey said, "the answer to whether they know where Rosa and Trish are is no. Sorry. Guess I won't be getting my private detective's license anytime soon."

"Don't be too discouraged. That's the way the game is

played," I said. "You just have to keep on asking, even if the answer's usually no."

"What the hell," Casey said, "you sound like me . . . giving one of my sermons about prayer."

Two rings. A click. "Leave a message." Beep.

That was it. Just, "Leave a message."

So I did. Then I lay on the bed in the room I'd rented on the southwest side near Midway Airport, in a motel that offered a "quiet nap rate." That meant you could rent the room for as little as four hours. The rate was the same whether the quiet nap was for one person or two. I'd considered a two-hour motel, too, but it looked a little sleazy.

It may not have been smart to call Karen Colter, but my hopes for getting Lammy and me out of our respective tight spots were riding on Rosa, and I'd used up all of my smart ideas for finding her. I had to trust that Karen wouldn't blow the whistle on me. She'd had other chances to do me in, and hadn't. Besides, from her comments that night in the van outside Gus's house, I knew she thought Rosa was right about Dominic attacking Trish. Karen liked Rosa, and she'd helped Rosa reach me. Maybe she'd help me reach Rosa.

A half hour later, Karen called back, obviously from a public phone in a busy place somewhere. She was willing to meet me. Seemed almost eager, in fact—maybe too eager for my own good.

I chose a Bohemian restaurant on Cermak Road in Berwyn, in the dining room on the second floor. The same huge portions were heaped onto the same wide plates as downstairs, with the succulent dumplings and rich gravies just as full of fat. But the upstairs room was smaller and quieter, and the booths—with their high, cushioned backs—offered more privacy. On top of that, it was unlikely there'd be a soul in the place who knew me except the owners—and they owed me big time.

So I was waiting in one of those upstairs booths by a front window, drinking cheap white wine, when I saw Karen arrive in a cab. I didn't see anyone behind her.

The first thing she said, after she tossed her leather coat onto the seat and sat down beside it, was, "How'd you get my phone number? It's a spec— I mean it's unlisted."

"I'm a private investigator, remember?" Actually, Herb Gatsby's people had finally gotten it for me, and I didn't know how. "Anyway, you're Rosa's friend and Rosa needs my help and I need Rosa's help. So I need you to put me in touch with Rosa." So much for small talk.

"And you take for granted I know where—"

"Try the roast pork," I said, as the smiling waitress came up, "with dumplings and red cabbage. Or sauerkraut, maybe. But here I'd go with the red—"

"I'd like a half pound, lean beef patty, well-done," Karen told the waitress, "and some cottage cheese and lettuce." She reached across and sampled my wine and made a face. "And bring me a dry white wine that costs about twice as much as that one."

"And you, sir?" The waitress was tall and thick and dark-skinned and, I decided, wild-looking like a gypsy—but a friendly gypsy.

"I'll go with the roast pork, and—"

". . . dumplings and red cabbage," the gypsy said. "I know. More wine?"

"Thanks," I said. "I'll stay with this stuff, though. Cheaper wine has fewer calories."

The gypsy left and Karen stared at me. "It's not true, you know," she said.

"Are you sure? I thought I read somewhere that wine—"

"I mean it's not true that I know where Rosa is," she said. "But I can find out, I think. And . . ." The gypsy was back already. She set two full glasses on the table, scooped up my empty, and hustled off.

"And?" I said, reaching for my glass.

"And I need your help, too," Karen said. "I don't wanna bleed to death on a hook in some meatpacker's freezer." So much for small talk.

"My help," I asked, "when you've got the United States government backing you up?"

"I knew you had things figured out, when you mentioned Anders' name the other night."

"You might be wired right now, for all I know."

"I'm not. You'll just have to trust me on that."

"Or . . . we could go somewhere and take off all your—"

"Not a chance." She was glaring at me.

"Just kidding," I said. "Anyway, you've already got the government on your side. What kind of help can I be?"

"I don't have the *government*. I've got Anders. And he's not on my side. He's using me."

"What have they got on you, anyway?"

"I'd rather not say. But it's . . . it's a big problem, and I've got kids. And if I wanna keep custody . . . well . . ."

"Fine."

"Anyway, I told Anders he had to pull me out because I think Gus is on to us, and—"

"Us? You mean *you*. Gus is on to *you*. But not certain, just suspicious."

"How do you know?"

"You'll just have to trust me on that. But what about Dominic? He's no genius. Is *he* on to you?"

"What are you talking about?"

"Dominic," I said. "Last name Fontana. Alias Hercules unchain—"

"I know who you're talking about, but . . ." She shook her head. "You mean, you don't know about Dominic?"

"Apparently not," I said.

So Karen explained. The gypsy brought our food and while

we ate she kept on explaining. I hadn't figured things out, after all. It wasn't Karen, but Dominic, that Anders was relying on to bring Gus down. When I told Dominic I knew his secret, he didn't realize I was talking about Trish. He thought I knew he was working for the FBI, a fact certain to earn him a slow and painful death if Gus found out. That's why Dominic freaked out and went after me.

Karen was just the go-between, posing as Dominic's girlfriend. Anders wanted her to be able to come and go, not living with Dominic, so he'd convinced Tina to put her divorce on hold and let Dominic come back and live at home.

"How did he do that?" I asked.

"It was Tina who first gave the FBI what they had on Dominic. Anders had promised to protect her. Then, once Dominic was away, Anders told Tina she hadn't been enough help and he couldn't protect her if Dominic found out she'd talked to the FBI. He even kind of hinted Dominic *would* find out. But he said if Tina let Dominic back home for a year, that would give Anders a chance to get something serious on Gus—and maybe even somebody higher up. If Tina did that, Anders said, he'd put her and her daughter in a protection program and move them somewhere safe."

"So she tried to save herself and her daughter. And now—thanks to me—she's dead."

"Thanks to you?"

"I think someone saw Tina talking to me, and told Anders. Then Anders told Dominic, and . . ." I suddenly remembered Dominic's alibi for Tina's killing. "Of course, Dominic didn't smash Tina's head against the vise that night in the garage. He was with you the whole time. Right?"

She lowered her head. "I lied. I . . . we all do what we have to do."

"Anyway," I said, "what's different now that makes you want out?"

"Anders is finally waking up that Dominic's not going to be any real help, even though Gus trusts him enough. Gus thinks Dominic went to jail to save his butt. Except that was all a setup. Anders had something on Dominic, way bigger than that gambling business, that nobody—not even Gus—knew about. So Dominic cut a deal, all part of Anders' big plan. But even if Gus lets Dominic in on anything important, Anders knows now that Dominic would never make a good witness. He's too, I don't know, unstable, I guess. And then that thing with Trish . . . So Anders is gonna try one more thing, something risky, which probably won't work because Gus is too careful, and it'll end up with both Dominic and me dead. The thing is, Anders doesn't care. He's been after Gus so long it's like he's obsessed. Plus, he's pissed-off out of his mind because his plan's going nowhere. He blames me, and Dominic, and even you."

"Why me?"

"He can't admit it's his own fault. So you're just one more thing that's screwing up his plan. He wants you locked up. And me and Dominic he's just gonna walk away from, leave us hanging out there. He says he won't, but I know he will. Deep down, Anders isn't that much different from the people he's after, if you ask me."

"So what are you looking for from me?"

"Jesus, I don't know. There's so many things. I mean, I need to convince Gus I'm not an FBI plant, so he doesn't kill me. I need to prove to Anders, or someone, it's not my fault the plan didn't work, so they don't just leave me out there with Gus and Dominic. And I need to keep Dominic from killing me before Gus does if Anders drops us." She paused. "At least I gotta do *some* of those things, anyway. Or maybe I just need a way to get my butt outta town in one piece."

"And you think I can do any of that?"

"Probably not, but you're all I got. And you'll try. That much I know."

"How do you know?"

"Because, first, you're up to your behind in this anyway, so what's the difference? Second, I risked my neck—twice—to save your skin. You owe me already. Plus when I put you in touch with Rosa you're gonna owe me even more. And you're not the type to walk away from a debt."

"I'm not sure that's a compliment," I said. "Trying to repay every debt can drive a person crazy."

"Oh," she said, "that's another reason. Anybody crazy enough to help a loser like that Fleming guy, against Steve Connolly and Dominic Fontana, must be crazy enough to help me, too."

That one I was sure I shouldn't take as a compliment. I was going to tell her that, too. But then I saw something in her eyes. I'd seen the same thing in Tina's eyes, but I was surprised to see it in a hard case like Karen. I'm always surprised—which is always foolish. Because what I saw in her eyes was fear, and nobody who's sane is immune.

She caught me looking, and she knew what I'd seen. And then she gave up. She let the tears flow into her eyes along with the fear. "I've always been real strong," she said. "Always the tough one, that's Karen. But it's so hard being on your own all the time, you know?"

"Yeah," I said. "I know."

"I had these kids, and their father was gone, and . . . anyway, I did something real stupid. I . . . I took some money, from a bank where I worked. I thought I was helping my kids—two of 'em. Boys, you know? Still little guys. And now here I am. I got caught and now here I am. And I'm scared I'm not ever gonna see my babies again."

CHAPTER
36

KAREN TRIED THE SAME avenue I'd tried, only her real last name was Colonelli and she spoke pretty good Italian and maybe that's why she was successful. By Friday she'd found out from one of Rosa's friends where Rosa was hiding.

It made perfect sense once I heard where she was. Rosa obviously hadn't planned her getaway, but she'd acted shrewdly once she made her sudden decision. She wanted Trish with her, away from Chicago and Dominic—and even Steve—while she tried to figure out what to do. They'd run from the rectory with the bingo money she'd taken, and nothing else but the clothes they were wearing. Knowing the cops would be looking for her, she must have gone straight to the Greyhound station. She selected an out-of-state destination that offered plenty of places where a woman and her granddaughter could stay several days at a time without drawing attention to themselves. Orlando might have come to my mind first. But Rosa's idea was better.

No one would have pegged her as much of a country music fan, and that may have made Branson, Missouri, even more attractive as a place to hide. Taking a cab from somewhere near the rectory, she could easily have made the bus that leaves downtown Chicago at midnight, heads all the way south to Memphis first, and then switches back up to Branson, arriving at six-thirty in the evening.

I called and found Rosa more than willing to talk to me. Although she was one tough lady, and not your ordinary grandmother, she was still plenty worried about what she'd done. She was staying in touch with one of her rosary cronies, but had been gone nearly five days and knew she'd have to act soon. Both of her own daughters were dead, and she was determined to provide a better life for Trish, and for Lisa, too, the teenage daughter of Tina and Dominic.

Rosa told me she knew she needed Gus's help. She planned to meet with him, she said, not only to reveal Dominic as the child molester, but also to try to convince Gus that Steve wasn't capable of being the parent Trish needed. She seemed to be trying out her ideas on me.

Aware that he counted Dominic among his more loyal people, Rosa knew that Gus wouldn't easily accept the idea that Dominic, not Lammy, had attacked Trish. That's where I came in. She hoped I'd found some evidence to support her. I assured her the meeting was a good idea, and said I had facts, things I couldn't talk about on the phone, that would help convince Gus. But I'd have to be at the meeting, too.

I didn't tell her I'd have my own agenda, and one that didn't entirely match hers.

"I don't know if it's good for you to be there," she said. "Gustavo may not want a stranger—"

"I'm not a total stranger to Gus," I said. "What I have to say is important. It will help you get what's best for Trish. Also . . ." I paused. "Also, it's the only way I can help Lambert Fleming. And it was *you,* Rosa, after all, who told me I had to help him because nobody else would."

So together we worked out sort of a plan.

Of course, our plan had lots of what the military people call contingency factors, and the rest of us think of as loose ends. In other words, we didn't quite know how things were going to work out, but had to go ahead anyway. One of the longer loose ends I could see, and Rosa couldn't, was hanging out there precisely because Rosa was mistaken about one important thing—something I'd finally become convinced of.

But it didn't seem helpful for me to tell her just then.

So it was Rosa's and my joint plan—slightly modified, and loose ends notwithstanding—that had Casey at the wheel of the Voyager on Sunday afternoon, waiting to drop Lammy and me off at Gus's gate and then drive off in a hurry.

One modification Rosa didn't know about was that Lammy was coming along. I hadn't planned on that, either. I couldn't see his presence causing anything but problems, but I've been wrong before. And he begged me to let him come. He was scared to death about what would surely happen to him if I wasn't around—a very reasonable fear—and he figured if I was going down he might as well go down, too. Those were my words, not his, but I knew he was thinking along those lines. On top of all that, he wanted to help save his own damn life, for God's sake, and who was I to take that away from him? Those weren't his words, either. Or mine. They were Casey's. So I figured the man of God had spoken—or something. Lammy came along.

Rosa got Gus to agree to the meeting, and to have Dominic and Steve there. She'd wanted to ask Gus's permission for me to be there, too. She said he usually gave her whatever she asked for. I rejected the idea. First of all, Gus might have said no. Secondly, I didn't want Gus telling Dominic or Steve I'd be there, or want the two of them thinking I had any arrangement with Gus. But mostly, I wanted Gus himself in the dark. He'd be less likely to interfere with my agenda.

I wouldn't have trusted Gus to take out last year's garbage without his looking to see what was in it for him. He would do whatever he thought was in his interest, and it would be better to catch him unaware. I'd apparently earned his respect, more or less, and told Rosa she could speak up on my behalf after I was already there. That, plus his not knowing whom I might have told where I'd be, made me believe Gus would have no inclination to harm Lammy and me. That is, unless something went seriously wrong—which I was seriously hoping wouldn't happen.

Gus's estate was adjacent to a country club, and was itself the size of a nine-hole golf course. A high wall, coated with white stucco to match the house, ran all the way around. We waited in the Voyager on a side road about a half mile down from the iron gate that controlled the only entrance, Lammy in the front passenger seat and I sitting on the rolled-up sleeping bag in the back. It wasn't quite as late as I'd hoped it would be, and the sun was still up, when Dominic rolled past. He was talking on his cell phone, maybe telling Gus he was nearing the gate. I wasn't happy that Karen was with him, even though I'd known it was likely. Then a few seconds later came Steve, in the Ford van.

Lammy and I had to go in right behind Steve. Otherwise, we'd have to climb over the gate, or over the wall with its original topping of broken glass and its recently installed razor wire. I didn't think I could do that, and Lammy certainly couldn't. Casey pulled out behind the van, keeping his distance. When Steve turned into the entrance drive that led to the gate, Casey accelerated.

"Don't get too close," I said, "he's gotta wait for the gate."

"Are you nuts?" Casey kept his foot on the pedal. "The gate'll be open already, for Dominic."

By the time we pulled even with the driver, Steve was already through, and the tall, iron-barred gate was sliding closed.

"Go!" I shouted. Lammy's door was quicker to open than the sliding rear door, and he was a couple of steps ahead of me, which was where I wanted to keep him. "Run, Lammy!"

The Voyager's tires spun on the cleared pavement as Casey sped away and I charged after Lammy. I was proud of him. Despite his bulky coat and boots, he must have been moving faster than he had in years. He made it through the slowly narrowing space with a couple of feet to spare. Steve's van was already into the woods and out of sight.

I'd have made it through the gate, too, if I hadn't slipped on a patch of snow, hard-packed and as smooth as ice. I lost maybe two seconds. But that was enough. The gate clanked into place, trapping Lammy inside, staring out at me through the bars—terror-stricken.

"Don't worry," I said. "I'll climb over."

And I did. I'll never know how I made it up and over. Like Lammy, I had on a winter coat, thick pants, and leather boots. My gloves were leather, too, and they gave me some grip on the cold, slippery bars. Like the wall itself, the gate was twice my height, the bars maybe four inches apart. At the top there were fancy curlicues and sharp points and some old-fashioned barbed wire. But I made it, with only a few tears in my clothes and one scratch on my cheek. I had to. I was more horrified at the prospect of my leaving Lammy alone in there than he was.

I dropped the last four feet to the pavement. "See?" I said, between gasps. "Nothing to it." I was nearly hysterical myself, and Lammy looked ready to burst into tears. I actually thought maybe I should hug him.

But I didn't want to give the idea we were scared to whoever was manning the monitor for the video camera fixed high up on the wall, pointing down at us. I kept my face turned away from the lens and pulled Lammy close to the wall under the camera.

Meanwhile, Gus's militia was already arriving.

Actually, I was happy to see the open, cabless Jeep bouncing out of the woods toward us. Better to have Gus's usual security guards get to us before Dominic or Steve, since the guards were more likely to notify Gus and less likely to just shoot us on the spot. But then Steve's van appeared, too, right behind the Jeep.

The guards—two thugs in matching snowmobile suits and semiautomatic rifles—climbed out of the Jeep and Steve stood by as they searched Lammy and me, very professionally, head to toe and everywhere in between. All they found was the

Beretta under my arm. They'd have found anything else there was, too, which is why there wasn't anything else.

"I'll take that," Steve said, reaching out for the Beretta.

"No fucking way," the man answered. He checked the magazine. "Damn thing's fully loaded. Mr. Apprezziano don't let no guns but his on the property. Even you don't bring no fucking piece in here, Mr. Connolly. You know that."

"Listen, you dumb sonovabitch. Give me the fucking jagoff's gun. I'm taking it in to Mr. Apprezziano so he'll know just what this asshole was up to."

"But we got our orders," the other man said, stepping close to his partner. "We gotta—"

"Fuck your orders! I'll have both your asses, you don't give me that goddamn piece." Steve, taller than either of them, leaned toward them and spoke very slowly. "Who the fuck you think I am, some two-bit fucking security guard like you?"

Gus was the big boss, but the guards knew Steve was far higher on the ladder than they were. He wasn't Italian, so he'd never be *made,* but still, he'd married into the family. He was a physically big man, too, and he exuded power. Besides, Gus was up at the house . . . and Steve was right here, in their faces.

The guards gave in . . . which in the end turned out to be for the best, for a reason no one could ever have dreamed of.

Lammy and I rode to the house in the back of Steve's van, sitting on the bench seat. One of the guards sat in a captain's chair swiveled around to face us, and the other followed behind in the Jeep. It was the same ride, in the same vehicle, I'd taken five days earlier, and the same road I'd walked out on after my visit with Gus. But it seemed shorter this time.

It was still light out—although it wouldn't be for long—and I noticed for the first time that the carpeting in the van was blue. We bounced up and over the little hump-backed wooden bridge, crossing the stream. Looking out the window, I didn't see

or hear any guard dogs, but knew they were around somewhere. I'd seen a tangle of thick leather leashes, and a couple
of muzzles, lying on the floor of the Jeep.

Steve parked the van beside Dominic's car and we all climbed
out. The Jeep pulled up and the driver waved a cellular phone
at Steve. "Mr. Apprezziano says to bring these two in to him," he
called. "Says he's in the library."

CHAPTER
37

If Gus's library wasn't as large as my entire apartment with the inner walls removed, it didn't fall short by much. There were even lots of books. A couple of walls full of them—from waist-high on up almost to the beamed ceiling, plus a couple of those ladders that run on wheels along rails so you can get the topmost volumes down. From the bottom shelves down to the floor, all the way around, were hand-crafted cabinets made of what I took to be birdseye maple, stained a golden color.

Of course, the very thought of Gus settled under a floor lamp in one of the comfy-looking chairs that were scattered around, cradling a volume of—let's say—Cooper's *Leatherstocking Tales* and transported to the pristine forests of upstate New York, was ludicrous. My guess was the lamps Gus used most in his library were the ones in the tanning bed that sat in one corner with its top up, looking like an open casket at a wake.

Besides the easy chairs and their floor lamps, there were four well-stuffed sofas, several library tables with carved legs and lion's claw feet, lots of table lamps of various styles, and even a huge—and, I suspected, interior-illuminated—globe.

It was plenty warm in the room, although there was no fire burning in the white brick fireplace. The predominant smell wasn't old books, but Old Spice aftershave—which I wasn't especially fond of, and which therefore I attributed to Dominic Fontana. His left arm was hanging in a narrow black cloth sling, and he wore a gray suit with a sort of a shine to the fabric. He was standing with Gus beside one of the library tables. The table was obviously used by Gus as his desk, because it held a telephone and a green-shaded desk lamp and several copies of racing forms in various colors. Gus himself was decked out in black-and-green plaid pants and a brown wool cardigan, unbuttoned, over a cream-colored shirt.

The two men were standing near the opposite end of the room from the door we entered, and beyond them was a wide, tall set of windows. The view was to the south, where the expanse of snow on the yard glowed with a rosy tint in the dying light of the afternoon sun. Gus wasn't enjoying the view, though. He'd spun around when Lammy and I stumbled into the room, pushed forward by Steve. After waving Dominic down into a nearby chair, Gus stood for a long moment, not saying anything and clearly not enjoying this view, either.

Goldilocks was there, about ten feet this side of Gus, his hands deep into the pockets of a dark blue blazer that he wore over a white shirt, open at the collar. When I got my balance I nodded to him and he nodded back, as though we were both happy to see a familiar face—and maybe we were. There was other muscle in the room, as well. Two average-sized, hard-looking men I'd never seen before—they could have been twins, actually—both wearing dark suits and narrow ties. Gus's version of secret service bodyguards. One stood off to our left near the fireplace; the other behind Gus, to the side of the windows beyond which the snow was already fading from rose to gray as the rapidly waning afternoon gave way to evening.

Not far from Gus and Dominic, at one end of a sofa that could have held three more people with room to spare, a solemn little dark-haired girl in white sneakers, light blue pants, and a pink sweatshirt sat with her hands locked between her knees, her body pressed close against the side of a thin, gray-haired woman in a plain black dress and flat-heeled shoes. The woman's arm was around the little girl's shoulders. Something about the look on Rosa's face said that Trish was under her protection now, once and for all, and she wouldn't give her up to anyone. Not Gus, not Dominic, not even Steve—not while Rosa had any breath left in her.

And, I decided, not while I did, either.

Everyone stared at everyone else, until finally Gus spoke up. "Steve," he said, pointing our way, "you know nobody brings a weapon into my house."

"Sorry," Steve said, and then tapped me on the shoulder with the Beretta. "But I took it off this—"

"Put it in your pocket."

"Jesus Christ, Mr. A.," Dominic said, "that's—"

"Watch your mouth, both of you," Gus said.

"Sorry," Dominic said. "But Steve's got—"

"Yeah, I know. Steve's got the pervert. I see that." Gus turned toward the sofa where Rosa and Trish sat, then looked across the room at the man near the fireplace. "Raymond." His voice was strong, but not harsh. "Take the child out of here. She should not—"

"No," Rosa said, staring at Raymond and freezing him in his tracks. She turned back to Gus. "I told you, Gustavo, I have something to say. I told you I would wait to say it until Steven arrived. Now he is here, and that this unfortunate young man is with him I take to be a sign from God. I wish to speak in front of him, and everyone."

"Whatever you want, Rosa. But not the child. She should go. Look at how she's starting to shake." It was true. Trish still sat pressed to Rosa's side, staring down at her hands between her knees. Her body was trembling visibly. "She shouldn't even have to be in the room with this . . . this scum," Gus continued. He was pointing at Lammy. "Dominic's lady friend's watching TV back in the old housekeeper's room, behind the kitchen. Raymond can take Trish back there."

"No," Rosa said. Her voice was strong. "I will not let anyone take her from me."

"Well then, take her yourself, for God's—" He stopped. "Take her yourself and leave her there and come back and get whatever you got to say over with." He turned his head and looked out the window. "I don't like this."

Gus was losing patience, and Rosa seemed to sense that she ought not press him too hard, certainly not in front of so many men. "Gustavo, please," she said, pleading, dropping any hint of challenge. "I beg you. Let her stay. I need her to stay." When Gus didn't answer, Rosa went on. "And it's good that this Fleming man should be here, too, because . . . because he is not the one who causes this child to tremble."

"What is this?" Steve said, speaking up from behind Lammy and me. "What the fuck is she—"

"Shut up!" Gus roared. Then, in a softer, but still ominous tone, he added, "In front of your own daughter. Think, for once." Gus seemed happy to have someone to be mad at besides Rosa. "Everyone . . . shut up and sit down."

"Sorry," Steve said. Then he grabbed me by the shoulder. "What about this guy?"

"I thought I said to shut up and sit down," Gus said. Then he pointed at Lammy and me. "You," he said, "go on over by Raymond." He gestured to our left.

Lammy and I walked across and sat on a couch by the fireplace, facing Gus. Raymond stood behind us. Steve took a chair beside Dominic, opposite Rosa and Trish. Gus sat, too, on a chair behind the library table. Goldilocks and Raymond's twin, like Raymond, stayed on their feet.

"All right," Gus said. "My sister Rosa has something she wants to say. She says it's very important, so we're all gonna be quiet and listen. Everybody understand?" When no one said anything, Gus nodded. "That's good," he said. "Go ahead, Rosa."

"Very well," Rosa said. She pulled Trish tighter against her side. "Dominic and Steven know, but Gustavo, you maybe do not know, that this poor child has scarcely spoken one word to anyone—not since she talked to the police on that night when . . . on the night of the incident, when the police and the lawyers kept pressing her to say who it was who attacked her. Finally she satisfied them, but since that night she will not repeat what she said, will not explain any further. Nothing. Not to the police. Not to the lawyers and their social workers. Not even to me. And I know why this is so." She paused. "It is because she is afraid. She is afraid because . . . because she did not tell the truth that night, about who attacked her."

Both Dominic and Steve were on their feet at once, but Gus lifted his hand. "Sit down."

Only two words, but both men obeyed. Men of violence, both still young and strong, probably both psychopathic. But when Gus spoke, they obeyed. And when they did, Raymond let out a long low breath behind me. They might be family, but Raymond had his own responsibilities.

"Rosa," Gus asked softly, "what are you saying? That the child lied?"

Trish's head was bent back and she was staring up at Rosa, her eyes wide, her little body rigid with fear.

Rosa twisted around until she was facing Trish on the sofa. She took the little girl's hands in her own and held them in her lap. "Don't be afraid, child. Nana will take care of you. You can say the truth now. Only answer the questions that I ask, and it will be okay."

"My God, Mr. A.," Dominic said, "the woman's gone crazy. We all know who it was."

"My little girl would never have lied about something like that," Steve said. He leaned toward Rosa and Trish. "You didn't lie, did you, honey?" The child said nothing, kept her eyes only on Rosa. "Trish! Look at me. I'm your daddy. Please." Steve's voice was rising. "Goddamn you, Trish! Look at me."

"Rosa's gone crazy," Dominic repeated.

"Shut up, both of you," Gus said. "I won't repeat that again. And you, Rosa, do not make a fool of me."

231

"Trish," Rosa said, ignoring her brother, "tell Nana who it was. Who did the bad things that night? No one will hurt you. I promise."

Trish opened her mouth as though trying to speak, then closed it. She tried again and finally, on the third try, she said, "I can't." Her voice was high and thin, tremulous, but clear in a room that was otherwise as silent as death. "He made me promise. 'If you tell,' he said, 'I will kill your nana.' Please . . . don't make me tell."

"Kill me?" Rosa said. "That's what he told you?"

Trish didn't answer. She was shaking again, and she threw herself forward, pressing her face into Rosa's lap.

"It's all right," Rosa said. "You don't have to say who it was. But I want to ask one other thing. Raise your head, Trish, please, look at Nana. Just for a minute."

Trish slowly lifted her head. There were tears on her cheeks.

Rosa gently turned the child's head our way, and then pointed at Lammy. "Do you see that man, Trish?" she asked. Trish nodded and Rosa said, "Tell me his name."

"His name . . . his name is Mr. Fleming."

"Okay. And Trish, was it Mr. Fleming who . . . who did bad things that night?" Trish was trembling uncontrollably now, and her breath came in gasps. But Rosa was determined. "If it was not Mr. Fleming," she said, "I won't ask you who it was. I promise. I just want to know if it was Mr. Fleming. That's all. Was it Mr. Fleming?"

Trish's lips were moving, but again she couldn't get any words out. It didn't matter though, because the shaking of her head was very clear. "No," she finally managed. "No, not Mr. Fleming."

There couldn't have been a person in the room who didn't know that Trish, whatever she'd said before, was telling the truth right then. No one moved or made a sound for a long time.

"My God." It was Gus who finally broke the eerie silence. "Make her say who it was then, Rosa. Make her tell, damn it."

Trish turned slowly and stared at Gus, both her hands covering her mouth.

"No," Rosa said. "I promised." She wrapped her arms around the child. "Trish," she said, "everything is okay. You must go now. Go with Raymond. He will take you to watch the television with Karen. Raymond is a good man."

I knew better than that, and so did Rosa. But she knew, too, that Raymond would protect Trish with his life, or give that life up—painfully—to Gus. Raymond looked at Gus and Gus nodded. "Take her back to that room where Dominic's puss . . . Dominic's lady friend is," Gus said. "You got the key, right?"

Raymond nodded.

"So leave Trish there. Then you stay nearby, in the kitchen, till I call you."

Raymond went across, took Trish awkwardly by the hand, and walked her to the door. Trish looked back over her shoulder at Rosa all the way, tears running down her cheeks, but said nothing.

"It's all right, Trish," Rosa said. "You like Karen, and Nana will be with you in a few minutes."

Trish nodded solemnly, and left the room with Raymond.

At a gesture from Gus, Goldilocks took Raymond's place behind Lammy and me. Meanwhile, I kept an eye on Dominic and Steve. Both of them sat silently, unmoving, as though frozen in place by the obvious truth of Trish's words.

It was Dominic who spoke first. "Jesus, maybe it was a neighbor. Or maybe some bum passing through. Yeah, that's it. One of those homeless people."

"This is all bullshit," Steve said. "Trish wouldn't lie. Not that night, and not now. But she's confused, out of her mind from what she's been through." He turned and stared at Lammy. "It was you, all right, you fucking cocksucker. Goddamn freaking—"

"No!" Gus's soft voice cut through the room. "The child is not confused. Rosa is convinced of that, and I am convinced also. Trish is afraid, but she is telling the truth. She lied before, because someone frightened her." He paused. "Someone still frightens her."

"Yes," Rosa said. "And who? It could not be some stranger, someone passing through, because a stranger would not know the one thing that would most frighten the child. The threat of taking me away from her."

"It was Fleming," Steve said. "He lives on the block. He knows Trish's mother is dead. He could guess what would scare her the most."

"No," Rosa said. "You heard the threat the man made. 'I will kill your nana.' Would this poor Fleming know to say that? Who would say such a thing? Not a stranger. Not even a neigh—"

"Wait a minute," Dominic said. "Mr. A., what the hell is she talking about? Rosa, what are you saying?"

"I am saying I know who it was that abused my granddaughter. I know who pulled down her panties and . . . and did those things. I know who must be sent away to prison." Rosa was on her feet now, moving forward, stretching out her hand, pointing her finger like an avenging angel.

Everyone knew it was Dominic she was accusing. It was Dominic the angel had selected. I might have intervened, right then. But during my whole time in that room no one had spoken my name, no one announced my presence. That seemed important at the time. So I decided to wait.

If I had spoken up, things would have turned out differently. Probably not any better, just differently.

CHAPTER
38

"You, Dominic," Rosa said. "You are the one."

The blood drained from Dominic's tanned face, leaving only the pallor of fear and death. "Rosa," he said, "how . . . how can you say that? Trish could not have told you that."

"But I know it. And soon, when she feels safer and stronger, Trish will say so to everyone."

Steve stood up and stared down beside him at Dominic, then turned and walked over to the windows and stood looking outward into the darkness—or maybe at his own reflection in the glass.

"But it wasn't me," Dominic pleaded. "I was—"

"Quiet," Gus said. "Rosa, why do you say such a thing? Please, sit down." When she took her place again on the sofa, Gus continued, "You know that Dominic is close to me, Rosa. He has proven himself loyal to me, to the business. You know Dominic went to prison rather than betray me."

"I know nothing of such business matters, Gustavo. I close my ears to them and do not wish to hear of them. I know only that Dominic is my son-in-law and that . . . that his wife, my second daughter, is dead now also, and—"

"See, Gus," Dominic broke in, "she's freaked out over Tina's death. She's off the deep—"

"Rosa," Gus said, "are you saying also that Dominic killed Tina?"

"I know he is a vicious, evil man. I know how he used to beat Tina. But that ended in the past, and I have forgiven him for that." Maybe Rosa believed she'd forgiven Dominic, but the venom in her voice betrayed her and I finally understood what

I'd been unable to understand till then. ". . . beat my Tina many times," Rosa was saying, "but I do not know that he killed her. I leave that to the police, and to God. Nothing will bring Tina back, and now I have no daughters, no children. Only my grandchildren, Trish . . . and Lisa, too, if it is not too late for her. I will protect them." She took a deep breath. "It was Dominic who attacked Trish."

Steve turned away from the window and looked at Rosa. "What proof do you have? Trish didn't tell you who it was, so what is your proof?"

"We all know Trish was at Dominic's house," Rosa said. "I left her there myself, with Lisa. Tina was at work. Later, Lisa went to her room to talk on the phone, perhaps one of those boys who call her constantly. Trish was left to watch the television by herself, and Dominic was the only other person in the house. Trish told the police that when her father was late picking her up she was bored and decided to walk home." Rosa paused and looked around. "Does anyone who knows Trish . . . you Steven, or Gus, or Dominic . . . does anyone believe Trish would do such a thing?" There was silence. "No. It is not possible."

"Wait a minute." Dominic started to stand up, but at a warning look from Gus he sat back down. "Wait a minute. You all know what my . . . what Karen told the cops. She was with me the whole time."

"Karen was not truthful with the police," Rosa said. "Poor Karen. I have come to like her, even though she is your . . . your woman. She and I have talked, most often when I would leave Trish at your house, or pick her up. But she was not there that night. Lisa said she wasn't." Rosa turned to Gus. "I do not approve of this Karen . . . and her relationship with my daughter's husband. But the marriage of Dominic and my Tina died many years ago. I can tell Karen regrets becoming involved with Dominic. I can see she fears him now, too." She turned back to Dominic. "She would say whatever you told her to say."

"But she *was* there." Dominic's voice was rising in pitch, becoming strident. "We were . . . well, I can't say in front of you what we were doing. But she was *there.*"

"Lisa told me she was not."

"Well, then, she must have come later."

"No," Rosa said. "Something Karen herself told me—not purposely—makes me know she was not with you. It was that same night, during the confusion, before she talked to you. She told me she had gone shopping. She lost track of the time and afterward she hurried to your house because you would be angry. When she arrived, Trish was already gone."

"She told you that?" Gus asked.

"Yes," Rosa said. "Karen was not at Dominic's house until after Trish ran home . . . until after Trish ran away from him."

"Karen couldn't have told you that." Dominic was shouting now. "She was with me."

That was Dominic's big mistake, right there, although he was too slow to recognize it yet. Everyone in the room believed Rosa was telling the truth about what Karen told her. I believed, because Karen had told me the same thing. The rest believed because they knew Rosa wouldn't lie. And we all knew that Karen had had no reason—on the spur of the moment, not knowing the significance of what she was saying—to make something up to tell Rosa.

Dominic should have admitted, right then, that Karen wasn't with him, admitted he had Karen create the alibi because he was afraid someone might suspect him. Then he should have stuck to his denials and trusted that Trish wouldn't identify him. But he didn't, and that's what turned the tide—certainly as far as Gus was concerned. Surprise, disbelief, disgust, anger—and who knows what else—passed over Gus's face. For a moment even he was speechless. He was standing now, staring at Dominic the bodybuilder, who seemed to shrink in size before the old man.

Dominic understood, finally, that he'd lost Gus, and he pan-

237

icked. He jumped up and ran toward Steve. "You gotta believe me, buddy. I didn't do—"

Steve's look stopped him. It was a look, not of anger or disgust, or even hatred—but of nothingness. A cold, deep vacant look. His hand was inside his sport coat and when it came out it held a dull black semiautomatic—my Beretta.

"No!" Rosa cried. She turned to Gus. "Dominic must be turned over to the authorities. Do you want him killed here? The police would only turn it around, would put it somehow upon your head."

"She's right," Gus said. "I don't need something stupid happening here." He stopped for a few seconds, rubbing the tips of the fingers of his right hand back and forth across his chin. "Dominic," he said, "have you brought a gun with you into my house?" When Dominic looked surprised, Gus added, "Do not lie to me."

"No, Mr. A. I swear I would never—"

"Search the fucking sonovabitch, Gus," Steve said. "If you don't, you're crazy."

Gus turned on Steve, his face twisted in anger. "Who are you? Who are you to come into my house, in front of my own blood, and order me what to do?"

"I . . . I'm sorry," Steve said, visibly shaken by Gus's rage.

Watching Dominic, I saw a change then—very subtle, more a matter of posture than anything else. He may have begun to believe things were going to work out all right for him after all.

"Come here." Gus was gesturing to Goldilocks. "Take this . . . take Dominic out of my sight. Take him to the kitchen and leave him with Raymond."

Goldilocks pushed Dominic toward the door. I was as certain as Gus was that Dominic would never have brought a gun into that house. But still I'd have sworn Dominic was hiding something. Maybe it was that "one more thing" Karen said Anders was going to try. If it was what I thought it was, maybe Dominic's belief was well-founded. Maybe things *would* work out right for him, after all.

But then everything changed. Just as Goldilocks and Dominic got to the door, Gus switched gears. "Wait," he said. "Steve, *you* take Dominic. And do not harm him, you understand me? Leave him with Raymond and then come back here."

Steve shook his head and started to say something, then apparently thought better of it. Goldilocks stepped aside and Steve, prodding Dominic in the small of the back with my Beretta, moved him out of the room.

When the door closed behind them, I spoke up for the first time since Steve had pushed Lammy and me into the library a lifetime ago. "That was a mistake, Gus," I said, "if you really want Dominic turned over to the cops, I mean."

"Shut up, Foley," Gus said. He was sitting down again, and he looked very tired. "What makes you so smart about ev—"

One explosion. Unmistakably a gunshot, from not so far away. Then two more, exactly like the first one, in rapid succession. Then one more, not as loud. Then nothing.

Goldilocks and I got to the library door together, but Steve was already coming our way. We backed up as he came into the room. He closed the door, walked over to Gus, and laid the Beretta on the table. Then he sat down in the nearest chair.

Running footsteps could be heard, and Raymond came in. "It's Dominic," he said. "He's dead. Somebody—"

"He turned on me." Steve spoke in a monotone. "He had a piece, a little revolver. I think he *wanted* me to kill him. He . . . he admitted he went after Trish. He came at me and I had to kill him."

I had to admire Steve. He was a quick thinker, all right. And he'd just pulled off an award-winning performance. I wasn't sure that I could do as well—even though, unlike Steve, I'd be dealing with the truth.

CHAPTER
39

RAYMOND, A PRETTY QUICK study himself, had made sure the door to the housekeeper's room was locked before he ran to where the shots came from. Gus had him give Rosa the key, and sent her to check on Trish and Karen and to assure Trish everything was all right.

Once Rosa was out of the room, Gus turned to Steve. "Jesus Christ, you really fucked up." Gus had abandoned the language code he'd been enforcing in front of Rosa. "We got a goddamn dead body to account for now, thanks to you."

"I told you. He went for me with his backup. I couldn't help it."

"Right. That's why the little popgun was fired last, huh, asshole?" Gus was no dummy.

"I . . . I don't know what you mean," Steve said. He'd apparently used up all of his quick thinking for the day.

"Bullshit," Gus said. "Dominic wouldn't have brought a gun into my place in a million fucking years. That second piece hadda be yours. Dominic tried to rape your daughter and you killed him. Simple as that. I can understand that. I don't like it, but I understand it. It's the fucking cops gonna have the real problem with it."

"Forget the cops and leave it to me," Steve said. "I'll put that fucking freak where nobody finds him. Permanently. Nobody's gonna care if he's dead or alive, anyway."

"Don't worry," Gus said, "I'm gonna leave it to you, all right. And you're gonna see to it his goddamn body doesn't bloat up and rise to the top of some lagoon somewhere next spring."

He paused. "Damn. Dominic was loyal, even if he had shit for brains. But a kid fucker, my God. Lisa's better off living with Rosa—or even *you*—than with him. Besides, you're right. Nobody's gonna care if he's dead or alive."

"You're wrong," I said.

"You stay out of this," Steve said.

"You're wrong, Gus," I repeated. "Somebody cares. Somebody cares a lot. And if my guess is right, those somebodies are probably already on their way here."

"Who cares a lot?" Gus demanded. "And what the fuck guess are you talking about?"

I turned and started for the door.

"Hold on." That was Raymond, stepping in front of me, showing Gus he was on the job.

I spun back toward Gus. "Listen to me. That person you wanted me to check out? I did, and she's not what you thought she might be."

"What's he talking about?" Steve asked.

"Shut up," Gus said. "Go on, Foley."

"She's not who you're looking for, but I know who is—or was. On top of that, you've got maybe fifteen minutes before the Feds send an armored truck through your gate if I'm right. The way we'll find out is by checking Dominic." I paused. "And I suggest nobody talk while we're at it."

"Shit," Steve said, "this guy's—"

"Shut up," Gus said. "I know what he's talking about. The rest of you stay here with the door closed. Foley and me are gonna go take Dominic's clothes off."

So we did. Or at least we tore open his shirt. That was enough. We found the expensive little transmitter taped to his smooth bronze skin, a few inches above his right nipple. We found two bullet wounds in his chest, too, but those were on the left side. There was also a little chrome-plated revolver lying on the floor beside his body—the gun Steve fired the fourth and final shot from and dropped there—after he'd blown a hole in the back of Dominic's skull and then put two more slugs into his chest. The tiny device Dominic was wearing appeared undamaged, and was probably still sending whatever it could pick up to some ear-rattled technician in headphones sitting in some distant dismal room—if we were lucky—or maybe in the back of a panel truck somewhere closer by.

Gus and I crouched beside the body, and neither one of us said a word. Finally, Gus stood and looked down, shaking his head slowly, as though in disbelief. I stood, too, and watched as Gus leaned forward, mouthed a few silent words, and spat— three times—into the dead man's face. He turned abruptly and walked back toward the library. I lagged behind a moment, then followed him.

Back in the library, Gus called everybody up around his desk—except for Raymond. Gus sent him to get Rosa and bring her back to the library. Meanwhile, the four of us—Gus, Steve, Lammy, and I—sat down. Lammy's face was shiny with sweat and far whiter than I'd ever seen it, even when he showed up in my dreams, but there hadn't been a peep out of him since Steve pushed us into the room. Raymond's twin and Goldilocks, who apparently didn't get paid to sit, stood by the window and the door, respectively.

Gus picked up the phone, punched out two numbers, and waited. "Yeah, it's me," he said to whoever answered. "Get to the gate and stay out of sight and call me if anybody shows up." He hung up.

Raymond came back with Rosa, then left again to keep an eye on Trish and Karen.

"So," Gus said, "we got a problem. We can't ditch the body. We're—"

"Why the fuck not?" Steve said.

"Watch your tongue! My sister's here."

"Yeah, but—"

"We can't ditch the body because Dominic's wired, you fool. The FBI or some God . . . some other agency's been—"

"Then we gotta get outta here," Steve said. "They're gonna find out I shot Dominic."

"We don't gotta do anything except stay put," Gus said. "Whoever it is already *knows* you shot Dominic. You're gonna have to tough it out. Self-defense. And if that doesn't work, maybe manslaughter or something. This was the man who tried to rape your little girl. You lost control, didn't know what you were doing. So we sit and wait, and cooperate." He paused. "Maybe we even call nine-one-one."

"Wait a minute," I said. No one had mentioned my name in the presence of Dominic's listening device, and I didn't want cops running all over the place before I got out of there. Anders would have my license—or worse—if he thought I had a role in blowing his game. "There are some things you need to know. Important things."

"Oh?" Gus said.

"Yes. First, Gus, you were wrong about Karen. She's not the one you had to worry about. Dominic was."

"Yeah. Dominic. But maybe the broad, too."

"We'll come back to that. But there's something more important." I turned to my left. "Rosa," I said, "Gus was wrong about Karen. But you were wrong, too." Rosa opened her mouth, then clamped it shut without saying anything. "You were wrong about Dominic."

You could see in her eyes that Rosa thought I was crazy. She *knew* she was right about Dominic. She knew it deep down in her soul, the same soul where she'd long ago convinced herself she'd forgiven Dominic, convinced herself she hadn't hated him with every breath she took since the first time Tina told her Dominic used her as a punching bag. She *knew* her judgment wasn't warped about who had attacked Trish.

She was a strong and honest woman, Rosa was. Maybe even

243

a holy woman, although that's hardly my area of expertise. But she couldn't live with the idea that evil might be hiding deep inside her, couldn't abide the thought that she could harbor such hatred as she did for the man who used to pummel her daughter in retaliation for his own inadequacies. What she'd refused to look at in herself for so long—the hate that festered below the surface—finally blinded her.

Rosa wouldn't lie. But, having convinced herself it must have been Dominic who was Trish's attacker, she couldn't see the truth. She'd easily convinced Karen, who already despised Dominic. She'd convinced me, as well, at least for a while. Then, when Rosa stood in Gus's library and extended the finger of guilt, Dominic hadn't known how to defend himself.

"Rosa was mistaken, Gus," I said. "Dominic knew that. And I know it."

And one other person in that room knew it, too, better than anyone else.

CHAPTER

40

"I SAW THIS GOING down differently, Gus," I said. "I thought you'd follow Rosa's advice, let the cops handle Dominic. You caught me off-guard when you switched, and had Steve take Dominic out of the room."

"Get to the point," Gus said.

"I guess you figured why bother the police and the court system. Why not let the victim's father take justice into his own hands? It's faster, cleaner. Especially when the executioner can be persuaded to dispose of the remains." I paused. "You surprised me, and you knew what you were doing. You knew it was unlikely Steve could resist the opportunity."

"What I know, and what you know," Gus said, "is that the so-called system doesn't always bring justice."

"Right," I said, "we all know that. But using the system did get Lammy off. That was justice, because he's innocent. And you know what? Using the system would have gotten Dominic off, too."

"What are—"

"He's full of shit," Steve said. "What are you listening to him for?"

Gus didn't answer him, so I continued. "No sensible person would use the word *innocent* in the same sentence with *Dominic,* so I won't either. But the system would have gotten him off anyway, at least about attacking Trish."

"Sure. His newfound friends would have taken care of him," Gus said.

"Maybe. But even if they abandoned him—which they might

have—Dominic would have gotten off. I guarantee it. Because Dominic didn't go after Trish, not any more than Lammy did. What—"

"But he did," Rosa said, "we all know he did."

"What you know is what you told yourself," I said. "People believe you, Rosa. You accused Dominic . . . so he must have done it. Just like everyone on the block thought Lammy did it, because Trish accused him. Would Trish lie? Then Lammy must have done it. Would Rosa lie? Then Dominic must have done it."

"But Trish *did* lie, out of fear," Rosa said. "I did not lie."

"No, you didn't lie. But you were mistaken. And I'm telling you Dominic would have gotten off, even without the Feds, if Steve hadn't gunned him down from behind." I turned back to Gus. "Steve did that, not because he's an aggrieved father. Uh-uh. Steve did that because he didn't want anyone bringing out the truth."

Gus did nothing but stare at me, but tension radiated from him and spread through the room. Both Raymond's twin and Goldilocks moved closer.

"What you are saying," Rosa whispered, "it cannot be. Not the child's father."

Steve started to stand up. "You can't—"

"Sit down," Gus said. "I wanna hear the man out."

"Fine," Steve said, regaining his composure. "Fine. But is he saying I tried to rape my own daughter? The one thing I have left in this life that means anything to me? Because if he is . . ." He paused, then turned and leaned toward me and spoke in a strangely calm, low voice. "Because if you are, whatever happens, whether anyone ever believes you or not, I swear to you, I'll spend every day of the rest of my life coming after you—you, and this lard-assed pervert friend of yours, and the priest, and anyone else who's important to you. And you haven't learned the meaning of the word *pain,* my friend, until you get what's in store for all of you."

I stared back at him. He was a liar, through and through, but a fierce coldness grew in my chest because I knew he wasn't lying now. This threat was his last chance to stop me from destroying what little hope of a life he might ever have. But it was more than a threat. It was a promise—a promise as real and dark as the menacing emptiness in his eyes. And I was afraid. Afraid for Lammy, for Casey, for everyone. Afraid for myself.

Maybe there was another way. Maybe Rosa could take Trish away and make a new life somehow and the truth wouldn't have to come out. Maybe fear would back me down.

"So," Steve said, "are you saying I tried to rape my own little girl?"

I took one deep breath, in and out, before I answered. "I'm saying whatever it was—attempted rape, or the stupid, brutal fondling of a child by an abusive, alcoholic father—whatever it was, it was you. And I'm saying . . ." I paused, hating what was coming next, but not knowing any better way. I stared into his eyes. "And I'm saying I invite you, Mr. Connolly, to spend your days coming after me, or anyone I'm close to. Because when you do . . . I'll see you won't have many days left to spend."

There was a long silence then. In reality, probably just a few seconds, but still a long, long silence.

Finally Gus spoke. "What is your evidence?"

"You'll find," I said, "if you read her statements, that the one thing Trish was most afraid of saying was that what happened to her happened in a garage. To anyone who wanted to listen, she might as well have announced that it *did* happen in a garage."

"Jesus," Gus said. "You think that's gonna stand up in court?"

"Not at all," I said. "But it convinced me. So I kept at it. Trish said her pants were pulled down and she was pushed to the floor. Later she changed *floor* to *ground*. But her clothes weren't wet. Then she claimed it was inside the enclosed back porch, but everyone knows this wasn't true. That whole area is rough

247

and broken concrete, and Trish didn't have a scratch on the backs of her legs or her buttocks. So where was it? In the house?"

"It was Dominic," Rosa said, "in his house."

"With Steve due to pick her up?"

"I don't know," she replied. "Maybe Steven called Dominic and said he'd be late or some—"

"That's right," Steve said. "That's exactly what happened."

"Oh? So then Dominic felt free to attack Trish . . . with Lisa right there in the house? And Karen expected to arrive any minute? Not likely."

"This is all bullshit," Steve said. "He's making it up as he—"

"I want to hear the man," Gus said. "Shut up!"

"Trish's denials convinced me that it *did* happen in a garage. So, I thought, probably Dominic's garage. Later, when the cops showed me photos of it, I saw there was plenty of room in the garage, but the floor there is concrete, too. Not as broken up as at Lammy's, but rough enough, and filthy. There'd have been scratches on Trish's body, and traces of dirt and oil. But there were none. So . . . what floor? What gar—"

The phone rang. Gus picked it up and listened. "All right. No, nothing. Just stay out of sight. And call me if anything happens." He hung up. "Go on," he said.

"Everyone agrees," I continued, "that Trish would never have left Dominic's just because she was bored."

"That's right," Rosa insisted. "And Steve called and told Dominic he'd be—"

"That can be checked out," I said, "by phone records." Whether it could or not, a look passed over Steve's face that told me I was right, and that I only had to keep on pushing till he broke. "I say Steve didn't call. And I say he wasn't late. He *did* come. He picked Trish up in his van and drove home with her, into his garage. That's where it happened. I don't know how far he went with her before he let her go, or she broke away."

"It could not be," Rosa said. "It was later when Steven got home and—"

"Maybe he sat in the garage," I said, "or maybe he—"

"Shut up and let me think," Gus said. He pointed a finger at me. "Steve's garage. What's that floor made outta?"

"Concrete, for chrissake," Steve said.

"And the van fills the entire space," I added, "with hardly room to get out of it. But there's plenty of room—and a carpeted floor—inside the van."

"He's still making this up," Steve said, but he got no answer from anyone.

"No," I said. "The cops took Trish's clothes. Their lab found no blood, no semen. That's what they were looking for, to start with. But they had a perpetrator identified, anyway, and there was no rush to go further at that point with the clothes. Lammy's lawyer, though, is the super-cautious type. And even when the charge was dismissed, she had the clothes analyzed herself. The child's pants had traces of fiber on them. Fiber that matches the fiber in the carpeting used by the conversion company when they customized Steve's van." I was making it all up now, although Renata had *talked* about having the clothes analyzed. "Fiber with the same blue dye."

"They would match," Gus said. "Trish mighta rode in that van every day."

"But . . ." Rosa's voice trailed away. She was staring at me.

"But what?" Gus demanded.

"That . . . that was the first night she wore those jeans," she said. "I remember. They were a Christmas present, and she begged me to let her—"

"That's something I didn't know," I said. "But I do know they found fibers on Trish's jeans, inside and outside—and on her underpants as well." I paused. "Trish was inside that van, parked in Steve's garage, when her pants—"

Steve was fast for so large a man, and his lunge carried him

249

the few feet to the library table before anyone could stop him. In one motion, he scooped up the Beretta and hit the table, slamming it into Gus and sending him toppling over backward in his chair.

All of us were on our feet instinctively, but Goldilocks was the closest, and the first to make a move. Steve turned and fired once. Goldilocks stopped in his tracks, one hand clutched to his chest and the other drawing wild circles in the air, like a man wobbling on a tightrope. He never got his balance though, before he toppled heavily forward onto the floor.

Raymond's twin had a gun in his hand, too, but by then Steve was behind Rosa. Without a clear shot, the gunman hesitated. And when he did, Steve shot him as well—twice. Both slugs tore into his chest, and one of them must have opened an artery. The man lowered his chin, as though he were studying the dark, dark blood that spurted and foamed from his shirt front. But by that time he wasn't seeing anything at all. And he never would— not in this world.

CHAPTER

41

By the time Gus was back on his feet, Steve already had his left arm wrapped around Rosa's neck and was inching his way backward across the room, dragging her along with him.

"Jesus Christ," Gus said, "think about it, Steve. Whaddaya got left? Two fucking cartridges, that's what." Gus didn't miss much, but I wondered at first why he said that. "You can't kill four people with two shots, even four unarmed people," he said. "Plus there's cops outside the gate, probably waiting for word to bust through, with a million more on the way. You got no—"

"Shut up!" Steve was shouting. "For once in your goddamn life, shut up and let me think."

Gus flinched, just slightly. The look in his eyes said that, if he survived, he would one day make Steve pay for shouting him down. But when he spoke his voice was calm. "You're right," he said. "You should think about—"

"I said shut up!" Steve was just one step short of uncontrolled panic. His voice was twice as loud as it needed to be. Thinking wasn't coming easily, and that was about our only chance. His eyes swept frantically from one dead body on the floor to the other, and I knew what he was looking for. But there was no gun in sight. Both men must have fallen on their weapons.

". . . think about it. I can still get you outta this," Gus was saying. "Otherwise you got no chance. Trust me."

I knew Gus wanted to keep Steve's mind busy, keep him from figuring out how he could get to those guns. I also knew trusting Gus wasn't going to get Steve out of there alive.

Even Steve knew that. "If I got any chance at all," he said, "this is it." He jammed the barrel of the Beretta up under Rosa's chin. "One of my shots is all it'll take." Steve's gaze shifted nervously from where Gus and Lammy and I stood together, as he dragged Rosa backward with him toward the library door. When he got there he stopped, then moved about six feet to the side of the door. "You tried to trick me with that two shots and four people to kill bullshit. Dumb old fucker. You think I forgot Raymond's out there somewhere?"

"I don't think anything," Gus said, "except you'd be smart to let me help you get outta—"

"Shut up! Call Raymond in here."

"Raymond!" Gus called out in a loud voice. "Raymond! Get in—"

The door flew open. Raymond burst through, in a low crouch, his gun sweeping the room. He froze, bug-eyed, when he saw Steve using Rosa as a shield

"Come on farther in," Steve yelled. "And drop the gun or Rosa's dead."

Raymond moved into the room. But he didn't drop his gun. "Mr. Apprezziano," he said, not looking at Gus, but watching Steve drag Rosa with him to the open door, "what do I do?"

"That's my sister, for chrissake. What you do is you let the sonovabitch walk outta here."

Raymond hesitated, then started to tuck the automatic under his suit coat.

"Uh-uh. Toss it on the floor," Steve yelled. "Over this way."

Raymond glanced at Gus. "He wants my gun. Maybe he's empty, or almost empty. I can—"

"No!" Gus roared. "Do like he says."

"I don't like it," Raymond said. "With my gun, he might kill us all."

"He's right, Gus," I said.

"No," Steve said. "Nobody else in here needs to die. I'll let Rosa go. But I need Raymond's gun if I'm gonna have a chance

252

outside this room. Tell him to toss the gun to my feet. Once I get it . . . I'm outta here."

"Raymond," Gus said, "do as—"

"Gustavo, no. This man will kill everyone." Rosa's voice was strong and clear. "I understand now. Steven killed Monsignor Borelli. He called me at the rectory to say he was coming to pick up Trish. She began to cry and I didn't know why. I could tell Steven had been drinking and I told him no. He said he was coming for his daughter, that I must stop interfering. Then he hung up. I cannot believe how blind I was. Trish was attacked by Dominic, I thought, but now her father is drinking every day and this is why she cannot stop crying and trembling. So I took her." She paused. "He must have come and killed the priest." She tried to twist her head to look at Steve. "You would rape your own daughter . . . and then murder a priest, a holy—"

"Shut up! That wasn't murder." Steve yanked Rosa closer to the doorway. His voice was trembling, but still loud. "He wouldn't tell me where you were. I only shoved him, and he fell, and—"

"And Tina, Gustavo," Rosa said. "Steven murdered her also. She must have seen the truth I could not—"

Steve pulled his arm tighter around her neck and Rosa couldn't talk. "She's crazy," he said. "I had nothing to do with Tina. That was Dominic. He got pissed-off at her for some reason I don't know. He told me he hit the bitch a few times and . . ." He paused. "Anyway, no more talk. Gus, tell Raymond to give me his gun and I swear to you . . . no one will be killed. Otherwise . . ."

I leaned toward Gus and spoke softly. "Whatever you decide, don't believe him."

Gus just waved me off. "She is my little sister. Give it to him, Raymond," he said. "Just do it."

Raymond stood motionless for a few seconds, then leaned and tossed his gun gently forward onto the floor. It slid along the polished wood, and stopped only a few feet short of where Steve stood in the open doorway.

"Good," Steve said. He crouched to the floor, pulling Rosa clumsily down with him. Then he withdrew the barrel of the Beretta from Rosa's neck, angled it upward, and shot Raymond—dead center, just below the throat.

Raymond stared at Steve. "Goddamn you," he said, his voice hardly more than a harsh whisper, "you fucking mick." He took one short, hopeless step forward. Still in a crouch, Steve was ready to fire a second time, but he didn't have to. Raymond opened his mouth. Maybe just an unconscious reflex, or maybe to curse Steve again. Either way, no words came out. There was nothing but a terrible gurgling sound, and then Raymond crumpled to the floor.

At the same time, Rosa let out a loud moan of a sigh, and passed out. The dead weight of her body sagged against Steve. For just an instant he struggled to keep his balance. Then he shoved her away from him, grabbed Raymond's gun with his left hand, and stood up.

It was only when I heard Lammy's frightened gasping beside me that I suddenly felt him clinging to my arm. I shook myself free. Steve was facing us, a pistol in each hand and a grin on his face that showed he'd left sanity far behind. My Beretta was still in his right hand—the barrel aimed directly into my face. "You should have stayed outta this," he said. "But maybe you'd rather watch your fat friend die first." As he spoke, he slowly swung the gun and, when it was aimed straight at Lammy's chest, he squeezed the trigger.

The snap of the hammer, as it fell on an empty chamber, came as a surprise to Steve. But not to me, or to Gus. We'd both counted the first six shots from the Beretta. Then the old man conned him with the suggestion that he had two shots left, not even knowing what the trick might be worth. And Steve—the gun freak—bought it because he wasn't thinking.

While Steve recovered, tossing aside my gun and switching Raymond's to his right hand, I threw myself hard into Lammy's side. He crashed into Gus and the two of them went sprawling to the floor. Steve fired twice, and the crash of breaking windows came simultaneously with the second blast. Meanwhile, the phone began to ring. And somewhere amid the roaring barks of the semiautomatic pistol and the shattering glass and the phone ringing—and all of that nearly drowned out by Gus's screams of pain—I shot Steve.

The little chrome-plated revolver I'd picked up near Dominic's body was a .22 and it didn't pack much stopping power. But still, Steve dropped down onto one knee. Raymond's gun was on the floor beside him, dropped and forgotten for the moment, as Steve clawed at the buttons on his shirt. I grabbed Lammy and pulled him with me toward the door, scooping up the empty Beretta on the way.

Rosa was gone. In the confusion, she'd moved quickly out of the room. Her brother, though, was going nowhere. Gus was lying on his face, and he wasn't moving at all.

CHAPTER

42

THE PHONE WAS STILL ringing as Lammy and I raced down the hall toward the kitchen. When we got there, Rosa was standing in the open door to the housekeeper's room. Trish and Karen peered out from behind her.

"He'll be coming in a minute," I said. "You still have the key, Rosa?"

"Yes."

"That phone must mean the police are coming. Lock yourselves in till they get here," I said. "But don't tell them I was here. If they find out, I'll go to jail." When none of them answered, I said, "Okay?"

Rosa may have nodded. Or maybe I imagined that . . . or hoped it.

"I think Steve will come after Lammy and me." I paused. "But in case he doesn't, and if he has a key . . . take this." Rosa cringed as I reached past her and handed the little revolver to Karen. "It won't be long. Don't worry. You'll be all right."

Rosa stepped back and pushed the door closed, crossing herself as she did. Maybe she didn't believe my assurances, and figured they needed more powerful help.

Lammy and I had been wearing our coats the whole time. My body had adjusted to the indoor heat, so when we stepped outside, the twenty-degree air hit like a shotgun blast. Lammy was searching frantically through his coat pockets. "Here," I said, and gave him my gloves.

The security lights showed that a sidewalk leading to a door in a large, barnlike garage behind the house had been shoveled, but everywhere else the snow was over a foot deep. We ran down the walk as far as the garage. The door was locked, though, so we turned left and into the snow. It was frozen solid on top, but broke through when we put our weight onto it, so the going was slow. If we could just get around to the rear of the garage, at least we'd be outside the circle of floodlights.

We'd gotten as far as the corner of the building when the back door of the house banged open. I glanced back and saw Steve in the doorway, his arm extended. I pushed Lammy around the corner and dove after him. Chunks of wood flew away from the corner of the building even before I heard the shots. I scrambled to my feet and chased Lammy toward the rear of the garage and into the darkness.

Steve wasn't far behind. We could hear him crashing through the snow.

Once around the corner to the back of the garage, we broke away from the building, toward the dark woods maybe ten yards away. There was no moon and the security lighting didn't reach this far. Still, our tracks in the snow would be easy to follow, even in the dark. If we made the trees; though, we might lose him.

We were into the underbrush and trees by the time he came around the corner to the back of the garage. He sent two shots into the area where our tracks led in, but we'd taken a right-angle turn as soon as we entered and were out of his line of fire. The frozen snow wasn't as deep under the trees, but with each step the crunching sound announced our position. I grabbed Lammy's arm. We stood perfectly still. I couldn't hear Steve moving, either. Finally, leaning to my right and peering among the tree trunks, I saw him. He was out in the open, silhouetted against the snow and the white garage, his gun hand raised. He was standing still, too, obviously trying to get a fix on just where we were, waiting for our next steps to give us away.

For a long moment I stayed focused on the hunter—motion-

257

less in the clearing, listening for his prey. He could have gathered up every gun in the library, and there was no telling how many rounds he had. We all waited. There seemed to be no sound at all, beyond the quiet breathing of Lammy and me. Gradually, though, I became aware of other sounds. Faint shouts, coming from far beyond the other side of Gus's house. Plus the distant roar of an engine—alternately revving up, then dying down—and intermittent metallic crashes. They were breaking open Gus's gate.

I watched Steve turn his head a little and knew he was listening to the same sounds. He took one step along our path toward the woods, then stopped again. "Foley!" he called, loud and clear. "I'm whacking you, asshole. Both of you. I don't give a fuck if I go down myself, but I'm taking you cocksuckers with me."

With my hand still holding Lammy's arm, I felt him tighten up even through his puffy ski jacket, and I suddenly remembered how angry I'd been when he insisted I take that coat back to the store. He was terrified now, and ready to bolt. I squeezed his arm more tightly.

"Don't move," I whispered. "Not yet."

Steve stood silently, hoping for some response to his threat. He took one more step, then waited again. He was out of my view now, but I could hear he wasn't moving.

"Lammy," I said, still whispering. "We have to split up. When I start running, you *walk*, as quietly as possible . . . that way." I pointed deeper into the woods, in the opposite direction from the garage. "Keep on till you come to the wall that runs around the property, then follow it to your left, all the way to the gate. You'll be safe. The police are there."

"Yes, but . . . are you—"

"I'll try to join up with you." That wasn't true. "But if I don't, remember, I'll be in big trouble if the police find out I was here." I wondered if Lammy saw the inconsistency in what I'd

258

said. If Steve didn't bring me down—about a fifty-fifty proposition, at best—I wasn't going toward the cops if I could help it. Anders would blame me for the collapse of his scheme. "I run *this* way," I whispered. "And, no matter what I yell, you walk *that* way. Got it?"

"I . . . I guess so."

"Now Lammy!" I shouted. "Follow me!" I took off, running, stumbling, crashing through the frozen snow, taking as many crunching steps as possible, making as much noise as I could, as fast as I could. I glanced back once and saw Lammy headed in the other direction.

I knew eventually I'd come up against Gus's wall, too. And I knew his entrance road crossed a bridge over a stream that ran through his property. The stream had to get under the wall somehow, or through it. My plan was to follow the wall to the spot where the stream went out . . . and see if I could join the stream.

Maybe I'd fooled Steve into thinking Lammy was with me, and maybe he'd just decided he wanted me more. Whichever, he was coming after me. At first he ran parallel to me, staying in the cleared area. But as I angled away, he had to come into the woods, too. I heard him crashing through the brush. A gunshot exploded. I thought I heard the bullet whistling past me. And if I didn't hear it going past, at least I didn't feel it coming in.

He was armed and I wasn't. But he had a bullet lodged inside him somewhere and I didn't—not yet. I didn't know just where the .22 slug had entered his torso, but I was amazed at his stamina. Psychotic rage may have had something to do with it.

It was very dark, nearly impossible to see. I kept plunging forward, not worrying now about making noise enough for two. My legs were turning to lead and it would have been a struggle just running in the snow, even without the undergrowth grabbing at my knees and a thousand low-hanging branches slashing my face. You'd have thought a smart guy like Gus would clear away the trees and brush on his property to give his people a better view—and a clearer shot—at intruders. But maybe that wasn't so important, what with the dogs and . . .

Jesus! The dogs.

I heard them, then. Barking, yelping. In the distance, but drawing nearer, it seemed. I wanted to stop and listen, to determine whether they were actually coming our way. But I had to keep chugging ahead. Steve was maybe twenty yards behind, I thought. Too tired to zig and zag. I had to hope the trees and the darkness, and his need to keep running to stay close to me, would keep him from firing more shots.

My breath came in great sucking gulps now, bitterly cold breaths that seared my lungs. I could hear Steve, gasping and grunting and muttering as he plowed after me. I thought I was in great shape, but somehow this wounded drunk of a man was keeping up with me.

And now there was no question about it. The dogs were on their way. Not from behind us, but from somewhere off to the left.

Suddenly I broke out of the woods. I was face to face with the high, stuccoed wall, about fifteen yards away. The woods had been cleared, leaving a strip of open land running all along the wall. I turned right and ran parallel to the wall, but staying just within the trees. The baying of the dogs grew louder. I veered to my left, to the edge of the clearing, and slowed a little to look back. They were coming. Two that I could see. Long-legged, dark shapes, visible against the snow in the cleared space between the woods and the wall. They had their own problems, sometimes breaking through the frozen crust and floundering, sometimes skidding along across the top.

I accelerated again and, just as I did, a sharp, howling wail rose up from behind me, a shrill cry of pain—from Steve—and

I heard him crash to the ground. ". . . fucking ankle!" he was screaming. "I broke my fucking ankle. You gotta help me!"

I kept going, though, running clumsily along the edge of the woods, driven now by a new fear—the dogs—and fighting the impulse to climb up a tree to escape them. Finally, up ahead and across the cleared space, I saw what I was looking for. A dark opening in the white wall, a half-circle cut out close to the ground, where the stream went through. From that distance, it was impossible to judge how large the opening was, and too dark to see what sort of fence or screen covered it. I turned that way, plowing into the deeper snow outside the woods.

Steve kept screaming behind me, and there was no question that his cries were genuine. He was hurt and he was down. The dogs must have sensed that, too. Their baying had gone up in pitch, turning more furious—and perhaps more gleeful at the same time.

I forced myself to keep going. My lungs were on fire. My one chance to escape the dogs was that they'd get first to Steve, and be too busy to bother with me. Finally, though, I had to stop to get my breath, and found myself shivering uncontrollably, even though my clothes were soaked with sweat. I could still hear the dogs, but couldn't see them. They were in the woods. And what I heard wasn't baying or barking anymore, but snarling, growling.

"The fucking dogs, Foley," Steve cried. "You gotta help me. They'll tear me apart."

He was a stone-cold killer, with no more concern for my life than the dogs had. His desperate demands for help infuriated me. I wanted to hate him. I *did* hate him, goddamn it. He deserved whatever he got.

But Jesus, those dogs . . .

CHAPTER

43

I TURNED AROUND AND stumbled back toward Steve, along the path I'd broken in the snow.

When I got there the dogs were moving in on him, slipping among the trees in the darkness, excited, snarling and snapping at each other. They slid in and out of sight, so that first it seemed there were three of them, or even four. But I kept watching and there were only two. Dobermans, I thought. Steve was flat on his ass in the snow, both legs straight out in front of him, his right foot pointing at a weird angle to the leg. He was waving his gun back and forth, trying to draw a bead on the creatures moving through the snow and brush around him. He hadn't seen me yet, and I couldn't decide just what to do.

It was decided for me. One of the dogs caught my scent. It stopped, sniffed the air. Swiveling its head from side to side, whining, honing in on me as though with radar. Then, with the whine dropping into a throaty growl, the dog began to walk my way. I didn't move a muscle and it probably hadn't seen me yet, but it kept on coming—stalking me with stiff, tentative steps. Its companion was still focused on Steve, but this dog was locked in on me.

It was useless to turn and run. Maybe if I took off my coat, I could wrap it around my arm and . . .

The instant I moved, the dog snarled and rushed toward me. "Stay!"

The voice came from my left. A strong voice. Confident. A voice the dog seemed to recognize as having authority. The creature stopped, turned its head. Still snarling, but with a new, almost questioning tone. A tone that asked: Whose voice is this?

I knew.

"Stay!"

The same voice. Lammy's voice. He stumbled forward through the underbrush. Not toward me. Directly at the Doberman, who didn't back away, but was silent now. The other dog stood still and silent, too.

"Jesus," Steve called out. "What the fuck is—"

"Shut up," I said.

Lammy spoke directly to the dog closer to me, but clearly had the other one's attention, too. He was talking nonstop. The words were nothing unusual. "Stay . . . good dog . . . atta boy . . ." The same words everyone uses with dogs. "Atta boy . . . easy . . . get back . . . good dog . . ." But the message had more to do with the tone, the inflection, it seemed, than with any rational meaning. I remembered Lynette Daniels' comments about whether dogs think, and about intuition and instinct— and Lammy.

Whatever did it, the closer dog turned around to slink away and join its partner. Half hidden in the trees, they stood together, on the other side of Steve from us. Motionless, emitting occasional ominous throaty comments.

Lammy stood beside me. He was shaking visibly, despite the confident tone he'd used with the dogs. "I got scared when we split up," he said. "I'm sorry."

"Yeah," I said. "Well, you don't have to—"

"We gotta go now. These dogs, they're smart animals. But I'm going against their training. And they don't know me."

"What about Steve?" I asked.

"I'll tell you, motherfucker." That was Steve, still sitting in the snow. I turned . . . and stared into the barrel of the pistol he held trained on my face. "I'll tell you what about Steve," he said. "Steve's gonna blow your fucking brains out, unless this faggoty freak here sends these goddamn dogs away and you get me outta here."

The dogs started snarling again.

"I can't." Lammy's voice was soft, tentative.

"Don't give me that shit, you prick," Steve said. "Get rid of the stupid goddamn fuckers." One of the dogs started barking furiously.

"Be careful," Lammy said. "You're making them ner—"

"Do it!" Steve yelled, jerking the gun in his hand. "Do it, or I blow fucking Foley away."

The dogs were shifting around again now, with louder, more menacing growls, snapping at each other again with excitement. And moving closer to Steve all the time.

"Do it," Steve screamed. "Get rid of them!" He was beyond control. He waved his pistol at the dogs. They had separated now, and were moving around him, whining and barking strange, soft barks. "Do it, you motherfucker!" he screamed, and swung the gun back in our direction.

I yanked on Lammy's arm and pulled him down with me and Steve's shot went into the woods. We half-crawled, half-stumbled backward away from him, watching in horror as one of the Dobermans leaped forward at him. He fired two shots. The huge dog whirled away and dove back into the darkness, whimpering.

Steve looked our way, but couldn't spot us. Lammy and I both turned and ran as best we could. There were two more shots, followed at once by a furious cacophony of snarls and yelps and yapping barks—mindless, bestial sounds that were dissonant accents against the high keening screams of a man whose flesh was being torn away.

Lammy and I kept on running.

CHAPTER

44

YOU COULD HARDLY CALL it running, really. Lammy—overweight and flabby—was practically dead on his feet, and I had to half-carry, half-drag him along. Stumbling, tripping, dragging our feet through the snow. But we made it to where the stream went through the wall. The semicircular opening was about three feet across, and blocked with vertical iron bars set into the wall at six-inch intervals, their pointed ends extending down almost to the frozen surface of the stream.

We crouched on our haunches in the snow and stared at the bars. From a distance came the sounds of cars, probably on the drive from the gate to Gus's house.

Then suddenly, from closer to where we'd left Steve, an unfamiliar male voice called out. "Rocco! Tony! Get over here." Damn, I thought, three more of Gus's thugs. But then the man shouted, "Stay, Rocco! Stay! Good dogs." A few seconds of silence, and again the same voice, this time filled with fear and shock. "Oh my God! Holy Jesus Christ almighty! I'll . . . I'll go get help. C'mon, you two." We could hear him crashing through the brush in the other direction, taking the dogs with him.

I stood and looked back toward where the frozen stream left the woods. Most of the way across the clearing, it seemed, maybe four to six feet across, narrowing down just short of the opening in the wall. Where it passed through the opening, it ran along a man-made canal of concrete.

When a stream narrows, I thought, it must deepen also—at least a little—to accommodate the flow.

Hanging on to Lammy for balance, I stomped my foot on the

ice and broke through to the water underneath. Then I waded right in, to see how deep it was. In its rounded concrete stream bed the water was still not much more than a foot deep below the iron bars.

It was also very cold.

"If we take off our coats and lie on our backs, we may be able to slide un—" I stopped and looked at Lammy. "Well," I said, "maybe *I* can, anyway."

CHAPTER
45

It was more of a squeeze than a slide. The concrete stream bed wasn't as deep as I thought it was and I got hung up for a while on the iron points. But once I was through to the other side, Lammy stuffed my coat between the bars. I was in a clump of trees beside a fairway on the golf course that abutted Gus's estate, already running as I struggled to get my arms into the coat. Lammy's hat, and my own gloves that he'd given back, were stuffed into the coat pockets. So the coat and the hat and the gloves were the only dry things about me.

I hadn't been thinking much about pain while I was squeezing under the bars—or maybe the icy water anesthetized me—and I didn't know how deeply the points of the bars had gouged into my flesh until after I'd gotten Casey on the phone and he drove me back to the motel and got me soaking in a tub of hot water.

Casey told me later that I was huddled in the tub, shaking and sobbing, when he left me there and drove back to see if he could find Lammy. I told him the sobbing part had to be bullshit.

The next day, Lammy described how he followed the wall to where the FBI had crashed through Gus's gate. He said there were a couple of huge tow trucks and lots of police cars and other cars "parked all over the place." People from the surrounding area were walking around, "and some TV people were there, with really bright lights." Lammy claimed he walked right out the gate and nobody paid any attention to him.

Some of the cars that were parked all over the place had their motors running. He "wasn't thinking so good," and he was so cold and tired he decided to crawl into one, except most of them were squad cars. He finally found one that wasn't, he said. It was "just a plain, dark-colored, four-door car," and he laid down in the backseat. He fell asleep, but two men woke him up and told him they were federal officers and this was their car. One was a mean-looking man with black hair that came to a point over his forehead. He started "yelling and screaming" at Lammy when he found out who he was, and demanded to know if I was around.

Finally Lammy couldn't even talk and just started "crying like a baby," he said. So they eventually took him in an ambulance to a hospital and the doctors made them leave him alone for a few days. He had hypothermia—and eventually pneumonia.

Lammy doesn't exactly have a vivid imagination, so you had to believe he didn't make up the part about sleeping in Anders' car.

OVER THE NEXT WEEK or so, no matter how many times they replayed their tape of what Dominic's wire had picked up, and no matter how convinced they were that I'd been one of the people in Gus's library, the Feds couldn't find anything solid to back up their belief.

Gus had been hit in the left hand by one of Steve's shots. His hand was pretty well destroyed and he had a heart attack that put him out of the picture for a couple of days—and gave him lots of time to talk to his lawyers. He didn't tell Anders, or anyone else, about my being there. In fact, he didn't tell much at all about what really happened, just that Steve had—understandably, Gus claimed—lost it a bit when he found out Dominic had tried to rape his daughter. I figured it wasn't Gus's practice to be of help to the authorities. Besides, he probably wanted to handle Steve in his own way if he ever got the chance.

The Feds threatened to charge me with a crime—interference with a federal investigation or some such thing—which gave me a good excuse to refuse to answer any questions. According to Renata, Anders was beside himself at losing Dominic, and blamed it on me. He was absolutely serious about getting my license lifted, at least, and preferably getting me a vacation at a prison farm for a while. I stuck with my right to remain silent and let Renata talk to Anders and his friends.

Nobody interrogated Casey about it, thank God, because he'd have had a hell of a struggle about whether to tell the truth and send me to jail. No one asked Trish, either, because it was months before she said anything again to anybody, even to Rosa. I never found out exactly what Lammy and Karen and Rosa said. They all must have lied, but I decided not to hold that against them.

Steve Connolly was a different story. They managed to save his life—for what that was worth. The .22 slug had just buried itself inside him somewhere between a couple of ribs, but the dogs did the real damage. His face would be horribly disfigured, and none of the reconstructive specialists promised much hope, even if there'd be someone to pay for the years of reworking it would take. Within twenty-four hours after surgery, he was strong enough to tell the entire world that I was there at Gus's, but he was raving and had to be kept in restraints most of the time, and no one was much interested in what he said. Later he clammed up, after Gus got him a lawyer, too.

Ten days after the carnage at Gus's place, Renata had her last meeting with Anders, the one where he threatened to have me indicted, despite the difficulties he'd have proving anything. She said she laughed at him so hard he changed his mind. There was probably more to it than that, but I wasn't there and that's what she told me.

Dominic's wire hadn't picked up anything about Steve being the one who attacked Trish, and that didn't come out from anyone. Why should it? Dominic was dead and, as far as we knew, didn't care about his reputation. And telling the whole world that it was her own father who tried to rape her wouldn't help Trish any, and it sure wasn't going to happen again.

Even the people who claimed they could understand how a father might freak out and shoot the man who tried to rape his little girl had to admit Steve had gone off the deep end a little too far. He'd seemed to admit on the tape that he'd killed Monsignor Borelli, too. But he'd been looking for a missing child, and the priest had such a bad heart it wouldn't have taken much stress to blow it. At any rate, Steve was going to spend an awfully long time—maybe a lifetime—locked away somewhere. Or maybe Gus would carry out his own version of justice—or vengeance.

If that ever happened, Steve would be sorry the dogs hadn't finished their job.

CHAPTER

46

"Isn't this a lovely old-fashioned village, Malachy? Look, that could be the bank where James Stewart worked. In that Christmas film, I mean."

"Uh-huh," I said.

We were somewhere in Ohio. Or maybe it was Pennsylvania already. Sunlight sifted through the leaves and fell in patches on the grass in the town square. It was warm, early September.

"Have you had any news regarding that unfortunate woman?" After God knows how many hours of driving in silence, the Lady wanted to talk. "The one who robbed a bank. Carol Colter."

"*Karen* Colter. You're slipping, Helene." We were on our way to visit Lammy, so it wasn't surprising the Lady was thinking about what happened more than six months earlier. "And she didn't *rob* the bank, exactly," I said. "It was theft. *Robbing* implies going in with a gun or some—"

"And her two little boys," the Lady said. She swung her old Lincoln Town Car into a hard right turn to get back on the state highway. "Have you heard anything?"

"Not much. I had Herb Gatsby take a look. You remember Herb Gatsby?"

"Oh yes. The private detective. I always intended to invite him for dinner. He must have such interesting stories to—"

"He just runs an agency. Anyway, Karen got her kids back. And then disappeared again. Herb says—"

"Oh look!" the Lady said. "A sign for the interstate. I suppose we should get back on."

"I guess, if we're gonna get to New York before the semester's over."

"I do hope your Lambert does well. I wonder how he's adjusting to the school."

"Actually, I called him last night. He loves it. Even his voice sounds different—a little, anyway."

"You called him? Last night? But we didn't check into the motel until nearly midnight. Those hot dogs and French fries made you sleepy and you wanted to stop."

"Right. And when I got to my room, I fell asleep right away. But I woke up about two in the morning and called Lammy."

"Oh my. Wasn't he sleeping?"

"Sure. But he deserved it. He woke me up first. By showing up in that dream again."

"You mean the boy in the river. Did you see his face this time?"

"The face is never clear. He's sort of transparent, like a ghost. But it's obviously Lammy."

"How can you be so certain?"

"It's obvious. It's a boy in a basketball uniform—reaching out to me. I really thought he'd go away once I helped him. But he keeps on showing up. And it's not just the French fried potatoes."

"You told me he didn't make the basketball team, so maybe it's not Lammy at all."

"It's Lammy, damn it." My voice came louder than I'd intended. "Excuse me. But it *is* Lammy. I keep him out of jail. I save his life. And now I've got him started in dog grooming school. So why does he have to keep showing up? Still acting like he wants me to pay attention to him?"

"Maybe your ghost keeps showing up because it isn't who you think it is, Malachy," the Lady repeated.

"You keep saying that, Helene."

"I know, but the boy keeps appearing in *your* dream, after all. So . . . maybe the boy who wants your attention is you."

I stared across at her, but she was on the expressway entrance ramp and she kept her eyes on her driving. "You know, Helene," I said, "sometimes I think you read too much."

She smiled. "Anyway, one couldn't really say it was *you* who got Lammy started in dog grooming school. As I recall, it was *my* suggestion. Then your new veterinarian friend, Dr. Daniels—who's very, very nice, by the way—found that school in New York that would take him on short notice. And it was Casey who actually talked him into giving it a try. Really, all you've done is supply the money."

"Yes. Well, actually it was Gus Apprezziano's money. I thought I should give it away because I never really earned it." I leaned my head back to try to get some sleep. "Anyway . . . Helene?"

"Yes, Malachy?"

"I'm kinda glad you like Lynette Daniels." I smiled. "I called *her* last night, too."